OPERATION NICARAGUA

COLLIN GLAVAC

First published by NIMA 2021

First edition

Title: Operation Nicaragua

Format: Paperback

This publication has been assigned: ISBN: 978-1-7776578-0-2

Title: Operation Nicaragua

Format: Electronic book

This publication has been assigned: ISBN: 978-1-9991631-9-8

Cover design by MiblArt

Please sign up for our newsletter, watch the book trailer, and stay tuned for more at: www.collinglavac.com

For my support network — my family, friends, and friendly strangers keeping me afloat as I bob along.

PROLOGUE

Aaron Miles didn't know that he was going to die today.

He did know, however, that the information he'd stolen was the most volatile he'd ever delivered. Snatching it from under the noses of Cuban intelligence might be praiseworthy, but Aaron could only care about not getting caught. The first twenty-four hours of espionage operations were the most crucial and the most vulnerable time for spies. He checked his watch.

"This is it?" his compatriot asked, looking at the sheet of information he'd been given. Aaron didn't know his name. He didn't know Aaron's. It was best that way.

"It's enough," said Aaron in a low tone, repressing the urge to look over his shoulder. He'd been doing this job long enough to know the best way to get caught was acting suspicious.

"It's a single page — where's the rest?"

Aaron hunkered down in his booth and gestured for the man to keep quiet. They had elected to meet at the *Nostrovia*. It was the only retro-Soviet restaurant in Havana and the designated share-point for Russians in his spy network.

A server walked by. Neither of the agents spoke until she passed.

"That's all I could get."

The other agent didn't reply.

"I've been here too long already," Aaron said quietly. "I have to go."

The other agent nodded reluctantly, but there was nothing more to say. Aaron looked out the window to admire Cuba's pastel buildings, but found his eyes lingering onto others crumbling with their scaffolding exposed to the street. The slums sat next to such beautiful buildings, most split in two so families could live one atop the other. Poverty was no secret here.

Aaron downed his drink in one go, left American dollar bills for payment, and got up to leave. He watched the other man tuck the delicate paper into a pocket before being satisfied enough to walk out the door.

The afternoon was hot but Aaron felt a chill. He tucked his hands in his suit jacket pockets and decided on a brisk pace, one not so quick as to bring attention, but not so slow to make him linger.

He had to get to the American embassy. This last piece of intel had finally fallen into place. He had solved the puzzle. What lay before him was something so destructive, he could hardly believe it existed. Once at the American embassy, he could count his mission as a success, and some of the burden would pass on. He would finally be able to rest easy.

He fell into step along the *Malecón*, the famous and beautiful walkway and seawall that stretched along Havana Cuba's coast. It passed through the three neighborhoods of Havana and was known as its 'living room.' In the evening, the Cubanos would come out to watch the sunset or to drink and dance. Aaron had a feeling that he wouldn't be enjoying the sunset from the *Malecón* that evening.

After a few minutes of wary walking, he stripped his jacket and turned to face the coast, allowing himself to do a discreet one-eighty to make sure he wasn't being followed. But Aaron's only company along the *Malecón* were the fishermen standing on the seawall, and the seagulls screaming to one another. He threw his jacket over his shoulder and walked past two fishermen laughing and untangling themselves from seaweed that had blown over the wall with a crashing wave. He found himself staring at the fishermen. Had he ever been so carefree? He wondered if he'd ever have that luxury again. Another wave crashed over the seawall and the spray of salt grazed him, breaking him from his reverie and urging him onward.

Although he was in a hurry he had decided not to take a cab from the restaurant. If he were being watched or tailed, surely Cuban counter-intelligence would send their own agent to pick him up in a car, and he would have no way of knowing and no way out. He was left to watch the old nineteen-fifties and sixties cars roll by instead. Cuba seemed to be a land lost in time. America's embargo on new cars meant that bright and pastel colored Fords, Chevys, Buicks, Dodges, Plymouths, and Studebakers cruised down the modern six-lane highway. Cuba brought in Chinese and Russian cars now, but pride still rested on American oldies which were painstakingly maintained. Off to his left down a dark alley, Aaron could see one of the many 'cannibalized cars' left stripped on the curb, its parts taken to make more precious antique cars run. A whole industry had emerged. Cuban locals, who made twenty-five dollars a month could now charge fifty dollars an hour to take foreign tourists for a spin in their vintage car.

The *Malecón* was lined with monuments, each telling a part of the history and culture of Cuba. He walked past them as they sprung up along his route, like beacons leading him toward the embassy. He paused at the monument dedicated to the crew of the *USS Maine*. It was a long wedge-shaped structure with two tall pillars protruding from the center, all in blinding white marble. He gave himself a second one-eighty look around as he circled the statue.

"Remember the Maine! To hell with Spain!" Aaron whispered with a chuckle. It was the old adage cried during the Spanish-American war. Americans had sent the *USS Maine* to Havana Harbor during the Cuban war of independence and she sank.

Back when Cubans liked America, he thought.

To this day many Cubans thought the Americans sank their own ship as an excuse for war.

Wouldn't be the last time they did that, Aaron smiled ruefully, and continued on his way.

Cuba had been the victim of three wrestling superpowers. Each time the island was 'liberated' they seemed to find themselves under a new thumb. Spain, America, and the Soviet Union had all treated Cuba as a colony-prize, to be taken and controlled. He was certain that sentiment contributed to what he'd uncovered in the *Dirección de Inteligencia*. But that would have to wait.

He was nearly there. As he grew closer to the Vedano neighborhood and the embassy he saw the *Hotel Nacional de Cuba* looking down on him from Taganana Hill. It was a building that held many secrets. Fidel Castro and Che Guevara had led the defense of Havana during the 1962 Cuban Missile Crisis from a series of tunnels and bunkers sprawling under the complex. Aaron hoped they would never be used again.

He crossed the *Plaza de la Dignidad* toward the José Martí Anti-Imperialist Platform. The American embassy came into view, obstructed by dozens of flagpoles flying black flags. A gust of wind picked up from the ocean and sent the flags into a frenzy. Aaron looked up at the ominous ripple of flapping fabrics.

The sound of a silenced pistol shot interrupted his thoughts.

Aaron's eyes grew wide with surprise and then with realization. He brought a hand to the bullet wound in his chest. He hadn't seen who had shot him. Aaron only had a moment to lay eyes on the embassy before collapsing to his knees, then the ground. His final struggling breath disappeared on the turbulent ocean winds.

"Filthy American," the Cuban agent whispered, chewing on a toothpick and tossing it to the ground. The Cuban was dressed as an

American tourist. He raised the camera hanging from his neck and snapped a picture of the agent's body. He looked over his shoulder in the direction of the American embassy and gave the building a dark look before moving away from the scene. He had known Aaron Miles was a spy working in Cuba. But he didn't know what information the spy was on his way to deliver at the American embassy. That didn't matter to him. This was only the beginning.

He placed a call as he moved.

"*Sí?*" came the reply.

"It is done."

"Good. Now we need to talk to the other American."

The Cuban grinned. "Barry Bridges. Take care *amigo*." He hung up and casually retraced Aaron's steps along the *Malecón*.

The Cuban had gotten one thing wrong. Aaron Miles was a spy, but he wasn't American. There was no way to learn that now, and it made all the difference.

CHAPTER 1

Barry Bridges lived in the trendy city of Menlo Park seated in Silicon Valley. His mansion was hidden behind a tall hedge and magnolia trees, tended to by a weekly gardener. The living room of his palatial mansion was lavish and pristinely maintained, but Barry didn't notice. He had a maid but drew the line at having a butler. That would just be snobby. Regardless, he was glad for his privacy at this moment.

"This is bullshit!" Barry yelled at the television screen. A too-pretty news anchor was talking about him — spreading *bad news* about him. With mounting frustration he turned up the volume.

"The eyes of the American public are on Barry Bridges' controversial app *Anono* and the scrutiny it will be receiving next week," the anchor-woman continued. "Bridges was called to testify at an upcoming Senate hearing regarding the use of his app. *Anono* has been implicated in a number of highly publicised cases over recent months. The Federal government has concerns that further threats to the American public could be developing behind the veil of anonymity the app provides."

Barry raised a fist. "They said that this story wouldn't be going public until after the weekend!"

"Bridges, who made his name with the popular financial platform *E-Buck,* has since raised the eyebrows of cybersecurity watchdogs and financiers, after releasing *Anono* two years ago. As digital security concerns grow, the app's promise of complete anonymity through its chat service has proven attractive for the average consumer. With government and business data-collection at an all-time high, *Anono* has taken the digital marketplace by storm attracting several high profile investors."

"Uncle Sam can go fuck himself!" Barry cried at the TV. He turned it off and tossed the remote on the couch. "They're making me sound like a comic book villain!"

He hadn't noticed his super-model of a personal assistant (and sometimes lover), Sandy, standing behind him.

"I told you not to turn on the news. It won't do you any good."

"I need to know what they're saying about me!"

"They're saying you're a comic book villain," Sandy replied, a wry smile on her lips.

Barry couldn't help but grin as he felt his anger ebb away. There was only one person who could talk to him that way and get away with it. And he had to admire the situation for what it was.

"Free marketing," he said to Sandy, her smile widening as she nodded her approval. "I think we should order in tonight."

"We ordered in last night," Sandy said, idly smoothing a crease in her white dress.

"I know. Take-out is the best. I just want to stay in."

"You have to go to Washington to talk to the lawyers."

Barry sighed and threw himself onto the couch, slumping into the full-grain leather cushions. "I called it off. I said we'd get together next week."

"But the hearing is next week!"

"Exactly. They'll have more fire under their asses and it'll be fresher in my mind."

Sandy picked up a tablet sitting on the kitchen table and scrolled through the news feed. The media was having a feeding frenzy, and nothing had even happened yet. She tried to think of something to say to Barry to knock some sense into him. But sense wasn't something Barry was known for.

"I know what I need. Another think-retreat."

Sandy cringed. "You don't need another think-retreat. You already had a think-retreat."

"No, that was just a retreat."

She gave him a sour look.

"It doesn't count." He hopped up off the couch and gasped. "I'm going surfing."

Sandy blinked and put down the tablet. "You're not going surfing."

Barry rushed toward her and kissed her on the nose. "I'm going surfing. For a think-retreat."

"Out of all the times to be going surfing-"

"Think-retreat."

"...okay, of all the times to be going on a think-retreat, this is not it."

"Why not?" Barry asked, moving to the staircase and bounding up two steps at a time. "Besides the lawyers!" he called.

"Nicaragua?"

"Best surfing in the world!" came a muffled reply.

Sandy rolled her eyes and grabbed the tablet again, idly pulling up articles while she made her way up the stairs. "There's a travel advisory!"

"It's Latin America, everywhere is a travel advisory!"

"Barry..." she found him in the master bedroom, tossing random articles of clothing into a small suitcase. "The country's unstable. There's unrest and kidnapping — government sponsored death squads for God's sake!"

"Hey, I've been there before."

"That doesn't make it any better."

"Which bathing suit?" Barry asked, holding two identically bright orange bathing suits up to his chest.

But Sandy wasn't done reading article headlines from her tablet and rattling off her concerns. "The students are blocking the roads from the airport. You'll never make the beach! Once they find out who you are, you'll be ripe for kidnapping by both sides."

"Both," Barry said, tossing both bathing suits in the suitcase. "Good call." He pulled out his cellphone and placed a call to his valet while scouring the closet. "Bring the car around. Airport. Oh and get me a ticket. Liberia, Costa Rica." He hung up, then turned to see Sandy pouting in the doorway. "Aw, come on. I'm flying into Costa Rica so that solves the airport issue. Cross the border at Peñas Blancas." He ran past her with the suitcase before she could protest. His surfboard was in the garage.

Sandy was waiting at the front door when he emerged again. He had that boyish grin and moviestar hair she noticed when they first met years ago on a private island, at a party that was a bit too wild and when she was a bit too young. The memory brought her conflicted feelings that she quickly shook away.

The valet had already pulled the car up out front. Sandy blocked the door. "What's the password?" she asked.

Barry leaned his surfboard against the stair so he could grab her by the hips and give her a passionate goodbye kiss. They parted slowly and he tucked the surfboard back under his arm.

"The weekend," he said, opening the door.

"Alright. The weekend."

Barry ran out the front door like an excited schoolboy catching the bus. Sandy waved and closed the door. She leaned against the wall and sighed, then moved to the kitchen and found herself a bottle of wine. She poured two tall glasses, pulled out her phone, and texted her lover to come over as soon as he could.

A couple of disappointing hours and half a bottle of wine later, there was a knock at the door. Sandy reapplied lipstick in front of the mirror to cover the wine stains (why did she decide on red wine?) and fixed her hair before opening the door.

She was surprised to find it wasn't her date.

"Hello?" she said.

"Hi — sorry to bother you," said the man at the door. He had a Spanish accent and a face she didn't recognize. "Is Barry home?"

"No," she said, far more aggressively than she meant. "No, he left a little while ago."

"Oh, where did he go?"

"He…" Sandy trailed off. Something wasn't right here. Maybe it was the wine, or maybe it was the paranoia of sneaking behind Barry's back, but Sandy didn't like this man standing on her doorstep asking where her idiot of a boss was. "That's none of your business."

The man gave her a dark look and Sandy felt fear rise in her chest. Maybe he was a private investigator or hungry journalist. She began to close the door quickly but the man slammed a strong hand on the wood and pushed his way inside.

"No!" she yelled. "Get out!"

The man closed the door behind him with a kick of his foot. Sandy swung a punch but the man caught her by the wrist. As she struggled against his grip, the man reached to his belt and drew a pistol with his free hand. The move was smooth and practiced.

"I asked you a question," he said, pressing the barrel of the gun against her forehead. "Where did Barry Bridges go?"

CHAPTER 2

There was a small house in El Gigante that all the villagers knew about. It was a typical Nicaraguan house, if not a little bigger and nicer than what most of the poor locals could afford. It was made of concrete block and sported a tin roof firmly joined to the walls. This sort of common roofing allowed air to circulate in the house but would also prevent high winds or hurricanes from blowing it right off. These natural threats were not uncommon in Nicaragua, along with vicious bugs and unrelenting heat, even if El Gigante was beside the coast. The luxury of a fan had been installed in the ceiling of the sitting area — the largest of three rooms in the house, the others being a cramped kitchen and a utilitarian bedroom — and the temperature remained cool. Mosquito netting hung from the ceiling shielded the bed from the night's attackers, and a backup generator ensured electricity through Nicaragua's constant power outages.

All the locals knew about this house, because their most interesting neighbor lived there. It was no secret. The resident was as much a part of El Gigante as the bugs were.

It was where the American *gringo* lived.

The American's name was John Carpenter.

He'd be quick to remind you that he was only half American, born on the Canadian east-coast before getting dual-citizenship, but these half-hearted attempts often fell on deaf ears.

"East-coast, west-coast, what does the difference matter? They are both coasts. Both have water," said Kervin.

John grunted. Of course there was a difference. He opened his mouth to object, but then the fisherman dug in his heels.

"Just like America and Canada. Same country. Both America. You are both because they are the same."

John tried to respond again, but their small, wooden fishing boat hit a swell and buffeted, causing John and the other fishermen aboard the small vessel to stagger. Kervin was a cousin of the captain (really just the man who owned the boat), and had immediately taken a certain shine to him. John helped with the nets and fishing a few times a week, and in return Kervin made sure to tease the *gringo*.

John steadied himself, then turned back to the petulant fisherman. Kervin was grinning back at him, clearly pleased with himself at having found a chink in John's armor. Most of the villagers and fishermen knew John by his stoic personality and invulnerability to insult.

So John grinned back. "And there is no difference between Nicaraguans and the *Ticos*. I am glad we agree."

It was the other man's turn to scowl, his face screwed up in a comically angry expression. 'Ticos' was slang for Costa Ricans, and Nicaraguans never liked how their neighbors looked down on them. Every country had their rivalries.

"Now you wait-" Kervin started.

"*Habla suficiente!*" the captain called. "*Enough talk!*" They dipped and crested a particularly large wave. Seawater splashed across the deck and John turned away as it slammed into his back. When he turned back around, he saw Kervin had taken it full in the face and stumbled, slipping to the floor.

John stepped over to the fallen man and offered his hand. The man took it sheepishly and he got back to his feet. He slapped John hard on the back.

"As long as we aren't *vómito Tomito,* eh?" the man said with another wry smile, jerking a thumb over his shoulder.

On the other end of the boat, one of the other fishermen was throwing up and holding his forehead, groaning in between heaves.

John gave the man's sleeve a tug. "Come on, let's get working on these nets. We'll need more fish to make up for what our friend can't keep down."

The other man laughed at that and followed John, getting down to work.

By the time the boat came back with its haul, the rest of El Gigante and its neighboring villages were waking up to join the early risers. There was no harbor or place to lock up the boat — just a spot on the beach where the boat rested until it went out the next day.

"Juan," the captain called to John. John was knee-deep in the water, helping to safely beach the boat.

The captain leaped off the edge and made a small splash as he joined the other fishermen in the water. He was holding a large red fish with a strong grip on the tail. It was the length of his forearm and width of his hand.

"Juan, for you," the captain said, holding it out to John.

He never called John by his English name, no matter how many times he was corrected.

John frowned and pointed at the boat. "Not the mahi-mahi? And I worked so hard."

The captain was taken aback for the split second before he realized John was joking. He wagged his finger at John as he accepted the red snapper. It was even heavier than it looked.

"*Mi mujer* gets the mahi-mahi," the captain said. They both laughed as John left for the village. He was sure the captain's wife would be a happy woman today.

When John first started fishing with the locals, they were concerned they would have to pay him. They didn't have money, at least not enough to be paying a *gringo* properly for their labor. But John didn't expect payment. He made more money than he knew what to do with. He didn't live a lavish lifestyle and didn't want to. He wanted to help the locals. He wanted to be one of them, as much as that was possible for a *gringo*. A fat fish once in a while didn't hurt either.

As he hit the dirt road on the way into town, a long train of cattle made their way toward him. He shuffled off to the side to let them pass. Unattended, single file, they slowly loped toward their pasture. He patted the last one on the rump and received a swish of a tail in return. He'd see the cows returning in the early evening, as he did everyday. The neighborhood dogs would be out then, barking and snapping playfully at the cows who turned in the wrong direction until they got their bearings and proceeded to head home.

John slung the fish across his back and made his way past the other villagers going about their day, surveying the shopkeepers and the friendly calls and conversation of the people slowly milling about. A pair of old women were yelling at someone down the street who was evidently a poorly behaved son. An ox-cart with a beautiful *chica* John always hoped to see rode on by, carrying produce to the local hotels. He gave her a wave, and she waved back. He held up his fish for her to see and she plugged her nose in turn before the ox pulled past.

With the road clear enough for John to cross, he walked up to his favourite small restaurant, *El Pimiento*.

"John, *buenos días,*" the owner said brightly as she stepped outside to dump a bushel of peppers onto a market stand. She wiped her hands on an apron and eyed the snapper in his hands with just a hint of greed.

John smiled back. "*Buenos días*, Eileen." He handed her the fish and she licked her lips.

"*¿Esta noche?*" she asked.

"Tonight," John repeated in English.

Eileen gave John a sweetroll before they parted. He ate it on his way back home, performed a rigorous workout, then washed the smell of fish off his hands and shaved. Once finished he retrieved one of the most expensive things he owned before leaving the house.

He carried the surfboard gingerly under his arm, hitting the dusty road at a jog in his bare feet. He kept his eyes on the ground, dodging the small piles of feces dotting the path from howler monkeys.

Playa Amarillo was a long wide beach with one end taken up by surfers while the other remained empty. The sand was fine and the wind was harsh. It was no good for sunbathing but it was one of the best places for surfing in the entire world. Tourists and surfing enthusiasts often went out of their way just to come to this particular beach and ride the waves. Nicaragua was a windy country in general, but the wind in southern Nicaragua was very unique. It blew offshore all day and everyday, grooming the waves, making the swells very consistent. John would never admit how much this beach had contributed to him choosing El Gigante for his main place of residence. Surfing was the only time he could truly clear his mind. It was one of the reasons he surfed nearly everyday, those moments of peace on the waves were the secret to his much sought-after stoicism.

While coming in and out of the waves, John would sometimes talk to other surfers and tourists. He didn't make a habit of it — he didn't particularly like being social — but it was necessary to appear amicable and normal enough, and sometimes it even proved a pleasant experience. Today he met a couple from France who were awful at surfing and gave up quickly, and then he had a brief interaction with a thirty-something American who had clearly surfed more than a few times.

After spending a little too much time on the beach, John looked up at the rocky cliffs that separated the beach from Playa Colorado. The one mile private beach behind blocked off a gated community where only the rich could afford anything.

The winds picked up as they always did in the afternoon and John turned away to shield his eyes from the sand's assault. He began to work his way up the beach to return home. He was glad he didn't live in Playa Colorado.

He watched his feet on the path as always. Now that early evening crept closer, a howler monkey screeched and was soon joined by a second. John risked a glance up into the trees. One of the monkeys tackled the other, shaking the tree violently before they both scurried up and out of sight into the canopy. He looked back down just in time to dodge and divert his footing from a small pile of feces. Another screech overhead prompted him to move faster.

After he washed and dressed, John went back to the *El Pimiento*, and sat at a small table on the street while Eileen brought him a snapper supper of fish tacos and *Toña cerveza*. He finished eating and sipped at the beer, watching locals head home for the day, and the younger ones begin to get ready for the nightlife. For a moment John thought of how different his own youth had been. Never going out to bars or clubs with girls and friends. The thought of a beautiful woman named Marcela flickered through his mind.

"*¿Qué tal tu día?*" Eileen asked, pulling him back to reality and taking his plate. *How was your day?*

John didn't know what to say. He was watching the two young men who were taking a table across from him. They each had an AK-47 slung across their back and the one was holding a red and black flag. He rolled it up as the other put his feet up on the table and leaned back in his chair.

"Hello? *Gringo*?" Eileen poked John playfully.

"¡*Señorita*!" one of the men called.

Eileen turned around and flinched when she saw the men and their weapons. They were *Sandinistas*; supporters of the presidential regime. These men probably belonged to a paramilitary group.

"¡*Sírvanos*!" *Serve us*!

Eileen looked back at John and he gave a small nod. She put his empty plate back down in front of him. "*Lo siento*," she whispered. *Sorry.*

John didn't reply. She rushed over to serve the two men. John watched wordlessly and folded his hands. His right hand had instinctively gone to draw his gun.

Once he arrived home in the evening he leaned on the door for a moment. Then he retrieved his laptop from his metal safe, sat on the scratchy couch in the living room, and opened the computer. Once loaded, he began a routine sweep and clean on the device, activated a medium level encryption software, and opened a document with a series of repeating templates. John worked for an organization known only to him as 'the Firm.' He was sure it was CIA, but this had never been confirmed for him. All he knew was that he worked for American interests. The Firm required John to fill in all the interactions he had in a day. What he talked about, with who, and at what times these things had occurred, no matter how trivial.

He stared at the forms in front of him, the screen casting a soft glow in the fading evening light. Sighing, he took the laptop off his legs and placed it on the small coffee table in front of him, next to a stale mug of coffee from earlier that morning. He picked up the mug, dumped the contents in the kitchen sink, and looked out the window.

The sun was setting on another idyllic evening in Nicaragua. He watched the beautiful ball of fire fall into the horizon, eyes lingering a while after, hands resting on either side of the counter. Grudgingly, he moved back to the couch and opened up the laptop again.

He stared at the forms, clicking through the different profiles. They were extensive. Absurdly detailed. Asking physical things like height and eye color, but also including lines and boxes for recording conversation.

He hesitated. None of his neighbors were spies. None of the locals here were insurgents. He didn't need to fill out paperwork and have the spooks in Washington run the names and occupations and facial recognition data to determine these things. But he also knew this wasn't about the locals. Not really. It was about him. It was a way to keep tabs on him. Keep him in place. Make sure he knew he was always on the clock. Even while he relaxed, he was always working.

He thought of all the people he had interacted with — Kervin and the other fishermen, Eileen, a few surfers, and the *Sandinistas*. He mentally walked through his entire day from the beginning, making sure to remember the smallest interactions, even waving to the *chica* on the ox cart.

Then he got to work, starting with Kervin from that morning.

CHAPTER 3

The neighbor's roosters started to crow at four-thirty in the morning. Their calls pierced the air like whining, petulant children. The cows started their mooing an hour later.

Despite the early hour, John liked the wake up call. He was an early riser by nature and it kept him from lazing about. It was part of his routine, which he craved.

John met up with the fishermen down at the beach before the sun was properly risen. He greeted them and got to work on fixing some netting when he was told they weren't going out today. The boat usually went out a few times a week, but not always. There was still plenty of other work to do to keep him occupied. He knew this from some of his earliest jobs as a teenager in Newfoundland. 'A lot of fishing isn't fishing,' his old boss used to say. He was a big-time lobster-hauler and had taken John under his wing for a summer job. It was one of the reasons John was so eager to help the fishermen here in Nicaragua. It was natural, and what was natural was like home.

After the nets were finished and Kervin had depleted his reserve of inappropriate jokes, John made his way back home to work out and get a bite to eat. There was no gym in El Gigante and he had no weights or training equipment, but John had learned years ago how to exercise anywhere. He lifted heavy jugs of water, planked on the floor, and ran along the cliffs before the air grew too sticky.

Although he ate out much more than any of the locals could afford, he still managed to do some cooking here and there. He broke out the eggs, cheese, and sweet plantains and cooked himself a small feast. All the ingredients were fresh thanks to the kindness of his neighbors. They always kept John well-supplied and he tried to do what he could to give back.

A knock at the door surprised him. He wiped his hands in a towel and moved toward the door. There was a small concealed peephole in the wood. When he saw who it was, he opened it.

"*Señor* Carpenter," the man said.

It was the village priest, *Padre* Castillo. He greeted John warmly and extended his hand. John took it and the priest shook it with both of his own.

"*Padre* Castillo," John replied. "*Que agradable sorpresa.*" *What a pleasant surprise.*

The priest smiled. He began a long conversation about the church that John attended every Sunday. Months ago one of the church's walls had collapsed from disrepair. John had helped with the repairs and had discreetly donated a tidy sum of money. They had been worshiping outside on the cliffs for safety in the meantime. The change in location offered a unique and pleasant experience, but it wasn't without its challenges. The priest wanted to be the first to inform John that all the repairs had been completed.

"*Ahora es tiempo de regresar a nuestra casa,*" *Padre* Castillo said. *Now it is time to return to our home.*

The priest produced a plate of roast pork he had hidden beside the doorway, neatly carved and piled high. John's eyes grew wide and he managed a genuine smile.

He accepted the plate in one hand, the towel still in the other.

"It is heavy," Castillo said, "use both hands."

"I have it," John said. "*Gracias.*"

The priest beamed at John and the food for a moment and then was on his way.

John struggled to balance the heavy plate but managed to get it onto the counter without too much trouble. He sampled a piece before closing the door.

Then he unwrapped the towel which had been concealing the knife in his other hand. He hung the towel back up in the kitchen. He looked at the knife for a moment, then returned his attention to the pork, slicing another piece to eat.

John sat on his front porch with a coffee before the morning was over, sipping the strong roast and mulling over his thoughts. Hogs roamed freely before him in his front yard, snorting at one another and rooting through the grass and dirt with their stumpy noses. Chickens and goats soon followed, making John think idly about how his mother would hate this dirty menagerie, and probably try to chase the animals away with a broom. John doubted any of them would budge if she tried. This was part of their routine, just as it was part of John's.

Every morning while watching the animals make a mess of his yard, John would think about his friend Brian, killed in action almost two months ago. He would think about the last time he spoke to him in Washington — the last time John had been in America — and the things Brian had been trying to tell him. Brian had caught wind of something very wrong happening in the brass of their employers. None of the operatives knew precisely who employed them.

It was hard to follow leads back to a source that wasn't supposed to exist. John knew something dirty was happening, but there was little he could do about it.

So he stewed in his thoughts. John rarely showed real emotion — some of the navy shrinks back in the day had expressed this as one of John's greatest areas of weakness and most necessary area needed for growth — but he could sit with his thoughts and pick them apart well enough. That was good enough for him. He might be sad that Brian was gone, and he might be angry that Brian was thrown away as a pawn in a needless game of geo-political chess, but those feelings didn't accomplish anything.

Manipulation was part of the game. He wondered how many other operatives like him had been through something similar. An op gone wrong, bad intel leading to someone's death, a cover-up and indifference from faceless handlers.

John wasn't without his own assets.

The first was a recording of Antiguan cartel leader Pablo Puentes confessing and revealing that he tried to shut down the operation of a sex trafficking ring only to have a mysterious American figure threaten him. John had been privy to the information because he was the one interrogating Puentes. But when he went to deliver the recording to his handler, he was told not to send it but play it for him. He was also warned not to send it to anyone else even if they had authorization. Clearly his handler didn't want anyone else knowing the dirt and didn't want a paper trail. So John played the recording, passing on the information — but he hadn't deleted the recording as ordered.

In the grand scheme of things, the recording wasn't a smoking gun. It was more like a drop of blood or fingerprint at a crime scene that couldn't be identified. It only confirmed what Brian had said — something dirty was happening in the background.

John was keeping something much more contentious in his back pocket.

In order to dig up dirt on the Puentes family and spur their tension into a self-destructive distraction, John and his partner Marcela had copied all the data off a laptop containing damning details of cartel activity. While they had only used this to set a single small bolt loose in the family's machine — a will skipping over the family's son and diverting power and funds to the de facto patriarch instead — there was an entire trove of data that had been swiped. Anything that had gone through that laptop, whether that be an email, a web search, financials, or files, anything at all was snatched up through a handy piece of Blackthorne tech called a 'wig. The 'wig was supposed to have been disposed of.

John kept it in a waterproof pouch strapped around his waist. Its familiar weight was there at all times.

Every night since he had left Marcela and Pablito in Antigua, and arrived back at his residence in Nicaragua, John would work late into the night, combing through the massive pile of data. It was tedious work, made more difficult from not knowing where to look or even what exactly he was looking for, but John had nothing but time.

His watch beeped. He pushed the stop button to end his alarm and downed his coffee, hoping the caffeine would be enough to get him through the afternoon. Late nights and early mornings had begun taking their toll. His porch contemplations were increasingly fatiguing for his mental state. His watch alarm was sometimes the only thing reminding him to carry on with the day.

John allowed himself one more minute which turned into five, then retrieved his surfboard.

His mind cleared as he raced the swells. He may have been a skilled surfer, but one huge wave had taken him before he had hopped the board, and he tumbled headfirst into the water. The water dragged him a ways off course before he surfaced, leaving him looking for where his board had gone off to.

A young man back on the sand waved to John. He wasn't Nicaraguan, probably not even Latin American. John shaded his eyes and saw that it was the American tourist he had run into on the beach the other day. He had picked up John's board and was calling to him, pointing at it.

"I got it *amigo*!"

John grunted. The man's accent was atrocious. He half-swam/half-trudged through the water until he could wade through the shallows and meet the man on the beach.

The man grinned with artificially white and straightened teeth. He probably had some expensive braces as a kid. John couldn't help but feel uncomfortable with the man holding his surfboard, but didn't show it. He seemed nice enough.

"Thanks," John said, reaching for it.

"¡ *Gracias*!" the man said, passing it over. "You have to say *gracias*!"

"Pardon?" John asked. He tucked the board under his arm and wiped water from his face. His nose was uncomfortably clogged but he wasn't about to snort in front of this stranger.

"You mean to say, *gracias!*" the man said cheerfully, talking loudly over the whipping winds. "We're in Nicaragua! You've got to speak the language, man!"

John assessed the man for a moment. He was physically fit but not strong, a little too handsome looking, and couldn't have exemplified American boisterous ignorance better if he'd been playing a part in a satire. John could tell the man's bright orange swimming trunks were from an abhorrently expensive brand, and his sandals may have cost more than his flight from wherever he had come from in the United States.

John held back a scowl, and mentally willed himself to keep back the half-dozen choice Spanish phrases that had risen at the back of his mind.

"I'll keep that in mind," he said instead. A second later he added, "*Gracias*."

The idiot man beamed. "Name's Barry Bridges. You might've heard of me."

John didn't reply.

"Alright. See ya *amigo!*"

Barry picked up his own board that was standing upright in the stand next to him and dashed into the water.

John watched the man as he splashed around. It was a little earlier than he normally finished surfing, but he decided it was time to go.

John would usually want to sit and eat a quick but proper lunch but he spotted some students playing baseball farther down the beach. He decided on some street food and picked up a *repocheta de queso*, which was similar to a quesadilla. He ate as he walked down the beach and joined the students on the sideline. He greeted them warmly and they waved back, although a few were too busy and focused on the game to give him a proper hello. John took no offense. If young people were so invested in baseball, the world must not be such a bad place, he thought. Many of the students were from the school that he did some volunteer language work at, so many of them knew him well.

Baseball wasn't his game, but after watching for a while the students insisted he join in. He ran two home runs and was starting to feel bad for the other team, but then they managed an easy out on a pop-fly, leaving him surprised and more sheepish than he should have been. Soon after he bade the students farewell and finally bought a latte, found a comfortable bench in town, and set his surfboard down to rest.

The drink went down easy. It was one of the highlights of the day and gave him the extra boost he needed to make it back home and get to work. Tito, his barista, could not be outmatched.

John was just about to get up from the bench and continue on with the remainder of his day when he caught someone approaching out of the corner of his eye. He was Caucasian and slightly built, with long pants, linen dress shirt, and hat. The man looked both ways before crossing the street and admired a monkey jumping across the tree branches up ahead as he sauntered over to John's bench. The man didn't look at John as he sat on the opposite end, and on the opposite side, each of them facing away from the other. The man didn't say anything. John kept his gaze ahead, watching the locals walk across the street, poking in and out of shops. Nicaraguans weren't lazy, but they had an enviable way of moving slowly through the world, hardly ever in a rush, with no one seeming like they had a busy schedule. It rubbed off on John and he had a longing to live like that. But he was always on the clock. Something always reminded him that the work never ended.

"Hello John," the man sitting behind him said. His voice was soft and devoid of any noticeable accent.

John kept his gaze steady. "Dimitri. To what do I owe this pleasure?"

Dimitri pulled out a slice of tortilla bread, tore off a chunk and rubbed it between his palms until it crumbled apart. He scattered the bread at his feet and the wind blew it away as sparrows flocked to poke at the lucky crumbs fallen to the ground. Dimitri leaned back into the bench, like he was relaxing and enjoying the day. He removed his hat and placed it gently beside him, holding onto the brim with a finger so it didn't blow away.

"Cuba," Dimitri said.

The gears in John's brain started to tick, but he held fast. He needed more information.

"Tell me about your trip," John said.

"Active," Dimitri replied. "Very active. A lot going on there."

John leaned back into the bench as well, stretching his arm along the smooth wood of its top.

"As active as the Russians?" John asked.

Dimitri ignored the bait. "Dupont Circle. Your man and mine."

The words lingered in the air. Dimitri had delivered a message and John would relay it.

John found no issue with this, but it had been a while since he'd seen Dimitri.

"There's a nice new view on Laguna de Nejapa," John said. A tight smile formed on his lips.

"Oh?"

John could almost hear the other agent's eyebrows raise. "A Russian satellite station — and it just happens to be on a hill facing the U.S. Embassy."

Dimitri didn't miss a beat. "It's hard to get there though, with this student uprising. The Americans wouldn't be involved with that, hm?"

"Not at all. It's not as if they have proper weapons like the *Sandinistas*. Russian imports?"

Dimitri gave the smallest shake of his head. "We'd never do such a thing…though funny you mention that John, I may or may not be missing something from inventory. You wouldn't know anything about that?"

"Nothing. But that's not what you're here for."

A gust of wind blew through the park making John more aware of the sweat in his armpits and down his back as it cooled. Neither agent said anything for a long moment.

"Nice work in Antigua, John. Messy, but…" Dimitri shrugged, not finishing the statement.

John grimaced at Dimitri knowing his previous op. The Russians were everywhere. Some things didn't change. But this Russian in particular was one which he had a more personal history with.

"Cuba," John said slowly. "Why tell your American friend? What's in it for the Soviets — I mean, Russians?" he turned his head in profile so he could look Dimitri in the eye without directly facing him.

Dimitri held a blank look on his face. "Don't joke."

John's smirk evaporated. "What's in it for the Russians?"

"Who knows."

"We never do." John turned back.

"You know," Dimitri said, tossing the last of his crumbs out to the birds gathered and chirping at his feet. "It never ceases to amaze me how untrustworthy Americans can be."

"We trust people after we're given no reason to distrust them."

"That's a smart way of saying you never trust anyone."

"It is."

Dimitri sighed. The conversation was coming to an end. "It may seem surprising to you, but a kind and just world is in the motherland's best interest."

John didn't reply.

"Take care John," Dimitri said, standing up and brushing the remaining crumbs off his lap.

"Why so kind, Dimitri?" John asked, still staring straight ahead and not turning to look at the other man.

"Professional courtesy," and John thought he heard Dimitri finally crack a smile. "You know I'd hate to see my favorite *mysh* get caught."

John almost laughed out loud and turned again. "Oh, I'm the mouse? I seem to recall-"

Dimitri turned, and John could feel his gaze bore into him. John was taken aback by the seriousness there.

"This time, you are," Dimitri said, the smile in his voice replaced with steel. "But I am not the cat you need to worry about."

He fixed his hat on his head and the birds scattered in a flurry of wings and chirps. Dimitri walked away without another word.

John forced himself not to stare as the Russian left. The birds returned to pick at the scraps left behind. He sat for another couple minutes, stewing on the Russian agent's warning, and giving himself plenty of time before moving on with his day — just like his fellow Nicaraguans walking up and down the street with carefree ease.

CHAPTER 4

———

Mike Morrandon didn't particularly enjoy being bored, but he reminded himself that if his job was seeing little action, that usually meant he was doing it well. He was the Chief Operating Officer for Blackthorne, a clandestine CIA taskforce that held a scattering of elite operatives, agents, and assets throughout Latin America. They could be called upon to perform a variety of unique tasks with none of it tracing back to the CIA. This was partly because Blackthorne was under the Special Operations Group, a division tucked an arm's length away from the bulk of the mainstream CIA offices and activity, and dedicated to paramilitary operations when the higher ups decided intensive covert action was necessary.

So as Mike scrolled through regular reports from agents sending him routine check-ins and any potential activity that may be of interest to their handler, he did his best to be thankful that things seemed relatively quiet. Of course there were always things he needed to maintain and watch. He had to constantly keep a finger on the pulse. Right now he was trying to pay particular attention to a massive student protest in Nicaragua which he knew was stoked by the Political Action Group, a rival to his own department in Special Operations...

There was a knock on his door from Barker, his quirky but highly effective second. Mike's office was a tall glass-walled division from the rest of the 'command room,' the colloquial name given to the dark room of computers and giant wall-mounted screens, run by a couple dozen obsessive coders and computer freaks. The office was far too modern for his taste, but it helped validate his authority. Mike nodded for Barker to come in.

"An agent is calling in sir."

Mike stopped leaning back in his chair. "Who? Patch me in."

"John Carpenter."

Mike furrowed his brow. "I just read his report, it didn't say… nevermind."

Barker wrung his hands excitedly and made a slurping sound while watching Mike put on his headset. It was a strange habit that used to keep Mike on edge. He'd learned to deal with it, because as creepy as Barker may be, he was pretty much the only person Mike knew who could always be counted on to do his job well, and the only person he trusted at all. Besides, Barker helped keep the computer jockeys on edge.

He closed the door behind him and left Mike to the call.

"Esteban?" John asked.

That was Mike's code name. None of the operatives knew his real name. Or who they worked for, really. "Go ahead."

"I'm making an immediate report. Instance was just under ten minutes ago."

"Okay. Proceed."

"A Russian agent just made direct, face-to-face contact with me. Agent's name is Dimitri. Known Russian asset, Latin America region, further regional specifications unknown. Previous contact…"

"Yes, I know of your previous instances with Dimitri. Continue."

"The message was a warning to be wary of active Cubans."

"Anything else?"

"They want a meeting. Dupont Circle."

Mike paused, then recovered. "Thank you." He hung up.

He leaned back in his chair, laced his fingers together and thought long and hard about what John had just told him. He was interrupted by his phone ringing again.

Startled, he picked it up. There weren't many people who could call his office directly.

"Mike," a cool female voice said. "Let's have lunch at the Toutenbourg. I've got a nice window table." It was his boss, Director of the Special Operations Group — Linda Kim.

Mike sat up straight. "Yes ma'am. Be right there."

Then the line cut out.

Mike's furrowed brow caved into itself so deeply it began to hurt. He forced himself to stop before he gave himself a headache. He pulled himself together and rushed to open as many relevant documents as he could think of. Then he hit 'print all' and waited impatiently for the printer to spit everything out. He stuffed them in an empty folder, threw on his coat and left his office.

"Sir?" Barker asked as Mike emerged. He was wringing his hands again and waggling his eyebrows. They were like two caterpillars kissing one another.

Mike suppressed a shudder. "Cancel everything for today. You're in charge of the command room."

Barker stood a little straighter and gave a nervous grin. "Linda?"

Mike grimaced then turned to make his way to the elevators. "Linda," he muttered.

The restaurant was a short walk from the CIA headquarters but a drive from Mike's office. It wasn't his first time having lunch at the Toutenbourg, and it wasn't his first time eating with Linda, but it was his first time having lunch with Linda at the Toutenbourg. He didn't like either. The restaurant was far too fancy. Linda Kim was his boss. And rumor had it, this particular restaurant was where she sat down with colleagues to ream them out.

She was the most intimidating figure Mike knew, and it wasn't because of her appearance or even her position as head of the Special Operations Group. It was that Linda was on top of everything, and everyone, and didn't seem to require sleep or any other naturally occurring human qualities. Mike was very good at his job, but Linda seemed to exist solely to remind Mike that he could always be better. He supposed it was fitting she was his boss. He couldn't fault her for any of that. If good were good enough, Blackthorne wouldn't exist.

He spotted her after a man in a tuxedo took his coat and another host escorted him to the table. He was careful not to swing his briefcase as he passed a waiter carrying a tray filled with wine glasses.

"Thanks for showing up," Linda said, not looking up from her menu.

Mike sidled into his seat across from her with a sigh. "Hope I didn't keep you waiting. Dealing with a situation."

He didn't feel the need to tell her what John had been calling in about. Sometimes it was better to play intel close to the chest. Mike still wasn't completely comfortable with how information from his previous Antiguan op had been slipped under the rug on Linda's orders.

"Nothing you can't handle, I hope?" Linda looked up from her menu with her probing eyes, the rest of her face impassive.

"Under control."

Her eyes returned to the menu. "Good."

The sparring had begun so Mike put on his mental boxing gloves and stepped into the ring. He wanted to steer the conversation to see what information he could parse together before Linda took control.

"Any news on who's the new head of desk?" Mike asked.

The SOG Head of Latin American Affairs had been Paul Locklee, but he had been found dead in his office from apparent suicide a month ago.

"I'm sorry Mike, but I don't care more about this desk than I do Africa or the South Pacific. Sometimes you specialists forget there's an entire world out there. If you only knew what I was dealing with in Ukraine right now, it'd make Latin America look like a holiday. I mean, you should see the guy trying to handle the desk for Taiwan."

Linda wasn't wrong. Mike would consider retirement before taking on that post. China containment was the CIA's biggest procrastinating project since former Yugoslavia. As one of Mike's colleagues had said, 'it's a ten years later kind of problem.'

"Fair enough. There a reason we're doing this here and not your office?" he asked.

He had decided to poke the bear. And Mike was reminded, not for the first time in his CIA career, that he may be working for the largest most dangerous intelligence agency in the whole damn world, but that didn't mean he wasn't an idiot from time to time.

Linda blinked. "Because all the other intelligence officers are eating here, all the government officials, and any other important people who know or care about who we are, are going to see you sitting here with me. They will know that you go to bat for *me* and no one else. They will see that everything is quite straightforward in Latin American affairs, and the departments under Special Activities get along like a happy little family. It's to keep up appearances Mike. And even though it's all bullshit — and everyone knows it, by the way — it's one of the most important things about this job, and it's something I don't think you've ever taken the consideration of learning. That's always disappointed me, but there's a lot of that going around lately."

Mike was silent for a long moment. Then, finally, he decided to appeal to Linda's better nature.

"I deserved that," he said.

"You did," she agreed.

Mike had learned the secret to Linda Kim long ago. It was very similar to how he imagined marriages might work. Linda would give him crap, he would take it, and they would move on. Although he was still happy he hadn't married. Long ago Mike learned that Linda's harsh criticism was completely impartial and impersonal. By keeping this in mind Mike managed to navigate a much more productive relationship with her. Mike suppressed a shudder and thanked the CIA gods that Linda and him were on the same side.

Linda slid a photo across the table for Mike to look at without looking up from her menu. "Cuban intelligence sent us this."

"Cuban intelligence?" Mike glanced at the photo. A man was lying on concrete face down, a bullet wound in his back. Blood pooled out from under his body.

Mike didn't say anything as he tucked the photo into his pocket.

"The Cubans seem to think they caught one of ours," Linda said.

"He's not?"

"No. We don't know whose."

"But that's not actually what we're here to talk about."

Linda smiled and continued to read her menu. Mike didn't look at his own until he realized Linda wouldn't continue.

The waiter came by and they ordered their food. Mike took a swig from his glass of water. It had come from a purified bottle from some European company he had never heard of.

"Why is everything so expensive here?" he asked idly.

"We're not paying for the food, we're paying to be recognized as elites. Yes it's abhorrent. No, you're not paying."

Mike always appreciated Linda's bluntness with him. He knew she played more subversive games with people that weren't in her inner circle.

"What, I don't make enough?" It was meant to be a joke. His salary was generous, even without all the frills covered by agency expense accounts.

"No, you don't," Linda said.

"What, and you do?"

That finally cracked her armor and brought about a smile. "You have no idea."

Their meals came. Linda was having pork chops, Mike a salad.

"What the hell is that?" Linda asked, stabbing a knife in the direction of Mike's plate.

"What?"

"Are you a rabbit or something?" She sliced a piece of pork and chewed.

"You ordered pork chops for lunch?" he replied, trying to turn the question on her.

She shrugged. "It was on the menu."

Mike drooped a bit. "I'm watching the weight," he murmured.

"Uh huh."

Mike dug into the salad. Neither of them made reference to Linda's absurd metabolism and thin body-type. It was clear she enjoyed it to its fullest.

They didn't talk shop until they were finished and the coffee and tea had arrived. Mike wished they could still be eating and having a good-natured vent about the workplace. But work in the CIA never ended.

Linda patted her lips with a cloth napkin, signaling that she was ready to get down to business. "I have an assignment for you. A quick light job."

They're all supposed to be like that, Mike thought. "What do I need to know?" he asked instead.

"It's about Barry Bridges. You know who I'm talking about?"

"Okay," Mike said, somewhat surprised. "Silicon Valley guy. Big tech, big money."

"Correct," Linda replied.

Barry was a rising star in Silicon Valley, quickly becoming a household name from his controversial headlines. He was a champion of crypto-currency, but had begun to break out into the frenzy of new social media apps. *Anono*, his newest app, promised the most secure way to socialize anonymously. It was becoming one of the most talked about companies from Bloomberg to Forbes. Some surmised Bridges would be TIME's person of the year.

"Bridges is on our radar," Linda said. "I sat in on a long-winded conference regarding cryptocurrencies and security a month ago while you were running around in Antigua. The Fed is concerned about the rising popularity of a decentralized, deregulated currency."

"Difficulty tracking transactions. Besides tax issues, crypto's becoming the go-to dollar for crime," Mike said.

Linda always seemed to appreciate Mike's ability to move quickly through a conversation with her. "Exactly. Bridges has taken that concern and applied it to his social application."

"*Anono*?"

"Yes. Absurdly popular, and projections show that his user-base is going to double in the next year."

"I hate this millennial app bullshit but there's not much I can do about that Linda."

That failed to bring a smile to her lips. Linda took a quick sip of tea and frowned. "Bridges is set to appear in front of the Senate next week. Addressing concerns of criminal activity and what controls are in place to prevent this through his app."

"Okay," Mike shrugged. "What do you need me for?"

"Police reported Bridges' assistant was found dead yesterday evening. A close friend of Mr. Bridges found her lying in the front hallway."

Mike's eyes grew wide. "How was she killed?"

"Gunshot to the forehead. .45 by the looks of it, if that really matters to you."

"Robbery?"

"Pretty professional for a robbery. Nothing stolen." Linda put her tea down and leaned in. "I think someone put a hit out on Bridges."

"With the hearing next week…maybe a political opponent?"

Linda gave Mike a sharp look. "That's for the FBI to figure out. But seeing as how the hearing is next week, I want to make sure he doesn't suffer the same fate as his assistant. Unfortunately, no one is able to reach him and he's mysteriously run off to Nicaragua."

"Ah."

"I say mysteriously — we tracked Bridges' flight. He landed in Costa Rica and hopped the border in Peñas Blancas. We have on file that he's an avid surfer — he likes to surf at Playa Amarillo. Is Bridges where we think he is?"

Mike was already reaching for a portfolio in his briefcase to offer her. "My agent confirms this." John had reported on Barry's presence in the area in his daily report.

Linda waved away the portfolio with a flick of her manicured hand. "Good. Task your agent to get him to the airport and send him home."

Mike smoothed his expression from the scowl he instinctively moved toward. This was hardly a task befitting a black ops agent. Then again, it was hardly a true mission, just tapping local resources.

Linda read his mind. "We're stretched thin. And Nicaragua isn't the place to be a celebrity *gringo* right now."

"Yes ma'am."

"Be advised we are not notifying the Nicaraguan government of our projected activity."

"Ours or theirs?"

"Pardon?"

"Our government or their government?" Mike asked.

Nicaragua's current political situation was in a tug of war between American and Russian interests. It was the same old story, one without an end anytime soon.

Linda suppressed a predatory grin. "I said we are not notifying the Nicaraguans, Mike. There's only one government in Nicaragua." She paused for a moment, then continued, speaking under her breath. "But for your purposes, neither."

"Alright. Understood."

Linda smiled. It was as if a puppeteer had pulled two strings abruptly up on either side of her mouth. "That will be all. Go get some work done."

Mike nodded, reached for his briefcase and began to stand but hovered over his chair for a moment. "Um…ma'am — a question?"

Linda furrowed her brow. "Okay."

Mike settled back into his chair and folded his hands on the table in front of him. He felt himself begin to fidget in his chair but worked to compose himself. "Has there been any progress on the Locklee investigation?"

Before he had been found dead, Paul Locklee had revealed to Mike that a rival CIA department — the Political Action Group — had been financially backing a Guatemalan cartel off the books. John Carpenter's interrogation of cartel leader Pablo Puentes confirmed Locklee's story during their operation in Antigua. Mike and his operative were the only ones who heard the interrogation.

Linda raised her eyebrows. "Not this again…" she trailed off, but when Mike stayed silent and kept steady eye contact, Linda let out air. "I will say this, and that will be it."

"Okay."

"The internal investigative report of Locklee's suicide has a few missing pieces. When I pointed this out I experienced a little too much pushback."

"So, foul play."

"No, not necessarily foul play, whatever the rumors might be telling you. Just jurisdiction-snobbery and classification safeties. I can at least respect the latter. But there's a spill I need to clean up and shit rolls downhill."

The public knew Paul had died but they didn't know he had been wired money from Pablo's brother, Sandor Puentes. That part was internal knowledge now, and if not downright embarrassing, it was career-threatening for anyone close enough to the desk. If that information leaked any further it would have even worse repercussions for the CIA. Not just for budget approvals, but with a public opinion-mob and a global stage to consider.

So Mike had left his team mostly ignorant of these clandestine secrets to keep things localized, and cozied up to the PAG to dig up the rest of the dirt on them instead.

"That's it?"

Linda's eyes were cold. Mike felt a small bead of sweat emerge from the back of his neck and roll slowly down his back. He didn't answer.

Linda's voice was low, quiet, and made Mike think of a snake's hiss. "I am balancing a very fine line here. I am performing some very high level damage control, including preventative measures for loss of resources leaking into other interested parties. Every day I crawl through a den of wolves. And when I have unfortunate underlings performing against orders and outside operative parameters-"

"Linda-"

"Mike. You used Blackthorne resources to investigate our own. Then the man you investigated shot himself in his office. I didn't know I hired a dumbass cowboy to play sheriff. If that doesn't ring any alarm bells-"

"I'm being careful-"

"Don't interrupt. I have a dead head of desk, an increasingly hostile department feud, and now one of my best chief operating officers is ponying up to the Political Action Group for a piece of ass and a seat at the next mixer."

Mike closed his mouth and focused on breathing as slowly as he could.

"I won't be able to protect you," she continued without pause. "It's not that I won't want to. I won't *be able* to. Do you understand me?"

The words lingered. Linda's gaze was frighteningly still. And Mike stewed on those words. What was outside Linda's abilities? Linda was godlike in the cutthroat bureaucracy of the CIA.

"Yes ma'am."

With that reply, she warmed a little. Not much, but enough that she was back to being stern instead of threatening. Enough to keep Mike's sweat to a reasonable level.

"I understand you have concerns. There very well may be something very wrong going on. And I know you are probing the PAG with your boy-scout sharing intel act."

Mike felt like he'd just been punched in the gut. The breath he didn't realize he'd been holding whooshed out of him all at once. He managed to keep his poker face, but that was about it.

"I'd be lying if I didn't say I'm not hoping to leverage what you come up with," Linda continued, not noticing or not caring that Mike had just realized his secrets were nothing but. "But at a certain point, if you go far enough — which I suspect you will — we may be stuck licking our wounds instead of keeping chase. Just keep that in mind, will you?"

"Yes ma'am." Mike looked down at his shoes for a long time before saying anything else. "I'll get on all this right away."

"Please do," Linda said, sipping her tea delicately before quickly deciding to add more sugar.

Mike, understanding that their meeting was over, drank one more sip of water then got up, tucked his chair in, and thanked Linda for lunch. She nodded and savored the extra scoops of sugar she had added as he left. Soon enough she'd have to get back to her office and her computer with all its emails and feeds. Her phone had alerted her nearly ten minutes ago on some political developments that could aid her operative forces in Crimea, and apparently a bomb had gone off in Iran.

Those pork chops really were good, she thought to herself.

CHAPTER 5

―――――

Barry was having a very pleasant dream involving a beautiful young woman when he was rudely awakened to knocking on his door. It wasn't quite pounding, but the raps were firm and loud enough to make him cry out as he awoke. He took a moment to remember where he was — a luxury shack on the beach of Playa Amarillo — then managed to separate himself from his king-sized bed and tip-toed to the door.

There was no peephole. He pressed his ear against the door. The knocking came again and he sprang back, a hand holding his ear in pain.

"Ow!"

"Mr. Bridges?" a man's voice. It had an accent he assumed to be Nicaraguan.

"Uh *sí*?" Barry said, touching the door's latch to assure him the lock was firmly in place.

"Mr. Bridges I am terribly sorry to wake you up. I am *La Policia Nacional Nicaragüense*. Please open the door."

"What? Who are you?"

"Police. Can you please open the door?"

"What's going on?" Barry suddenly became conscious he wasn't wearing any clothing other than his boxers and began pulling on a shirt and shorts.

A pause. "The government is worried about tourist safety at this time and has sent us to protect high-profile travelers."

That didn't sound good. Barry remembered Sandy's warning before he left. After he got home he knew she'd give him a harsh 'I told you so.' He opened the door for the officer.

"What do you-"

The door flung open under the officer's boot, slamming against the wall, and throwing Barry to the ground. Barry tumbled to the floor and landed awkwardly on his arm, crying out in a mix of shock and pain.

"What is…why are you-"

The officer — who wasn't wearing any uniform Barry could make out — grabbed him by the ankles and dragged him toward the door. Then before he knew what was happening, a black hood appeared in the man's hands and enveloped Barry's head.

He was tossed into utter darkness.

Barry attempted to struggle. He didn't understand what was happening. He was still groggy and confused from waking up in the middle of the night, and was trying to process who this man was. He kicked but only hit the air, then swung his fists around. One of them connected with flesh but the man didn't react and Barry didn't know where he'd hit him. His other hand collapsed into the concrete wall.

"Son of a-"

Barry didn't have time to finish swearing. The man's fist collided with Barry's face. The sudden impact sent him reeling through the darkness. An instant headache spread across his brain. He felt like he was drunk with the spins as he tried not to throw up into the hood. It didn't help that he was definitely hungover to begin with.

"You are coming with me," the man snarled.

"What do you want!" Barry cried, his voice muffled through the hood. He tried not to cry, but he could feel the tears starting to burn at the back of his eyes.

The man didn't answer. He hauled Barry up onto his feet. But Barry didn't realize he was going to be standing so suddenly and couldn't catch his balance. His legs buckled and he collapsed under the weight of his own body, sending his knee painfully into the ground and then the rest of him toppling onto his shoulder. Not out of fight yet, Barry windmilled his arms and felt one of them slap against something solid, cylindrical, and hard. Wood or soft stone. It must've been the small front table beside the door. Not thinking or caring how this table could be used for his defense, Barry gripped the leg of the table and heaved it with all his strength at his invisible attacker.

There was a thud and an 'oof,' as the table connected with his opponent. Barry began to scramble away again but his calf was seized by pain that instantly stopped his efforts. An iron grip locked onto Barry's ankle and began to drag him on his back, one handed.

Barry raced to think of what else he could do. What else he could grab. Some sort of weapon. His grasping hands didn't find anything as he was pulled back in the disorienting darkness.

"Help!" he cried, feeling the weakest he had ever felt. He cried for help again, then screamed. No words, just screaming. Screaming incoherent things into the night, hoping someone would come to save him.

His voice began to grow raw and tears and snot leaked from his face. He realized he would probably die. He had sunk to the most terrifying, most awful place anyone could fall to. As Barry felt the man drag him out the door, he spread his arms and grabbed onto either end of the doorway, pulling his body back in a tug of war he could never win. Still, he held on. If he were to die, he would die trying to fight back.

That's when the gunshot rang sharp and crisp in the night. Barry's screams and struggles were immediately silenced.

A man's voice came somewhere high above Barry and it took a moment for him to realize the voice was talking to him. He couldn't make out the words at first. He couldn't see anything. Everything was black. His breath came out in ragged bursts, and the space around his head was stifling and hot.

"Get up," the voice said. It wasn't the same as the man who had been at his door that he had heard before. It was hard but not unkind.

Barry flailed before getting his bearings in the darkness. He had full control of his arms and legs and no one was holding him down. He sat up and clawed at the bag over his face.

He struggled for a moment before another set of hands started fumbling with the bag. Barry panicked, thinking his attacker was about to smother him. He spun his arms as hard as he could, trying to strike back blindly. He connected with something that felt like an arm but his fist was caught in the palm of the other man's hand and used to turn him over effortlessly. He was forced onto his stomach in a log roll as the stranger straddled him, pinning his arms and continuing to fumble with the bag.

Exhausted, but still struggling, Barry swung his legs to strike out with his heels. Light streamed into his vision and crisp night air washed over his face as the hood was removed. He gasped for air and rolled onto his back once he realized no one was on top of him anymore. He spent a moment blinking at the stars overhead and taking long deep breaths to collect himself. Then the man stepped forward and entered his view, looming over him.

He was early middle-aged and caucasian. He had salt and pepper hair and a clean-shaven face which made him seem a little more kindly, but the man's expression and piercing gray-blue eyes removed any thought that Barry was out of danger.

"Who are you?" Barry managed, before he coughed. Then he remembered. "From the beach!"

The man handed him a plastic water bottle. "I'm here to help you. But we have to go now."

Barry drank and tried to figure out what was going on. He coughed again. "I was attacked. I thought I was shot. Or going to get shot? Was that you?"

The man looked at him for a moment, as if deciding what to do with Barry. It didn't make Barry feel any better about his situation.

"No," the man said. He pointed to a large dark lump a few feet away from them. "That was him."

Barry followed the man's finger and traced it to a figure in dark clothing, lying face down in the sand. He barely recognized what he could see of the man's face.

"That…that's a police officer. He tried to-"

The man crouched and took back the water bottle. "No. Not police. He was trying to kidnap or kill you."

"Oh," Barry said. He looked to the man again, unease growing in his belly. "And what do you want with me?"

The man grabbed a hold of his arm and lifted him off the ground. "We've got to go."

"Ow!"

The man covered Barry's mouth and looked over his shoulder. "Quiet."

"I think I broke my arm," Barry said, looking down at the grip the other man held. He had landed on it awkwardly when he'd been attacked.

The man looked at the arm and loosened his grip. But instead of letting go, he ran his hand firmly up and down the arm. Barry flinched. The man locked eyes with Barry.

"You're fine. Let's go." He hoisted Barry to his feet before he could protest anymore. Then he began dragging Barry past the dead body and toward the foliage.

"Are you kidnapping me?"

"No."

The man loosened his grip again and eventually let go of Barry when it became clear he'd follow the other man.

"Who are you? What's going on?"

The man hesitated. He didn't seem to want to answer. "My name is John. I'm here to help you. That's all you need to know."

"But-"

The man wheeled on Barry and Barry shrunk back. The man's eyes seemed to glow in the moonlight.

"Those men are after you. You need to come with me. I'm not going to say it again."

"Who are-"

John pounced on Barry and he tried to scream but his mouth was covered with a firm hand. He started to kick his legs but the other man wrapped his own around them, keeping them in a deadlock.

Barry's panic was rising, but before he could manage anything else, a man was yelling and movement appeared from out of the corner of his eye. Two dark individuals ran across the beach, illuminated briefly by a tiki-torch burning in the sand. He didn't get a good look at the figures but they both wore dark clothing and held guns.

They were moving toward Barry's luxury shack.

John slipped his hand slowly off of Barry's mouth. Barry looked up at him.

John held a finger to his lips and Barry nodded slowly. He didn't know who these people were or what they wanted with him, but all he could do now was follow this other man who wanted to keep him safe.

CHAPTER 6

Mike's condo was in North Bethesda, ten minutes outside of Rockville, forty-five minutes from downtown Washington, and half an hour to Langley. It wasn't cheap, but nothing his generous government salary couldn't handle.

Mike was from New York, so anything bigger than a studio apartment felt like a luxury and downright waste of space. He wasn't much of an interior decorator either. If it was considered normal, Mike would've left the walls bare. He didn't know anything about art or style or design. After a friend had visited and seen the spartan space in which he lived, she insisted he hire an interior designer to make the place look acceptable for any visitors.

So he had gotten paintings that meant nothing to him. A couch that had cost too much. A dining table and chairs that he rarely sat and ate at. Mike was a loner, and he didn't feel bad about that. As much as the few friends and colleagues he spoke to would hound him about his long-lived single state of sadness, he could hardly be bothered with a relationship. His life was devoted to his work and dating took too much time. He'd had two awkward one-night stands and one more promising fling in the last two years, but nothing lasted. Mike didn't lament that. He had his condo and his paintings and his furniture to satisfy his meager social circle and spent his time ignoring it while making sure to install state of the art security cameras and systems. The work for the world's largest intelligence agency soldiered on.

But tonight of all nights, he thanked his friends who had encouraged him to spend the extra on the expensive condo and all its added frills.

"Oh…" Sara moaned as Mike kissed her neck. "I've been waiting for this all week."

His hands slipped under her thighs as he carried her away from the dining room table. Their food was half finished but the bottle of wine was empty.

She bit his neck and it threw his thoughts reeling, making him stumble and slam her into the wall. Instead of crying in pain, she cried in pleasure. Sara wasn't a gentle lover.

"I haven't felt this alive in years," Mike whispered.

He slid his hands slowly up her thighs, clutching at her as she threw her head and arched her back. Her brown curls fell like water down the back of her dress. A painting fell off the wall and hit the ground, threatening to interrupt the moment.

"Oh god, I'm sorry," Sara said.

"I hate that painting," Mike growled.

Sara squealed and threw her arms around his neck, trembling with anticipation as she let him carry her the rest of the way to his bedroom.

Mike was acutely aware that their love affair was completely unprofessional. Sara worked the Latin American desk in the Political Action Group. They had met during the Antiguan op and Mike had offered to share resources in an effort to build rapport and squeeze whatever secrets he could get.

That mutual benefit had become much more literal in a short amount of time.

He hadn't meant it to turn into sex — Sara was gorgeous and had the body of a rocket — but Mike had never been one to fall prey to temptation in the line of work. If he were easily corruptible, he would never have been put in charge of Blackthorne. But before he had shut the affair down, he decided it could be useful. If sex gave him a leg up in getting information, so be it. Figuratively speaking, of course.

They had woken up late and naked, anticipating a round two. Mike wasn't sure if Sara was hoping to get any off-the-record information from him the way he was, but when she spoke next he suspected it was so.

"Any good work gossip lately?"

"Not really, no," Mike said, not about to reveal that an unknown spy had been killed in Cuba. He gave her a stern look that made her laugh, then curled an arm around her shoulders. "Just the whole Locklee affair last month. Investigation still hasn't settled."

Sara frowned. "Right. You don't believe any of the rumours about Paul Locklee, do you?"

Mike felt his heartbeat quicken and searched Sara's face for any hints that she suspected him of digging for information. Her expression remained sweet and playful.

"You've asked me that before — and no, I don't."

Sara nodded. "Sorry, well okay. Do you want to do breakfast?"

"Not much of a breakfast person."

Sara frowned. "That's one way to turn a girl down."

Mike tucked a curl that had fallen in front of Sara's face behind her ear. "Work, actually. I just have a lot of work."

"I'm sure you have your hands full with the Barry Bridges thing."

Mike gave her a sharp look, surprised. "How do you know about that?"

She batted her eyes playfully, looking far too proud of herself. "Who do you think requested the op?"

An eerie discomfort gripped Mike as he processed Sara's words. *Linda didn't tell me it had been a PAG request.*

"I thought you were the one who sent out the hit," Mike grunted, only half joking.

Sara picked up her pillow and smacked him across the arm with it. "No! Are you kidding me? We need Barry!"

"Yeah? And why's that?"

Sara pursed her lips and held her head high, looking away from him.

"Oh stop being dramatic," he took her chin softly in his hand and turned her toward him. He looked into her eyes.

She kissed him and it lasted longer than he expected. Mike reminded himself not to let feelings complicate his real objective. Extract what information he could from Sara. He needed to find out who was making backdoor deals with Latin American cartels within the PAG. It would take time.

She leaned into him and pressed her forehead to his own. He felt her breath and her warmth wash over him. His libido was hungry for more.

"I need you to do me a favor," Sara whispered.

"What's that?" Mike grinned.

"When you get Barry back to the States…bring him to me."

Mike drooped with disappointment as he realized where the conversation was leading. "Bring him to you?"

"Yes. The PAG."

"What, are you going to torture him?"

"No!" she pushed him and he toppled onto his back, bouncing against the bed. Sara crawled over to him on all fours, giving him an excellent view of her breasts. "We want to talk to him. Before he goes to his lawyers and preps for the hearing."

"That sounds sketchy as hell."

Sara ran her hands up Mike's chest until she held his face. She stuck a thumb in his mouth. He bit down hard.

"Ow!"

Mike pushed her off him and sat up. "I don't think Linda would let me get away with that."

"Fuck Linda."

The words struck him like lightning. "If I got you Barry...what would you do for me?"

Sara wrapped her legs around Mike's waist and sat in his lap. "I think I could come up with something," she whispered in his ear, then kissed his neck.

Mike shivered but pulled her away. "Why are you so interested in Barry?"

Sara hesitated, looking back and forth between his eyes.

"If you tell me, I'll get him for you."

Sara let out a breath. "Okay. Fine. We are concerned about the results of the upcoming Senate hearing."

Mike raised his eyebrows but Sara didn't continue. "Go on," he prompted.

"If the committee finds Barry's app too much of a security threat, they will work to restrict its abilities and implement oversight."

"And you don't want that."

Sara smiled. "No. But if he is forced into that position — which we suspect he will be — we hope to have him deliver those oversights to our people on the committee."

"Our people?"

"Oh come on Mike, you know — people who are in our pocket."

"That doesn't sound ethical. I thought you guys were supposed to be international, not internal."

Sara snorted. "Don't be so naive. Besides, we all break the rules from time to time, don't we?" She gave him another one of those sweet-but-dangerous looks, and it made him feel like she could read his thoughts. She was obviously referring to when he investigated Paul Locklee internally — a serious breach of CIA resources.

"Why would that be so important to you?"

"I've given you enough."

Mike closed his eyes and cocked his head, making it seem like he was measuring a weighing scale in his head.

Sara sighed again. "Fine. We are interested because a lot of powerful people may or may not use the app. Happy?"

Mike had to stop himself from betraying any sense of surprise at this last statement...or accomplishment. He needed to escort Barry out of Nicaragua...but he definitely didn't want him falling into the hands of the PAG. Even if he refused, PAG would find a way.

"So. You'll bring him to us?" Sara asked, running a finger down his chest.

"Tit for tat," he said, grabbing one of Sara's nipples and giving it a not-so-gentle twist.

Sara squealed and swiped his hand away. Then, to his surprise, she continued to latch on to his arm and twisted it backward until he cried out and found himself dragged back down to the mattress.

Most CIA officers had some basic hand-to-hand combat training, but few kept up the practice. Sara clearly took it seriously.

She kissed his stomach as she moved down on him, but all Mike could think of was how this was not a woman he'd ever want to end up in a fight with. That would be deadly.

CHAPTER 7

John led the way into the foliage. They weren't following the path that Barry normally used to get onto the cliffs and take pictures and led to the road out of town.

He tugged on John's sleeve.

"The road is that way," he hissed.

John waved him off. They continued picking their way through thick plants and vines and trees that provided nothing but chilly darkness.

John wanted to stay in cover as long as possible. But as they grew closer to where his small house was located, he knew that couldn't last forever.

"Where are we going?" Barry asked.

John thought he had been clear about how much Barry needed to know and how little him talking would help the situation. He was already starting to form a headache.

John crept to the edge of the forest, where small shrubs and bushes provided cover but then gave way to grass. He held up a finger, sensing Barry was about to say something else. They both crouched silently, listening for the sounds around them.

A bird up above flapped its wings and disturbed the canopy, and a twig snapped somewhere a ways off, followed by the rapid dashing of small feet. All animal. No human sounds. But then John heard a whoosh and crackle from down on the beach where they had come from. An ominous light dotted the darkness.

"Stay here," he said to Barry, making clear this was a command.

John drew his Glock and took two steps forward.

"But where are you-"

John held up a hand again to silence him. He saw Barry's eyes flick nervously to the gun.

"I'm going to that building to get something, then coming right back."

He ducked his head then made his way forward without another word.

John knew Barry was already hyped up on confusion and nerves, and leaving him alone in a dark forest wasn't helping the situation any. If John wasn't back fast, Barry would bolt. So he'd have to be quick.

John's effects were stuck in his home. When he'd gotten the call from Esteban to retrieve Barry, he'd taken his tactical backpack which was bulletproofed but only held minor gear. He hadn't taken his go-bag, only used for survival purposes in a pinch. If he were going on a mission, John only needed his tac-bag, but this was hardly the case. Esteban had told John to retrieve Barry and escort him out of the country — he'd failed to describe the severity of the situation.

John crept forward slowly, each foot turned on a diagonal. It always made him think of a penguin. It might look ridiculous, but it let him sweep over ground with a steady motion with no break in between steps. Off in the distance, he might be a swaying tree branch or unnoticed altogether. The human eye notices patterns and distinct movements — rarely smooth, continuous motion.

He reached the wall of his house and pressed his back against the concrete.

He stopped, took two breaths, then listened.

Men could be heard yelling to one another down on the beach, and a chilling scream tore through the night. No gunshots. Not yet. But more bright lights were poking out through the dark, and John knew there was little time to spare before things grew worse.

He slid to the back window, unlocked the simple padlock with a house key, then lifted the heavy wooden flap and scanned his own house to see if anyone had already broken inside. It wasn't hard to break into his house, but he had nothing of value other than his gun, laptop, and some cash. The laptop and cash was kept in his safe. His gun he kept on his person.

John climbed inside, taking the floor silently with his feet. He padded over to his bed and got down on all fours to retrieve the go-bag tucked underneath. He dragged it out and slung an arm through a strap, then moved to his safe. It wasn't large, but it did the job. He spun the code on the dial and cracked the heavy metal door. The laptop lay on the bottom along with a few modest stacks of American cash and spare passports. He grabbed the laptop, locked the safe and stood to go.

The front door burst open in an explosion of splinters.

The man storming the room held an AK-47. It took him half a second to spot John in the darkness and raise the thing to aim.

John didn't have enough time to juggle the laptop to his offhand and draw his gun, but he had half a second to respond to the man's burst of fire. He threw the laptop at his enemy like a frisbee and swept his leg to knock the kitchen table over and dove for the floor.

Three rounds pumped into the concrete wall behind where he'd been standing a moment before, the holes appearing as if someone had hammered nails through a board. The initial rounds stopped short when the laptop collided with the man and he cried out in surprise.

The wooden table interrupted line of sight for the gunman but wasn't going to absorb any fire once the man recovered. John ignored the pain on his ribcage from hitting the floor and pulled out his gun. He scrambled forward on his elbows in an army crawl just in time for the man to resume his attack.

The AK-47 started up again, blazing rounds that punched behind John's feet, splinters exploding from the table as the rounds continued into the concrete wall. John didn't have a lot of room to maneuver with the tight confines of his small home.

More bullet spray. They blasted through the table in an erratic wave, whizzing over John and slamming into the wall again. The noise of the AK-47 thudded painfully in his ears.

Luckily for John, most people didn't know how to engage in a proper firefight.

The man was standing in the open, thinking that a continuous spray was a good enough tactic. Then again, the man probably didn't think John had a gun, or years of training, and if he'd aimed just five inches lower he'd have done some damage.

John decided to teach the man a valuable lesson.

He finished pulling himself forward, knowing that time wasn't on his side, and poked his pistol out from the end of the table. He didn't need to look at his target — the bullet spray's direction and the man's yells were enough to figure that.

He squeezed off three quick rounds, each at minutely different angles just to be sure he didn't end up clipping an arm and miss out on a real hit. The man fell to the ground with a muddled thump and the roar of gunfire evaporated into the night's silence.

John waited two breaths before raising his gun above the table and taking aim. No response. He took a peek through one of the holes in the table and saw the man out cold on the floor. Too many firefights ended with someone being less dead than the other thought.

John briefly checked himself over for wounds, found none, then climbed out from the table. He circled around, swept the room with his pistol, and honed in on the man on the floor.

Brown complexion. Muscled. No uniform, at least not a proper one, but he wore military clothing — and decent quality too. Some gear but nothing substantial.

That probably made him state-sponsored militia. Paramilitary.

John knelt and lifted the man's balaclava to reveal his face.

It was one of the young *Sandinista* men he'd seen at Eileen's restaurant.

"Dominic!" someone hissed from outside the doorway. "¿*Problema*?"

And that was the voice of the second.

John focused on the doorway but he held an arm out behind him, toward the door and his go-bag. He didn't have time to play hide-and-seek. More flames sprouted in the distance. The militia were burning the village, as he'd suspected. The fishermen and their boats, the tourists and their luxury shacks…perhaps they'd continue downtown. Gunshots dotted the distance, but more men were moving down the beach toward John's neighborhood.

The other militiaman calling for his friend grew silent. Suspicious soldiers were trouble.

John curled around the fallen table and knelt by his couch. The man entered, starting to sweep with his own AK-47.

John picked up a shell casing and tossed it into the kitchen. It clattered and the man brought his assault rifle about. He wasn't quite as trigger happy as John had guessed, so he heard John as he pounced.

A quick jab to the kidney and a hard forearm against the back of the neck had the man pinned against the wall in seconds. John stuck his Glock in the man's ribs before he could try to spin or somehow turn his AK for backward fire.

"Stay," John whispered.

"*¿Quién crees que eres? ¡Somos los propios hombres del Presidente!*" *Who do you think you are! We are the President's own men!*

John would keep that in mind. "Why were you after the American?"

The man paused and struggled, so John ground his forearm against the base of the man's skull, feeling vertebrae against his muscle and pressing the man's face into the concrete. John brought the muzzle of his gun up under the militiaman's chin.

"Orders," the man hissed again, spluttering against fear and pain.

Torches grew in the darkness of the doorway. More men coming to terrorize citizens and burn buildings. John had already stayed too long.

"*¡Inmundicia rebelde! Estudiante de mierda!*" the man continued. *Rebel filth! Fucking student!*

"Orders," John said.

Without looking at his captive held down in front of him, John pulled the trigger.

The militiaman's skull exploded at the top and his body crumpled to the floor. John had considered a silent twist of the neck instead, but he needed to buy more precious seconds for whoever was coming next into his home. Let them see how their comrade was killed and be suspicious. Let them be scared of someone with a gun.

But John couldn't stay. He could hunt these men for hours if he wanted to, but he didn't have the kind of blood-mad desire other men in the military often had, and he had a mission to complete.

At least now he had some intel.

He retrieved the laptop from the ground but found it inoperable — the screen was cracked and it wouldn't turn on. He tossed the thing back onto the floor in frustration. One of the men had probably stepped on it. He made for the window and hoisted his go-bag from the floor. More paramilitary were sweeping around outside, torches flaring and angry words whispered to one another.

John popped the window, made sure his tac-bag was on tight, and put one foot over the window, hoisting his go-bag off the floor. He'd managed to get all the supplies he'd need although it was a shame the laptop was scrapped.

The go-bag ripped open, its contents spilling out onto the floor.

John spun his head in surprise while straddling the window. The fabric around the zipper was littered with bullet holes, having taken a beating in the initial firefight. He was about to bend down to stuff it all in as best he could when a torch appeared in his home, lighting up the man's masked face with a haunting glow.

No time.

He dropped the bag and slipped out the window, sweeping left, then right with his Glock to make sure the coast was clear. Yells came from behind him — the militiamen finding two of their own dead. John ran off into the forest, into the safety of darkness.

The forest was difficult to navigate in the dark but John had no trouble finding Barry.

"Please! Don't shoot!" he was crying in between words. "I'll give you whatever you want!"

John was about to say something, then decided better of it. He walked closer to Barry until the man's face lifted in relief.

"Oh! Oh. It's you. Okay."

"This way," John said.

Barry pointed toward the beach. "My shack is that way."

John stopped moving and regarded him.

"My...things. They're back there."

John turned back around and trudged through the undergrowth.

Barry jogged to keep up. "Jake? It's Jake right? My things-"

"John."

"John — great name — my things are-"

John spun on Barry. He didn't have time for this. Neither of them did. In fact, Barry was in much more danger than John was.

"We can't go back. They're burning everything on the beach. We're leaving."

"What? But my surfboard!"

"Now."

"You got to go back for your things."

John looked at him with a dark expression. Barry got a full glimpse of what lurked behind the haunting eyes of a predator. He whimpered.

John grabbed the man's shoulder and Barry flinched, but John wasn't hurting him. He pulled Barry down gently into a crouch, and stayed there, pointing to a flame that had sprouted in the darkness. John didn't say anything, so neither did Barry. After a moment Barry looked at John and saw him staring, that same dark expression on his face. It was terrifying.

"Did you...are there more bad guys nearby?" Barry asked.

John didn't answer. He was watching his house burn. He had more than one property in Latin America. But only one home. And he hated that he couldn't do more for his neighbors. The lovely Nicaraguan men and women who treated him as their own, now screaming and burning and running for their lives.

No one had followed him into the jungle. John had been concerned about sentries or soldiers blocking exits but this was a terror op alongside a kidnapping. He didn't know who Barry was or why the Nicaraguan government would want him, but none of that really concerned him.

John stood up and motioned for Barry to follow close behind. Barry eyed the gun John kept pointed to the ground but obeyed.

"Who was he then?" Barry asked, his voice far too loud for someone trying to stay hidden.

John didn't answer right away. He was focusing on keeping his footsteps quiet, checking the night sky for any air threats, watching the beach for any other hostiles.

"Who was the guy pretending to be a-"

John raised a hand to keep Barry quiet. "I don't know. It doesn't matter."

"But-"

John indulged him, if anything just to keep the man quiet. "They were paramilitary from the Nicaraguan government. Maybe hoping to extort money. It's not uncommon." Though it seemed a bit of a stretch for John to be getting a call to interrupt a petty kidnapping. Barry was important enough to the U.S. as well as Nicaraguan authorities for them both to be putting such efforts in.

"Government? But that would be...that's not-"

"Not what? Keep your voice down."

Barry dipped his head and hunched, as if that would help his voice be quieter. He at least sounded quieter when he spoke again. "The government can't do that. It's not...you know, legal."

John grunted and Barry nearly bumped into him when he took a sharp turn. John looked at him and Barry flinched.

"When you're rich enough, powerful enough, or have something someone else wants, laws tend to change."

Barry didn't know what to say to that. John was surprised himself. He hadn't expected something like that to come out of his mouth.

Barry finally cleared his throat. "Well...I-"

"It's not my business. I need you to stay close, and stay quiet."

So the other man gulped. He was about to ask John why they had stopped again. John held a single finger to his lips then tucked his body into a crouch, then continued to creep forward slowly.

They'd reached the road. John didn't spot any sentries but didn't let his guard drop. They picked their way alongside the road but still in cover, staying just out of earshot of anyone who might be passing by.

"Look," Barry said, "a building!"

Up ahead was an old abandoned granary John had used as storage during an operation tackling gun smugglers for the Nicaraguan president. He'd captured enough arms to equip an entire company. That had been months ago. He was still waiting for someone to follow up with him, but he figured it was a forgotten file on a desk by now.

Although he didn't have a key, John considered breaking in and arming themselves.

He looked over his shoulder, in the direction of town. Maybe he could protect the village…

No. I have a mission. Don't stray from the path.

It was too late anyway. The *Sandinistas* would seize the makeshift armory if they got a whiff of what was really there. Better to leave the thing alone.

John ground his teeth. He was sweating from their trek but Barry was so sweaty he looked like he'd just gotten out of the shower. It was just as well that John had decided to rest for a moment. The sun was starting to peek up onto the horizon and poke through the jungle trees. He could make out the howler monkeys jumping from tree branch to tree branch now, no longer ominous dark figures of shadow.

"Rest here. I have to make a call." John said.

"Please don't leave me again."

John grimaced as he pulled out his phone. "I'll be within eyesight." *Just not within earshot.*

Barry slumped down onto an uncomfortable looking rock, looking downright dreary but not able to do anything about it. John tossed him a half-bottle of water that had been in his tactical bag.

He punched in the number, keeping his Glock loose but ready in his other hand.

The line picked up.

"Esteban?"

"Go ahead," came the familiar low voice of his handler.

"I have the asset."

"What took so long?"

"Paramilitary. Ordered by the president to kidnap Barry."

There was a pause on the other end, then John was put on mute. Esteban was probably giving orders to someone. John wondered if Esteban was trying to get him killed. He still suspected him for foul play in his previous mission in Antigua, and for having something to do with the death of his best friend Brian. But John wasn't sure where that left him.

The line returned and it was as if Esteban had read his mind. "I'm sorry John. I didn't have that information. Where are you now?"

John didn't know what to make of that. But it didn't matter right now. "In the jungle, mile and a half from the beach. No hostiles sighted here."

"It won't be long until they comb their way to your position. Too hot for extraction. Do you have transportation?"

"Yes."

"Get to the Costa Rican border."

"Understood."

John paused to see if Esteban would tell him anything else, but the line simply dropped.

He tucked the phone away and prodded Barry back up. The man was reluctant and exhausted.

"Are you going to get me out of the country?"

John wouldn't tell Barry anything he didn't need to know, but he could tell him enough to keep him from being too discouraged. "Yes. Let's get out of this jungle first."

Barry smiled and John nodded back.

"This way," John said, crouching and leading the way out of the jungle and toward the building.

It was just as well they didn't rest long. Gunshots rang out through the trees, scattering howler monkeys, barely heard above their screams.

John grabbed Barry by the collar one-handed and threw him with a backward toss, then went prone and slid through dirt and vines like a baseball player making a dive for home. John pressed up against the granary's wall, and edged his head out to see how far the enemy was, pulling his gun up to the ready once more.

CHAPTER 8

━━━━━

Mike knew he didn't like the cafe as soon as he walked in the door. The sound of lazy acoustic guitar and low murmur of college students attacked his ears. The smell of coffee and baked goods helped, but the damage had already been done. This was a trendy and artistic location and Mike didn't like either of those qualities.

It was his own fault for letting his assistant Barker choose the location.

The lanky young man sitting at the far end of the cafe's bar waved to him with a full length of arm. Barker was built like a scarecrow and had a similar grace. A young woman walked by the bar with her drink and nearly spilled it when she saw Barker staring at her.

Mike often wondered if his assistant was intentionally creepy or if it just came naturally, looking like a swamp creature and all. But he decided not to pursue such thoughts. He ordered the most normal coffee he could manage and slid onto a stool next to Barker.

"Nice spot," Mike said.

"Right? All the college kids come here. Open mic is tonight," Barker said.

Mike's sarcasm had evidently fallen on deaf ears. At least they were sure to avoid any of their colleagues here.

"Thank you for meeting me," Mike said after taking a sip of his drink. It was still too hot, and he burned his tongue.

"Boss, we work together everyday. Why are you treating this like a super secret meeting we shouldn't be having?"

Mike let the pause linger.

"Ooooooh. Very cool."

"Not the word I would choose but — wait, what the hell did you order?"

Barker looked at his drink like there might be something wrong with it, but failed to see what Mike was getting at. It was a tall cup with a mountain of whipped cream and chocolate drizzling. The straw barely managed to poke out from the monstrosity.

"It's my order. Mocha frap, double cream, double shot, triple the whip but hold the chunks." He narrowed his eyes. "I don't like chunks." He went back to sipping, and loudly.

Mike had no idea what Barker just said. He sighed and tucked in his stool. He propped his elbows on the bar and clasped his hands, resting his chin on them for a moment. It was his own damn fault for asking. Like anything in this job.

"We don't have a lot of time," he said. "I came back from a meeting with Linda."

Barker was all ears now. Still sipping away, but focused. He could read Mike's tone well enough. He was about to hear certain things that shouldn't be falling down the chain.

"She's got nothing more than the party line on Locklee. I'm not expecting anything to change there," Mike said.

"Is she covering?"

"I don't know. I don't think so. Linda's a straight shooter. But she knows more than she's saying."

"So we back off?"

"For now."

Barker took another long sip then gave his drink a disappointed stir, and made a small noise of disgust.

"What?" Mike asked.

"Chunk." Barker scooped it out with his straw, deposited the piece of chocolate on a napkin, then turned his attention back to Mike.

Mike blinked. "Our best option is still infiltrating the PAG. If we're going to get information from anywhere, it'll be from them."

"Sara?"

"Working on it."

"I'm sure you are." Barker gave him a sly grin and a wink which met Mike's dagger-like stare until he choked out an apologetic "Sir."

"How does everyone know about this?"

Barker shrugged. "I'm a spy."

"Who needs to get a hobby."

Barker shrugged again. They both took a sip from their drinks.

"I guess intelligence is my hobby," Barker said.

"Don't say that."

"Why? I mean, why do we do what we do boss? The pay isn't bad, the benefits are nice, but damn if I'm not looking over my shoulder every other day with the whole…business that went down last month."

Locklee. Neither of them wanted to say it out loud.

Mike hadn't revealed to his assistant what their operative John Carpenter had beaten out of Pablo Puentes, the cartel *Patrón* of Antigua. Someone in the CIA was pulling strings in the Puentes family, and when Mike and his team went poking around, the blame and evidence fell on Paul Locklee. Paul may have been an asshole to work with, but he wasn't guilty. No, Mike was looking for some deep corruption in the PAG's end of things. He shook his head.

Wheels within wheels…

Mike was sure Barker could put things together. Barker was sharp as they came. But as long as Mike didn't acknowledge anything for certain, Barker could be kept safe from the whole affair. Or so he hoped.

Why do we do what we do...?

Mike nodded and licked his lips, returning his thoughts to Barker's question. He'd thought about this before. He never realized he hadn't shared his thoughts with Barker. Funny how they could work so closely on the most sensitive missions and hardly know a thing about one another.

"I was in New York working as a detective," Mike said. "Liked the gig. Liked New York. Always wanted to put bad guys away as a kid. Did a lot of that until nine-eleven happened." He took a drink of coffee.

Barker's face dropped. "You were there?"

"When it happened? In New York, but not right there. Was on the island. Meeting a girl for a date."

Come to think of it, maybe that was the last girl I seriously considered. Ah well.

"That made you go CIA?" Barker asked.

"Pretty much. Wanted to save lives. And saving lives is good work. Protecting a country from threats is good work. But there is nothing that makes me work harder than knowing that someone else would do it worse. That they would fuck up everything. And they would." Mike paused to wipe his chin with the napkin sitting next to his coffee cup. "Does that make me a control freak? I don't know. I don't care. It's not the same reason everyone does it. But that's why I do the job. To do it *right*."

Mike's stare was hard. Barker squirmed in his seat.

"Alright boss. I just...it was a rhetorical question was all."

Mike grunted. "Let's pack this up. We don't have much time."

"This about Nicaragua?"

"No."

"Because there's not enough going on…"

"I know. Just listen," Mike said, taking the time to take another long sip of coffee as he collected his thoughts. He rifled in his jacket for the photograph Linda had given him. He laid it on the bar and slid it over, giving a discreet look over his shoulder to make sure no one was walking by or taking a glance. "Linda showed me this today."

"Dead guy."

"Dead agent."

"One of ours?"

"No. I'm positive he's Russian."

"On American soil? That's some drama."

"Even better. Cuba."

Barker swayed back and forth like an excited cobra, his eyes flicking from the photo to Mike like its tongue.

"So…the Cubans must be as confused as we are, but also angrier and feeling betrayed. Nice."

"The Cubans don't know. They think he was American. The photo is courtesy of Cuban intelligence — gloating, presumably."

Barker did some mental math. His eyes narrowed. "What was a Russian agent poking around at that was enough to get him killed? In an ally country?"

Mike nodded. "I was thinking the same thing."

"Bargaining chip for us?"

"Definitely. Russians want a meet."

Barker gasped. "They made contact?"

"Through Carpenter. Just before our Nicaraguan op."

"Huh. You want my opinion?"

Mike shrugged. "Sure." He didn't need it, but it was important to play the mentor once in a while.

"I'd say you're being drawn out."

Mike nodded.

Barker frowned at that. "That doesn't concern you?"

"Everything concerns me."

Barker giggled. "Right. Okay, I guess it just bothers me. You expose yourself and it proves you're connected to an active operative in Nicaragua. They know about our local agent, Carpenter — just as we know about theirs — but we don't know who their handlers are. Those stakes are a bit higher."

"They'll be coming out from under their log too, Barker. I'm counting on it."

"But they could easily send someone lower down the chain to pose as-"

Mike nodded in a way that stopped Barker short. It'd be rude if he had done it to anyone else, but they were close enough colleagues that they had their own secret language quirks that made communication between them work.

"You know Barker, when I first transferred over from crime to intelligence, I really bought into all that spy stuff. Oh, I knew all the things we see in movies are just in the movies, but I was still always looking over my shoulder and managing contacts through code. But after a while…"

The straw in Barker's drink slipped out of his mouth and he gasped in horror. "You got sloppy?"

"No! No, of course not. But after a while it stops being plans-within-plans. It stops being a message within a message. Sometimes two people just need to sit down and talk."

"And this is one of these times?"

"Yeah. But there's still some spy stuff for you to do."

Barker immediately sat up straighter.

Mike felt like a knight sending out his loyal squire to attend to some petty function. He didn't particularly relish that feeling, but when he was in charge, Mike knew things would get done. And Barker loved to play the loyal lapdog, as unsettling as it might be for anyone else.

"Oh boy, whatdya got for me chief?"

Mike suppressed the pain he felt when Barker made him feel like Santa Clause bouncing a kid on his lap. "Dupont Circle. They'll give us a clue. Something to signal who they are before they meet."

Barker nodded, sucking on the rest of his triple-sugar-double-dairy-monstrosity of a drink. "You got it boss."

"And Russian agents…well, they'll be crafty. Mostly just to show off. Look closely."

Again, that over-enthusiastic nod. Mike was silently thankful Barker hadn't made any children. They'd be creepy as hell. "When do you-"

"Now," Mike said. He looked at Barker's drink, grimaced, then got off his stool and moved to the cafe till to order a muffin.

To hell with my diet.

CHAPTER 9

———

"Oh my God! Oh my God!"

The rattle of assault rifle fire filled the air and bullets pinged off trees and concrete. John counted only two *Sandinistas* running toward his position, but more shapes were moving behind. He wasn't about to stand and fight. The enemy had cover and were gaining control of the area.

John and Barry had cover too. They'd be safe for half a minute.

"Come here," John said, slinking along the side of the abandoned granary and moving past Barry.

Barry was coughing and struggling to get up after being thrown to the ground. Dirt streaked down half his face and his pastel clothing hadn't done him any favors.

John approached a motorcycle leaned up against the wall. He did a quick glance-over to make sure everything was in working order as best he could, then climbed aboard.

"Holy crap! Are we stealing a motorcycle?"

Would you shut up? John thought. He shook his head at Barry instead.

"It's mine. Hop on."

"No helmets?"

Gunfire hit the building and Barry ducked instinctively. Men were yelling in angry Spanish, not forty feet away.

Barry climbed aboard without any more argument while John turned the key.

The engine gave a burp but didn't start.

Barry slapped John's arm, indicating they were running out of time.

John clenched his teeth and gave the key a second turn. The engine roared to life.

"Hold on tight."

John twisted the throttle and they were soon on their way, cutting through jungle and hitting the dirt road. In his rearview mirror, John spotted a group of dark-clothed and hooded paramilitary. One even held a red and black *Sandinista* flag. They were making no secret about their assault on the village.

It made John sad. Nicaragua was in turmoil and it wasn't going to fix itself anytime soon. With this attack the country had lost a beautiful place for surfing and a home to many innocent people.

They sped along the road for a while, and John could feel Barry shaking behind him. The man's arms were wrapped around his stomach in a deathgrip. John tried to avoid potholes and rocks as best he could, even if it slowed him down a bit. It'd be no help to have Barry any more panicked. In fact, John counted himself lucky so far. A panicked package was an unpredictable package.

"I bought this motorcycle a long time ago," John said, as he hit a steady pace and they reached a longer, straighter section of road. It wasn't maintained, but it connected to a few other small paths that cars had helped smooth over. "I let the village use it. It sits propped up against that old storage building — it used to be a granary — and we keep the key in the ignition."

"Why would you do that?" Barry asked. He seemed to be composing himself now. Somewhat, at least. John flicked his eyes at the rearview and saw the man's blonde hair flying wildly across his face as he tried to spit it out of his mouth and shake it out of his eyes with little success. Barry caught him looking so John looked away.

"So they can use it," John said.

They were nearly out of El Gigante and on the way to Route 1. There was a short bounce as they transferred from dirt to the paved road of Route 62. Banana and coconut plantations, fields of corn, and potato crops passed by on either side. Barry kept swiveling his head left and right as if he'd never seen Nicaraguan country before. Maybe he hadn't.

"Can you tell me where we're going?" Barry asked.

"Costa Rica. Once we get across the border it'll be easier to get you out."

"And go where?"

"Back to America." That was all John knew. He didn't know who was pulling the man out or what they wanted with him. He was just an agent making sure it happened.

"I'm from California," Barry said, putting on a nervous smile.

John didn't say anything.

"You know, that's usually when you say where you're from. And then we make fun of each other's states. And then we agree on something we do like about each other's-"

"Doesn't matter," John said.

"What?"

"It doesn't matter where you or I are from."

The drone of the motorcycle's engine filled the silence between them.

Barry huffed. "Okay, I get it, you're a super secret tough guy. Interpol or some shit. I don't care. Just figured you'd like to know something about the guy riding your ass."

John looked at Barry in the mirror, then looked away. The man was nervous and trying to fill that with something.

"Canada," John said.

"Canada?"

"That's where I'm from. East coast."

"Wow! Canada! Cold up there?"

"What do you think?"

It would take an hour and a half to get from El Gigante to the Costa Rican Border. They passed the little hamlets of San Cayetano, El Coyo and Tola. John figured they were making good time when Barry pointed at something in the distance, up on the road.

"What's that?"

John slowed down their approach.

It was a blockade.

Road tiles had been pried up one by one and stacked across the road like a thin castle wall. It was only chest-height but was effective enough to stop traffic and protect the dozen students milling about behind and hunkering down as John's motorcycle groaned to a crawl. Some held make-shift weapons, like homemade mortar launchers made out fused metal tubing, looking like small submachine guns. Blue and white flags hung about, and shields cut out of metal drum containers were being handed around.

"John, who are they? The ones that attacked us before?"

"No," John said as they slowed down. "Not *Sandinistas.* These are protestors. Against the government. Probably students from *Universidad Anunciata* and *Universidad Internacional Antonio de Valdivieso* in Rivas."

"Good guys, or bad guys?"

"Just be calm and don't say a word."

Student barricades weren't uncommon with the political tensions against the current government's rise. Oftentimes they would be set up to shake travelers down for money, food, or support in whatever way they could get it.

Barry was about to say something else so John interrupted him with the most assuring tone he could muster. "They don't usually bother *gringos*." But that didn't stop either of them from eyeing the crates of Molotov cocktails off to the side of the barricade.

As they pulled up, masked students streamed out from the barricade to surround them.

Barry flung his hands up in surrender. John stayed still. One of the students stepped forward, wielding an AK-47 — no doubt captured from one of the paramilitary groups terrorizing the country.

"*Gringos,* what are you doing here?" the young man barked out in English.

"*Hola. ¿Cómo estás?*" John said. He figured he'd play a tourist for as long as he could before having to draw his gun or speed away.

The student laughed and turned to the others surrounding John and Barry. "Oh, the *gringo* speaks some Spanish." He turned back to John, getting right up in his face. "What are you doing here?"

"We're just passing through, leaving Nicaragua as quickly as we can," John said in English.

"Ah. Costa Rican border, yeah? Sorry to say it is closed."

That was news to John. *Well shit*, he thought. He'd have to figure out a new extraction point altogether.

John turned his front wheel to indicate he was about to leave but the students weren't done with him yet.

"Ho! *Gringo!* Where are you off to now?"

John shrugged. "Managua. We'll fly out from there."

Managua was the capital of Nicaragua. It was the easiest answer and most plausible, even if John wasn't completely sure where Esteban would want him to go.

"Managua? Why, are you going to tell *El Presidente* about our barricade?"

This was starting to get ridiculous. "Look, we don't want any trouble," John said, raising his offhand and shifting the other to the back of his waistband. John stared down the dark eyes of the student. John could neutralize him quickly, but he'd have to get out of the line of fire of the mortars. That would be easy enough, seeing as how no one seemed primed to fire, but if someone else had a gun...

The eyes under the mask of the student holding the AK-47 narrowed into a smile. The young man reached a hand up and before John could figure out how to respond, the student brought down his balaclava.

"*Mi profesor!*"

John stayed frozen, still uncertain of what was happening. But out of the corner of his eye he saw a few other students relax their weapons, and one even rolled their eyes.

The student in front of him, barefaced now, looked familiar. He had a huge grin plastered on his face.

"Come on *Profesor.*" He handed the AK-47 to one of his compatriots. "You know me."

"Smiley?" John asked. "Jorge?"

"Yeah!" Jorge replied, laughing. "I'm sorry for the scare, I didn't recognize you at first, and when I did I couldn't help keeping up the charade." He flashed his teeth in a mischievous smile that gave him his nickname.

John could hardly believe seeing one of his old students. Then again, Nicaragua wasn't a large country and he had been teaching at the local school for years. The last time he'd seen him he'd been a small kid in the eighth grade. In front of him stood a young man.

"You...look different," John said, eyeing the AK-47 as the other students backed off. "I haven't seen you since..."

Jorge kept smiling like nothing had changed in the slightest. "I went to the *Universidad Nacional Autonoma de Nicaragua, Profesor!*"

"UNAN? Good for you, Smiley."

The kid beamed. "Civil engineering, too! But that was before they shut down the university. Had to come back home to help with the protests."

"Hey…" Barry piped up. "I know I'm not supposed to talk but what's happening?"

John jerked a thumb at Barry over his shoulder. "Old family friend I was showing around the country. But we're thinking it's time to go."

Jorge grew more somber at the mention of that. "Easier said than done."

"Who closed down the border?"

"*Sandinistas*. We set up our barricades to catch people before they can get to them."

John didn't want to ask what they'd been doing with their catches. But if the government had the border shut down it didn't matter if the students would let them through their barricade, even with Jorge's blessing. John would have to call Esteban and figure something out.

"Can you get to Ometepe?" Jorge asked.

John frowned. Ometepe was an island. They'd be cut off, but there wouldn't be any reason for the paramilitary to be there. It also happened to harbor a joint safe-house with the DEA. Previously it was used in the 80's for helping the U.S.-backed Contras seize control of the government. The revolutions never seemed to end.

"I wouldn't trust the ferry," John said, now second-guessing things.

Jorge grinned again and snapped his fingers. "Jorge has you covered. Do you remember Miguel?"

John thought for a moment. Seeing Jorge again had brought up a few memories from the past. Miguel was another of the students he'd taught in the same makeshift class as Jorge.

"He went into the priesthood," Jorge said. "He might be able to help you. He helps arrange transportation for *gringos* and families out of the country. I'm sure he could get you a *lancha*. And I know he'd love to see you."

John met Jorge's grin as best he could. Assuming Esteban agreed to the zone and could use it for extraction, they could be out of the country within a similar timeframe to what they'd originally planned.

"Thank you Jorge. I'll drop by on him."

John didn't have any more time to spare, but he managed to buy a couple water bottles, sandwiches, and a container of beans and rice off the students by giving a generous donation of American bills. It wasn't as if he were the only American funding the protesters against the government.

"So, we've got a way out?" Barry asked as he wolfed down a sandwich.

"Possibly. I've got to make a phone call. Then we head out."

John pulled out his phone, looked over his shoulder as he walked a little ways into the field off the side of the road, and dialed for Esteban.

CHAPTER 10

———

"Well? Anything?"

Mike had just gotten off the phone with John, setting up an extraction point on Ometepe. It wasn't his first choice, but things were heating up enough on the ground that he was willing to take John's lead. He looked up at his assistant. Barker's grin reminded Mike of a deep-sea creature.

"I think so, sir." Mike's assistant produced a pair of photos, dropping them on the desk for his boss to see.

Mike was sitting in his private office attached to the larger command room. The place buzzed with computers and activity from agents monitoring and facilitating operations in Latin America.

Barker continued to leer over Mike and his desk. He flicked a pair of eyes at the photos, then back to Mike, anticipation glowing dangerously in his assistant's eyes.

Mike picked up the photos. They were both variations of a man sitting on a bench, reading a newspaper.

"This is in Dupont Circle?" Mike asked.

"Yes sir. Snapped them from my car."

Mike stared at the photographs. There wasn't anything particularly odd about an old man sitting on a bench. If he spent some time with a picture he was sure he could do some deciphering, but time was of the essence and Barker was rocking back and forth on his heels like he was going to burst with excitement.

"Alright, go ahead."

Barker beamed. "Take a look at the newspaper headline."

Mike squinted. "Something about…a Russian trade deal."

Barker nodded.

"That's a bit of a stretch, isn't it?"

"It could be, but if you look closely at the date, it's five years old. It's not even a front page."

"Which someone would only notice if they were looking," Mike said squinting further, but unable to make out the details described. He looked up at his assistant. "Good work Barker."

Barker looked entirely pleased with himself. That was good. Mike needed to give the man more praise. He didn't need to ask how long it took Barker to scour Dupont Circle with nothing but a vague Russian connection. It must have been painstaking.

"He left something on the bench when he got up to leave," Barker said, pointing at one of the other pictures, showing the man half-exiting the frame.

Mike grunted.

"It's a chess piece."

Mike rolled his eyes. "What chess piece is it?"

"A pawn, sir."

Mike frowned. "Of course it is." He sighed, stood up, and retrieved his coat off its hanger, sliding both arms in and buttoning up. "Fucking spies and their theatrics."

"Sir?" Barker asked, drawing himself up and standing more erect than before. "Where are we going?"

"To play a game of chess."

* * *

Dupont Circle was bustling with people despite the chill in the air. It wasn't a gloomy day, but it wasn't comfortable either. Mike huddled in his coat as he crossed the street and entered the park in the middle of the big traffic circle. He couldn't help but feel like he was being watched. Of course, Barker was keeping an eye on him, but he still scanned buildings for hidden snipers or noted which idle pedestrians were stationary for longer than a minute. Old habits. He missed New York at times like this. In New York, the crowd was a shield. He could move smoothly through people like a boat in a river, letting the current push him along. In Washington, he had to pick his own way, and everyone seemed to be government. It was boring.

At least it's clean, he thought, spotting the chess tables and his man sitting alone near the end.

The man could be described as old but he probably had some good years in him yet. Thinning grey hair was combed back on a narrow head, glasses hid eyes staring intensely at the pieces laid before him, betraying no sense that he was waiting on anyone. Even when Mike sat down across from him, the man didn't look up.

Mike allowed the silence for a moment. A jogger passed by them, a husky towing its owner. Mike glanced at the woman jogging past, and continued to wait until he felt his time was being wasted. He cleared his throat.

"Do you like chess?" the man asked.

"No."

The man frowned. "Shame."

Another silence fell between them.

"Tell your man to back off," the man said. His voice had some gravel in it, but failed to cover the lingering authority in those words.

"What man? I came alone."

The Russian smiled. "The one feeding pigeons. He looks like he likes those pigeons a little too much."

Mike grimaced. He had argued with Barker to choose a different cover. Something farther off and more discreet. But Barker was too concerned for the safety of his boss. He had tried to get Mike to wear a bulletproof vest and wanted to be close enough to spring into action if necessary. And he liked birds.

Mike stared into the Russian's eyes. They were old, true, but contained a playful spark that didn't match the rest of his calm demeanor.

So Mike gave a curt nod, pulled out his cellphone, and ordered Barker away with a text. A moment later, pigeons scattered as Barker stood up — looking ridiculous in the bulk of layers he had insisted as identity cover — tossing the rest of the feed and walking away, not risking a glance over his shoulder.

The Russian smiled. "Good."

"Not quite," Mike said. "Yours too."

"Hm?"

"Your own agent. Get rid of her."

The Russian continued to stare at Mike, unamused.

"Jogger. She passed us a minute ago. The dog is a nice touch."

The Russian's smile faded. He waited a moment, debating whether to grant Mike his wish, before scratching the top of his ear. The jogger Mike had spotted made a turn on the pavement and reversed direction, exiting the park.

"Satisfied?" the Russian asked.

"Immensely," Mike grinned. But he wasn't so much satisfied as he was itching for business.

"Very well." The Russian looked at the board in front of him, looked up at Mike, then moved a pawn forward two spaces.

He didn't say anything else. He waited for Mike, expectantly looking up and down from the pieces.

"I said I don't play chess," Mike said.

"You said you don't like chess. But we all play chess," the Russian replied.

"Let me rephrase: I don't do metaphor bullshit."

The Russian looked pained. "If it weren't for metaphor bullshit, we'd all have to deal with the truth. And no one wants that."

'And ye shall know the truth and the truth shall set you free.' Those words greeted Mike every time he entered the CIA headquarters in Langley, engraved in a stone slab by the entrance.

Mike leaned forward, locking his fingers together over the table. "That's what I came here for. Not to play games."

The Russian cocked his head, waiting for something. Mike leaned back to indicate it was his opponent's move. The Russian picked up a pawn from Mike's side and moved it two spaces forward to stand off against his own.

"Not the opening move I'd make, but…" The Russian spread his hands and shrugged.

"Why did you contact my agent?"

The Russian simply looked at the board, reveling in the brilliance of the game and all the unmade moves that could be executed.

"Why did you want to meet?"

Still no reply. The Russian advanced a knight.

Alright, Mike thought, *I guess we're playing hardball.*

Mike pulled a knight from his back row of pieces, jumped his pawns and placed it firmly on its seat in a new square, again matching the Russian. "Why did your agent die in Cuba?"

The Russian's eyes snapped up and locked onto Mike's, no longer watching the board. Now it was Mike's turn to calmly appreciate the chess match unfolding before them.

He could play the game. He knew he had to play the game. But that didn't mean he had to like it.

"I believe it was an American agent," The Russian said slowly as he selected another pawn to support his first.

"Curious, when a Russian agent pretends to be an American."

"Wouldn't be the first time."

"Won't be the last."

The Russian smiled. "I like you Mike."

Mike bristled at the Russian agent across from him using his name so nonchalantly. It was no secret he worked for the CIA — it was only secret that he headed the Blackthorne taskforce, because Blackthorne itself wasn't supposed to exist. But finding out his identity that quickly…was a bit disconcerting. It all went back to what Barry had warned him about. Mike exposed himself by engaging with this Russian element. His meeting would reveal that he was an intelligence authority in Latin America, at the very least. That could be a valuable piece of knowledge for foreign counter-intelligence. But the sword was double-edged. The old Russian man in front of him revealed the same connection, which at least left them on an even playing field. Both of them were forced to trust the other.

Trust. A hot commodity in the intelligence world. Mike began second-guessing his lack of a bulletproof vest after all. He edged a pawn forward cautiously.

"I think we may be able to work together," The Russian continued, hesitating with his fingers before moving a bishop in a particularly long move toward Mike's side of the board. "That's why I wanted to meet. Mutual interests."

Mike slowly moved a pawn forward a space, noncommittally challenging the bishop. "I doubt that."

The Russian looked up, eyebrows raised.

"But I'm listening," Mike said, pressing down on the pawn's head before letting his fingers go.

The Russian nodded, contemplating Mike's words. Mike expected to be given a backhanded compliment on manners but instead the Russian spoke plainly.

"We believe it would be best to leave Cuba thinking that it was indeed an American agent who unfortunately died during an unknown operation." The bishop retreated to the edge of the board.

"Hard to keep a secret like that without an incentive. I'd be curious to know what the operation was. That might suffice." Mike moved his own bishop across the board, pinning the Russian's king.

The Russian didn't look up from the board. He made as if to move one piece, but elected for another. "Discussing the operation is on the table." He swiftly jumped a knight over pawns to block, but also to pressure one of Mike's pawns. "Provided you agree to certain discretions."

"Are you a defector?" Mike asked suddenly. He realized he should've asked sooner. Protocol for defectors were rigorous and treated seriously, and with haste. This would be a very different conversation if that were the case.

"Hardly."

"Do you speak for Russian intelligence?" Mike asked. He took a pawn with his own.

The old man rocked his head back and forth, considering the question. "Would you speak for American intelligence? The entire CIA?"

Mike frowned. They were both niche departments then. Both working for their nations, both intelligence, but it wasn't as if anything spoken here could represent any agency at large. And that meant any interests or any deals forged...well, nothing was binding.

Mike decided to play it safe and by the book. "I have the interest of the American people at heart."

"Ah, of course."

"I'm not interested in anything my agency wouldn't approve of," he amended.

"So which is it, Mike?"

"Which is what?"

"The American people, or your agency?"

Mike grunted. They were back to playing games.

"Can you say the same?" Mike asked.

"I am intent on keeping Mother Russia safe, stable, and prosperous, without making sacrifices that would compromise any of these qualities."

"Okay," Mike said, knowing when it was time to talk and when it was time to listen to a man express his life philosophies.

"And in my unique position within the…Russian framework, you could call it," here the Russian made an all-encompassing circle with his hands, "I am able to conduct certain dealings independently of the broader Russian government and intelligence, without betraying the motherland."

"You want a backdoor deal," Mike said.

"It is nothing seedy. Nothing that compromises either of our countries."

"But you wouldn't exactly want the rest of the CIA knowing what we're up to. Is that what I'm hearing?"

The Russian didn't answer. He pulled out his queen and brought her to the center of the board. Check. Mike found himself thinking of all the following moves that the queen could make, and all the possible counters he would have to set up in response. Then he cleared his mind, returning to the matter at hand. The chess game was a distraction and the Russian wasn't playing to win. He was toying with him. Mike chose a knight to block.

"Which arm of Russian intelligence would you so vaguely

represent?" Mike asked as the Russian silently moved a pawn forward in a forgotten part of the board. He was genuinely curious if this was diplomatic, internal, or something more military. Those or any other possibilities would decide how he'd proceed. Mike inched a pawn toward the Russian queen.

The Russian thought for a moment before moving his bishop defensively in front of his king. "I…fix things."

"You haven't come to me before."

"That's a good thing."

"Why's that?"

"That means I wasn't needed before."

"And you're needed now? We need you?"

"I'm only concerned with big problems."

"How big is big?" Mike extended another pawn to threaten the Russian queen. The Russian pulled her back immediately. Mike moved his bishop to give chase, and managed to capture a knight in the process.

The Russian pursed his lips, eyes not leaving the board. "Catastrophic." He took Mike's bishop with his queen.

Mike forced himself to forget about the game for a moment. 'Catastrophic' was quite the word. Mike found that Russians loved to toy with their prey, but they rarely exaggerated. Another cultural opposite that forced a gap between their two nations.

"I don't know what you were trying to do in Cuba. But it will take more than a vague threat for American intelligence to willingly pick up the blame. I don't do well with work slipping under the rug. What was the operation?" Mike punctuated the question by moving his knight to pressure the Russian queen.

The Russian picked up his queen as if to continue their game, but dropped it, and didn't bother to pick it up again. He pulled his eyes away from the board to finally look at Mike directly. His voice was harsh, and betrayed the barest hint of his Russian heritage. "We are both loyal agents. Both good agents. Both want to protect and serve our countries and people. Is it impossible to consider whether I know something that may help us both? That we could solve together?"

Mike held the man's gaze. It bordered on desperation. But Mike wasn't going to soften up for theatrics. Not now, not ever.

"Impossible? No. Very difficult? Unfortunately, yes."

Mike was already on a tightrope, digging into a conspiracy and playing Sara for information — all while an active operation was in effect. He couldn't give the Russians a favor for a secret Cuban threat they wouldn't divulge. He'd sooner send it up the chain for the brass to pressure the ambassador with. He could always cash in on the earned rapport in a pinch.

The Russian held the gaze a second longer, then his whole body drooped as he sighed and took on a deflated expression. It was an exhaustion held at bay while verbal fencing and a game of chess had taken precedence.

"Unfortunate. Yes."

They both stared at the board a little longer. Mike felt things were coming to an end. But he hadn't really got anywhere. If the Russian couldn't give him anything, he couldn't hand over the token advantage he held. That was his only bargaining chip. This could all very well be a desperate ploy to stop Russian embarrassment.

"What else is on the table?" Mike asked. He knew they were the wrong words before they were out of his mouth.

The Russian set his cane against the pavement and hoisted himself off his seat. "Discretion. Then we talk. Let me know if this is agreeable." The Russian placed a hand on Mike's shoulder as he passed by, almost making him flinch as he leaned down to speak close in his ear. "And soon."

"We're not done playing yet," Mike said. He thought he could draw more out of this character. This ending was too abrupt.

Which was by design he was sure. Leaving him wanting more.

"Oh, I never like finishing a game of chess," The Russian said, waving Mike's comment away.

"Why's that?"

"Then there is a winner and a loser."

"And?"

The Russian let out a long breath of air, his drooping expression revealing to Mike how old he really was. "Sometimes it's just enough to play the game."

Mike sat and contemplated the board until the Russian disappeared from sight. He didn't like how melodramatic so many of the old-guard liked to keep things. But he supposed a world war and the threat of nuclear fallout would create more eccentric spies. The idle thoughts were nothing worth dwelling on. Instead, he was surprised to find a business card in his pocket when he went to pull out his phone. Slipped into his pocket, probably when the Russian had gripped his shoulder. Clever. He'd give it to Barker to decipher.

He dialed for his assistant, dipping his chin into his coat to achieve as discreet a call as possible in a public park. Barker picked up immediately.

"Barker?"

"Sir? How did it go?" He sounded like he was out of breath, panting.

Mike decided not to inquire. "Later. I need you to assess any situations in Cuba. Activate our assets."

"Sir? I can do that, but the Nicaragua op is heating up."

"Of course it is." Mike wiped a bead of sweat from his face with a hand, wishing idly that he could do the same to his stress. "I'm coming."

"Sir, if you end up doing a meeting again I really think you should wear a vest. We have extras in the-"

Mike hung up and tucked his phone away, fingering the business card the Russian had given him. He couldn't deny the Russian was a professional. He had that much to be thankful for at least.

Yet for all their caution, neither agent had caught a nondescript car sitting on a sidestreet, far on the other side of the park. Sara Burnes sat in the driver's seat, snapping pictures of their meeting all the while.

CHAPTER 11

Jorge had assured John there wouldn't be any more blockades on Route 62 toward Ometepe. But they both agreed Route 1 and 72 into the city of Rivas would be guarded one way or another, and not necessarily by protesters. Although the Nicaraguan government could only cover so much ground, its paramilitaries and general supporters could be anywhere and were unpredictable. John and Barry knew that first hand from El Gigante, so they both agreed to take every precaution and cut a circle around Rivas on the back roads and enter San Jorge from the north. Once in the city Barry grew more concerned but John found himself beginning to relax.

Two *gringos* on the back of a motorcycle was a description the military could spot. But two *gringos* in a city full of Nicaraguans and *gringos* amidst the panic and tension of fervent uprisings spelled safety in numbers. As John took in his new surroundings and watched people mill about, he figured they were jockeying for passage to Ometepe or frantically cutting through the city after turning tail from border patrols.

They left the motorcycle in an alley and picked their way to the address of the church Jorge had given them. *Iglesia San Francisco de Asis* wasn't anything like a cathedral but stood out as a fairly wealthy building for the surrounding parish. Tall dependable brown bricks greeted John and Barry as they made their way up the front steps.

"Oh man, I feel like I'm going to get lit on fire if I go in there," Barry said.

John raised an eyebrow but didn't say anything.

"I'm not exactly the holiest dude, John. Just saying."

A pickup truck drove by with people standing in the back, screaming and waving black and red party flags. John frowned before opening the door and pushed Barry inside. He took a look over his shoulder before ducking in after him.

A quick cursory glance showed that no one was around. John dipped his fingers in the holy water fonts offered at the sides of the door and waved Barry to stop when he started to wash his hands in one. John slid his tac-bag off his back and carried it loosely in one hand. He'd rather be holding his gun, but that might discourage Miguel. Still, anything to stay alert to threats. They might be off the roads, but getting stuck in a building could lead to capture just as easily.

They walked up the aisle and John bent a knee at the altar and the crucifix hanging behind. A priest emerged from the back offices.

"Ah, hello," he said. "Welcome to *Iglesia San Francisco de Asis*. If there is anything we can do for you, please do not hesitate to ask."

The man didn't have a Nicaraguan accent which surprised John, but that didn't mean he was out of place. The priest could have grown up in Honduras or Costa Rica.

"We're looking for Father Miguel," John said in Spanish. "I'm an old friend."

"Ah, you just missed him unfortunately, *señor*."

John frowned. "Do you know when he'll be back?"

"Oh, perhaps in an hour? You're more than welcome to wait here."

John didn't reply. He wasn't sure if holing up to wait for Miguel was their best option. With their timeline, it might make more sense to just bribe someone on the ferry if any trouble came up. Everything depended on how fast the propaganda department could work across the country to get a message out to all government forces that they were to seize Barry and John on sight. The paramilitaries could hardly be controlled that way because they were unregulated self-formed militias, and most low-level national guardsmen would bow to a bribe if it were big enough.

As Barry wiped his shoes on the stone floor and walked around the church to stare at statues, John watched the priest walk back to his office. As soon as he did, John had his gun in his hand.

"What?" Barry asked, wide-eyed at the gun.

John walked over, light on his feet as if he were imitating a cat. He held a finger to his lips to stop Barry from asking anything further. "Something's not right."

Barry opened his mouth to say something else but stopped himself. He was starting to trust John and his instincts.

The priest hadn't bowed or knelt when he passed the altar and crucifix. Any Catholic priest would've done that out of respect without thinking. And although John could initially ignore the lack of Nicaraguan accent, these two things together created one suspicious individual. Anyone suspicious was dangerous.

"Go to the confessional," John pointed. "Stay in there. I'll see what our man is up to."

Barry followed John's eyes to the tall, dark, wooden boxes next to one another beside the wall. He opened the door and slipped inside.

"It smells really bad," Barry whispered.

John didn't answer. He already had his tac-bag on, wearing it in front of his chest for body armour. His Glock was in both hands, pointing forward, following the doorway leading past the wall and into the back.

Dusty sunlight came through windows down the hallway, layering the darkened doors on either end with calming yellow. John controlled his breath and picked his steps wisely, criss-crossing his feet as he moved, keeping even pace and swiveling evenly over each of the doors. There were six in all, and Miguel or this false priest could be behind any one of them.

John didn't hear anything behind the first, but a voice came from the second. He knelt and kept any nerves under control. It was a natural bodily reaction to grow uneasy in difficult situations. It was only a matter of controlling and channeling that into a higher sense of awareness.

Keep calm, move smart, aim true.

He crouched and pushed an ear close to the door, staying silent as dust motes danced around him in the sunlight.

"…I don't know who the other *gringo* is…yes American…"

The priest was evidently on the phone. John narrowed his eyes at the Spanish accent. It was much more prevalent now. Enough so that John could say with confidence that it was Cuban.

A Cuban in Nicaragua making a report to someone else.

"…looking for the priest…Yes…No, nothing else…"

"John!" Barry hissed from down the hall.

John tensed up like a porcupine ready to fire its quills. He snapped his head over his shoulder to see Barry poking his head into the hallway and taking a cautious step forward. John raised a hand for the man to stop and be quiet.

"…I don't know how long, but send them quickly…" the man was saying.

"We have to go!" Barry whispered. He jerked a thumb over his shoulder. "There's a dead guy in the confessional!"

Shit.

That would probably be Miguel. Whoever this impostor was, he had known John and Barry were coming to see Miguel. Had Jorge betrayed them?

Barry was a thorn in John's side, but he had to admit the man was right. Their best option now was to flee and find other passage to the island, or establish a new point for extraction. John tried not to consider that they were rapidly running out of options, and their enemies were slowly closing in on them on all sides.

There was too much to consider. Were the Cubans involved now? No doubt helping the presidential regime just as the Russians were propping up what they could, but even the Russians limited their operatives and didn't directly interfere.

The conversation on the other end of the door had ended abruptly. John couldn't hear the Cuban impostor saying anything else. There was the sound of shifting fabric and the creaking of a chair as the man might be standing up. The sound of a drawer opening…

"John?" Barry whispered.

John held up a finger, listening. As soon as the impostor opened the door and stepped out, John could have his gun against the man's temple, demanding answers.

The faintest *click* sounded on the other side of the wall.

Instinct screamed into John's system. "Down!" he yelled to Barry.

John hit the ground flat on his ribs as three gunshots tore through the door and wall where he had been crouching. Barry ran out of the hallway and disappeared into the sanctuary.

The door flung open and the impostor took a quick step outside the room to establish a diagonal sight line on John with his pistol at the ready.

But John had already spun onto his back and forfeited the time to get to his feet. Instead he pointed his own gun at the far end of the door where the impostor hoped to catch John unawares.

John fired two short bursts, but his enemy was well-trained, unlike the paramilitary he'd dealt with earlier that morning. The impostor ducked and gave the door a kick so it closed off John's visual in an instant. There was a pause on either end. John sucked in oxygen and rose to his feet without using his hands, keeping one out for balance and to push off a wall if need be, the other kept his gun trained on the door.

They were at a standstill. But only for a few breaths. The wall one foot in front of John sprouted a bullet-hole with a crack of gunfire.

A second and third sprouted, and John knew what game the man was playing. He was pushing John out of the hallway so he could get him off the door and secure an exit, but even with John knowing the man's plan he was still forced back. John retreated to the end of the hallway and back against the wall to the left of the doorway. Beside him stood the confessional, and Barry was right. It did have a smell emanating from it that John was all too familiar with.

The quiet of the hallway shivered with the sound of slow and careful footsteps, contrasting with the sharp cracks of gunshots that were still ringing in the air. John looked to find Barry, but he was nowhere to be found.

Shit.

Barry was his primary objective, but he couldn't search for him with this Cuban on his back. John kept his gun trained on the new diagonal sightline into the hallway, and rotated his body to face directly onto it, so any shots coming out would slam directly into the bulletproof plate in his tac-bag resting on his chest. He couldn't afford to get clipped or have a shot slide under the edge of the bag.

Another pause was felt between them. Attackers had an advantage because they knew when they would move and the defender had to react, buying the attacker a fraction of a second more time to get a hit in and end a firefight. But on a turn or an entrance into a new room, defenders could hug the wall and fire across the entryway. John's enemy couldn't fire through the wall to push him out of position again this time because the wall against his back didn't adjoin the hall. John was sure the Cuban would figure out some other trick. It was times like these John almost wished he carried a grenade or flashbang. If either of them were part of a proper fire-team in an urban environment, that'd be the obvious solution to their impasse.

The more present problem became clear to John in the few moments of tense silence between the two of them. John might hold the advantage for defending the door-gap, but the Cuban didn't need to charge it anytime soon. John was the one running out of time. And he had a feeling they wouldn't be alone for much longer. All the Cuban had to do was keep them there.

John made up his mind. The decision could jeopardize the mission, but he couldn't spare Barry the luxury of tagging along with a bodyguard anymore.

John snapped his fingers. "Hey," he called to Barry. He didn't want to say his name out loud. Barry didn't come out from wherever he was hiding until John called again.

"Me?" Barry asked, poking his head up from behind the altar.

John nodded, only seeing Barry out of the corner of his eye, only sparing a little thought for anything that wasn't the gap in the door and the reaction of his trigger finger to any movement.

"Watch the left, I'm going to smoke him out."

Barry was about to say something stupid, but John tapped the side of his nose and Barry actually managed to catch the gesture. *We're feinting.*

"Oh…uh, yeah. Yeah, you got it boss. I got the left. Oh yeah."

John resisted the cringe that came from Barry's poor acting, and held his hand to keep Barry where he was. John backed up a couple of steps…

And the Cuban dove through the entryway.

John squeezed off three rounds before being forced behind the confessional. The impostor had gone full-dive; fully horizontal and flying through the air like a bird, too fast and erratic and narrow a target for John to fully-anticipate. It would've been painful hitting the ground without support, but that also meant the impostor could get off his own three shots at John.

He was pinned again, but now his target was in the open and on the ground. He had to move fast before the Cuban decided to take a shot at Barry...

A shot flew by John just as he was about to poke out, clipping the edge of the confessional and causing splinters to fly. On an edge like this, bullets could bounce and ricochet in unpredictable and possibly deadly ways if the wood was strong enough, changing the direct trajectory of the shot. John decided to come right out, trusting his bag to absorb the first shot the impostor could get off, and down him before any others flew his way.

He jumped out and fired, but the man had already scrambled behind a pew, his head and gun the only things barely visible. They both fired again and both missed, John ducking into his own pew and he heard the other man pull his feet up from underneath. Smart. The first thing John was going to do was fire from below.

"Ah!" Barry screamed.

John thought he'd been hit somehow, so popped up immediately. But the impostor spun around in his pew, just as confused as John. Barry rose from behind the Cuban, giant golden crucifix in his hands. He gave a deranged warcry and brought the thick metal down on the man's head before he could raise his gun to answer.

A muted *thwack* sounded out, like a fist hitting a punching bag, and the man crumpled to the floor, his legs still laying on the seat of the pew.

John waved for Barry to get out of the way but Barry had the crazed look that came from adrenaline and battle. John recognized the expression well.

"Oh my God! I killed a guy! Oh my God!" Barry waved the crucifix around in the air.

John didn't spare a moment pushing Barry behind him and he kept his gun on the impostor's body as he got a closer look. Blunt force trauma to the skull. But the man was pulling in slow, shallow breaths.

"I guess you could say…" Barry was saying, "that he died on the cross."

John opened his mouth to reply but then thought better of it and said something else. "No, still alive."

Barry breathed a sigh of relief but didn't stop pacing.

John got down on his hands and knees, gun at the ready, and slapped the Cuban's face gently. But he was out cold. John would have to wait until he came to if he wanted to pull any information from him. And they didn't have that kind of time.

John snapped a photo of the man with his cellphone and sent it off to Esteban to see if they could dig up anything in their databases. He rifled through the agent's pockets and managed to find a phone along with his gun, but no wallet or identification. The man was probably an agent like John.

"Get him into the confessional," John said.

"What?" Barry asked.

"The priest. Bad guy. Get his legs."

That way if anyone came looking, it might buy them a few precious minutes. They carried the man over and opened the door.

The body of Miguel stared back.

John tried not to stare at his former pupil's grown up face. A clean bullet-hole pocked his forehead, and a thin trickle of blood had begun to dry on the way into an open eye.

To Barry's credit, he didn't throw up. He helped John shove the impostor's weight on top of the other body. He would still probably be out cold, but John wanted to see if he came to while they planned their next move.

He held out the impostor's gun to Barry.

"What am I supposed to do with that?"

The sound of an engine and tires coming to a fast halt came from outside the front of the church.

Barry jumped with fright and John brought up a hand to be silent and pointed to a pew. Barry took the gun from John and got down to the floor, taking cover behind a pew while John checked the door. John wasn't so sure it was a good idea to have given Barry a gun but he was running out of ideas and ways to protect the man.

Churches in much of the West didn't have peepholes. But with the tumultuous role churches found themselves in during various revolutions, many in Latin America came equipped with one by nature of the build.

John saw a pair of men in National Guard uniforms walking up the steps outside the door. A military truck was stopped on the road in front of the church, with four more men hopping out the back and checking gear as they moved.

It wasn't his first choice, but John needed to keep the doors shut. He snapped at Barry to retrieve the crucifix he'd used to knock out the Cuban agent, and slid the length of it through the handles of the heavy wooden doors.

"What do we do now John?" Barry asked, keeping in mind to stay quiet enough that the men outside wouldn't hear anything.

The door shook as the men tried to open it. John could hear the bootsteps of the other men from the truck joining their compatriots. That made six. It was only a matter of time before they gave up on the locked door and moved to pin them through a backdoor — there was sure to be more than one way into the church but John hadn't had a chance to do a proper sweep. That was one of the first things any operative instinctively looked for when entering a building.

Entrances and exits. Doors and windows. Sightlines for bullets going out or coming in.

"Is there a back door?" Barry said, thinking quickly.

"Yes, but they'll be on that soon. There should be a tunnel."

"What? A tunnel?"

"There are tunnels in a lot of the churches in Nicaragua."

"Oh, wait a sec, I read about that!" Barry ran back to the sanctuary. "I saw a trapdoor over here!" he pointed to the floor in front of him.

"You read about it?"

"I was bored on the way over. Saw some churches and their tunnels in a brochure. I'm a tourist. Barry saves the day," he said, nearly dropping his gun as he swept his arms.

John moved behind the altar where Barry stood and found the trapdoor at his feet. They weren't hidden as they once had been. John tasked Barry with getting it open and moved to the confessional. He opened the door. The impostor was still unconscious. Miguel's dead, haunting stare greeted John past the Cuban's neck.

John tucked his gun into the back of his waistband, put a firm hand on the Cuban's cheek and another bracing the back of his head. Then he gave a fast twist. The spin cracked the spinal cord and killed the man instantly. Then he brushed his hands over Miguel's face and closed his eyelids.

"Come on, John what are you doing?" Barry hissed, glancing back at the door. "Saying a prayer?"

John closed the confessional door and pushed Barry into the tunnel ahead of him. He grabbed the handle on the wooden cover and closed it to the sound of pounding fists on the church door. The door handles rattled against the golden crucifix holding their enemies off.

"Something like that," John said.

He sealed the tunnel shut.

CHAPTER 12

"Where does this lead?" Barry asked as they ran down the length of the tunnel. There was no light source. Barry had his phone held in front of him and John was using a small flashlight from his tac-bag. The lights bobbed to their uneven steps, reminding John of a strobe light.

"Main square," John said, careful to watch for rocks in the uneven ground. The tunnel was tall enough that they didn't need to crouch but Barry still felt claustrophobic. It was carved directly out of the dirt. Nothing was smoothed or supported with wooden beams, and no light fixtures had been built.

"This one dates back to the Battle of Rivas, when there was a military barracks in the plaza. Keep up."

Barry did his best to match John's pace. But he was still shaking with adrenaline, the sound of gunfire still rang in his head.

"Here," John said as he reached the end. Barry met him twenty paces behind.

A wooden ladder sat at the end of the tunnel. Barry shone his phone light to see it reach up into another trapdoor.

John tucked his flashlight in his mouth and grabbed the rungs. Barry took a deep breath and tried to steady himself for whatever was coming next. Neither of them thought they'd lost their pursuers so easily.

"Barry," John said.

"Yeah?" Barry looked up to see John standing at the top of the ladder, face a haunting glow and leering down at him. The man turned off his flashlight and tucked it away. Barry started to climb up under him.

John cracked the trap door. He was happy enough that it wasn't stuck or blocked. But tourists were often shown these tunnels so he had little to worry about in that regard. There were other things to be concerned about.

Through the slit of light, John took in a three-sixty of the plaza. There were some people walking around and motorcycles zooming past on either end of the square, but no government forces as he'd half expected.

John looked down to Barry. "Hide the gun," he said.

Barry's gun was sticking out of his back and was sure to attract attention. He fumbled to stuff the gun further down the back of his waistband and adjusted his shirt while struggling to keep hold of the ladder rungs. He frowned when he looked down to see how rumpled and dirty his expensive clothing had gotten.

"When I open this, we're going to run for it," John said.

"Won't that be conspicuous?" Barry asked.

"Yes. But the church towers in the square are a problem. William Walker posted snipers there in the second battle of Rivas."

"What? When was that?"

"1856. But the towers are still there, and I wouldn't put it past our friends to do the same. Come up here."

Barry struggled to stand next to John on the ladder, looking perplexed.

"You're going to go first."

"What? Why? That's not fair, you're supposed to be protecting me!"

John didn't react to the outburst. "It's safer for the first person. They alert the sniper, but it's the second person who gets shot."

"Oh. Uh, thank you."

"Get ready to run. Zig-zag. We're going to the harbor ." John hesitated, then pointed. "That way."

"Okay. I got this. We got this. Zig-zag."

John took a breath, and began to count to three, but that was when he heard a clattering at the far end of the tunnel. The harsh yells of men carried down through the dirt.

They were out of time again.

Barry snapped his head around to look but John hoisted the man's shoulder and flung the trapdoor open. Light poured into the tunnel. John kept his eyes away from the sun to stop himself from getting blinded.

"Go!" John hissed.

Barry scrambled out and John vaulted himself out and into the square right after. He wanted to keep the gap between Barry's exit and his own as thin as possible.

Crack.

Barry cried out as the cobblestones six feet away from them burst and flew up into the air.

A sniper.

"I said zig-zag!" John called.

Barry immediately pivoted and ran horizontally across the plaza. But he wasn't changing patterns fast enough to throw off a trained shot.

Luckily, the gunshot had startled much of the crowd around them into a panic. The square wasn't packed with people, but there were enough of them screaming and running in different directions, trying to get out of the line of fire, that John could use them to cover his movements.

"Those buildings!" John called and pointed to Barry. "The alley!"

He didn't know if Barry heard him but the man tore off in the direction John had spotted. Barry ducked into the alley and John was fast behind him. Barry was still in a mad sprint to get past the buildings and onto the street on the other side when John reassessed their situation.

"Barry! Stop! Wait."

John caught up to him and pulled him aside before he could hit the street. He pushed him against the alley wall, holding his shoulders steady.

Barry's eyes were wide and full of fear.

"More snipers?" he asked.

John shook his head. "No. But now we blend in."

John led the way before Barry could ask him any other questions, pulling him by the arm. They walked as purposefully as they could down the street without it seeming like they were on the run. Just two *gringos* late for the ferry. Nicaraguans and tourists passed through the road as they worked their way to the lake. Their pursuers would still have to sift through panicked people from the square.

They walked by vendors selling hand-carvings and jewelry and clothing. John kept his head scanning side to side and turned around to check behind him for threats when they reached a particularly large clothing stall. No one was following them. For now.

He grabbed two hats, jackets, and sunglasses off the stall and paid the merchant, giving an unnecessary tip. The woman tried to suppress her surprise at the good fortune of such a robust sale.

"Put this on," John said, shoving the clothing at Barry while putting his own disguise on. He had to pull the ballcap on tight before the wind took it away.

"These?" Barry said, looking at the shades. "This is a knockoff. And I'm going to look like I'm from the eighties in this jacket."

"Put it on."

Barry punched John playfully in the arm. "Hey, I'm joking man. Good idea."

John grunted and he pulled Barry along when he stopped to look in a vendor's mirror. John did another sweep, then pulled out his phone and a pair of earbuds. He left one ear hanging out so he could still listen for threats, then called Esteban.

The phone rang twice then picked up.

"Esteban?"

"Go ahead."

John didn't like calling his handler in the middle of a crowd but there wasn't time to get to a quiet location. And he had to update things as soon as possible.

"Got in a fight at the church. I sent you a picture of an impostor priest. He's Cuban. Got a phone and a gun but nothing else."

Esteban's deep voice resonated through John's earbud. "We ran his photo. Cuban intelligence."

John's eyes shot up at that and he took an involuntary look over his shoulder. The average person wouldn't think it, but Cuban intelligence forces were among the best in the world. Things had just gotten more dangerous.

"What are they doing in Nicaragua?" John asked.

"Asking the same question here."

Helping a socialist ally perhaps? But what help did the Nicaraguan government need? They wouldn't bring in Cuban intelligence to help with the protests. Soft influence, sure, but not boots on the ground.

Unless it was the other way around. The Cubans needed something from Nicaragua.

It had to do with Barry. John could think of no other more obvious answer. But why was he so important?

"Escaped through a tunnel with National Guard right behind us,"

John continued. "The agent called them in. We made it past a sniper in the square and now heading for the ferry."

John stopped, thinking if Esteban was in on things, and trying to get John and Barry killed, or capture Barry for himself. He still didn't trust his handler after Brian's death in Antigua, and the suspicious way he'd asked John to transfer information garnered from Pablo Puentes before his assassination.

But he didn't have a choice either. If Esteban really wanted him dead, it would have played out much simpler than this. John didn't know what to think. His job didn't include that kind of thinking. He knew there were puzzle pieces far above him, behind a secret curtain, and he wasn't privy to any of it.

He blinked and shoved all the conflicting thoughts from his mind. He couldn't afford to think of those things. Not right now. They'd mess with his head. Make him slip up. He had a job to do.

John passed by a tourist vendor promoting different activities and attractions in Nicaragua. He snatched up a ferry guide. "Assuming we get onto the ferry…" he flipped the pages to find the departure and arrival times. "We'll be at the safe-house in under two hours."

"I'll have air extraction ready for you. Notify me when you're on the island. Let's time this right."

"Yes sir."

"Anything else?"

John hesitated again. "Yes sir. I'm concerned Cuban agents may have infiltrated the student groups. There's no other way that agent could've intercepted us at the church so fast."

"Okay." Esteban's monotone of disinterest came out more as a question than an answer.

"Background checks?"

John could hear Esteban's exasperated sigh through the phone. "Thank you for the suggestion, John. Get Barry to the safe-house."

Another pause, then the line cut out. John dragged Barry from ogling a pair of pretty Nicaraguan girls who were eyeing him up and down.

"We are business colleagues in the tourist industry," John said, feeling for his wallet.

"What?"

They reached the line for the ferry and John tried to press up close and sink into the crowd. Most were tourists who looked more ridiculous than they did, which was helpful. Most sightlines would be blocked. But that didn't mean a truck of paramilitaries couldn't disperse the crowd and meet them head on.

"That's our cover."

"That won't match my ID," Barry said searching for his own wallet. "Wait, where's my wallet?"

John found his own missing from his back pocket as well.

"Pickpocket," John said, snatching a glance at the road of vendors behind them.

"What? When?" Barry spun around and looked back from where they'd come. "My wallet!"

It wasn't the first time John had been hit by a pickpocket. But it was the first time in a long time that he hadn't noticed. Maybe they were getting better. But it was more likely he was getting distracted.

While Barry lamented his loss, John unzipped a hidden pouch under his shirt and discreetly pulled out some *Córdobas*, the Nicaraguan currency. The fake wallet he kept in his back pocket only held forty bucks at a time.

As the line filed forward for people to buy their tickets and board the ferry, the itch of panic started to overtake Barry again. John didn't blame him. He was getting a bit of anxiety himself. There were few things worse than waiting when danger could be anywhere, with nothing to do about it.

"What if…I mean, won't they know we're getting on the ferry?" Barry asked. "They're looking for us!"

John nodded as he took a photo of the sky with his phone, blending in with the rest of the tourists around them. "It depends how far they've sent the message out. But I don't think they'll bank on us taking the ferry."

"Why not?"

"The island is isolated. It's the last place they'd think we'd run to. Makes more sense to book it northwest for Managua or somehow sneak through the Costa Rican border."

Barry didn't seem to find any comfort in that.

"Once we're on the boat, it's smooth sailing."

"Okay," Barry said. "Okay."

"Actually," John frowned. "Not really. Do you get seasick?"

"What? No way, I'm a surfer."

"Right. But-"

"Hey, I've been on the Alcatraz Island tour in San Fran. Twice." He lifted a pair of fingers to emphasize this.

"That's the only store that sells *medicamento para el mareo*," John said, pointing to a small store beside the water.

"I don't know what you just said."

John reminded himself that patience was a virtue. "Pills for seasickness." The wind tore over their heads and whipped at their clothing. One lady lost her hat and went running frantically after it. The ferry before them rocked back and forth. "I'm surprised they haven't canceled the ferry." Nicaragua's current rainy season was stormier than normal.

"Why don't you go get *'medicanto para la maro* '?" Barry asked. "I'm fine."

Barry folded his arms. "Alright, big guy. Then so am I."

A truck of *Sandinistas* drove slowly down the street, honking at passersby and warning people to get out of the way. Small flags waved on either side of the truck's mirrors and a man in the back waved a larger red and black flag at gawking tourists. John pointed away from them, making Barry keep his eyes forward. By the time the paramilitary truck had passed and their whoops and yells fell down the street and into the crowd, it was their turn to buy their tickets and board the ferry.

"Feels a little rickety," Barry said as they crossed the gangplank and hopped aboard. The small boat seemed to rock in response to their added weight.

John didn't respond. Tourists walked to the second level to press against the guardrails and look out onto the lake. John suggested they do the same. He wanted to blend in with the other tourists as much as possible and be far away from any guards inspecting the line.

Lake Nicaragua or *Lago Cocibolca* — its indigenous name — was the largest lake in Nicaragua. It wasn't comparable to the Great Lakes John was used to in Canada, but it still made up around ten percent of the entire country's territory.

"How long?" Barry asked, staring ahead into the horizon at the island of Ometepe.

Two large lumps rose from the land in the distance ahead of them. 'Ometepe' meant 'two mountains,' but the two lumps were actually dormant volcanoes. Ometepe was the only island in the world with two volcanoes in a freshwater lake.

"Just over an hour," John said.

The horn blew to signal their departure. That gave John and Barry a small feeling of relief. It would be much harder for anyone to find them now. And John still thought no one would be expecting them to make their way to the island. For the first time since last night, they weren't in immediate danger. True, they were still technically on the run, but at least they could rest their legs.

Well, John could.

Barry started looking pale in the face. He rocked back and forth on his heels and kept taking quick shallow breaths.

John gave him a questioning look.

"I'm fine," Barry snapped.

The wind had continued to pick up with a fury since their launch. John was surprised they hadn't cancelled the ferry altogether and turned around. The swells reminded him of the angry Atlantic off the Newfoundland coast. One of his earliest lessons as a child was to respect the Ocean's fury and understand it wouldn't respect him back.

"The first time I took this ferry I thought it was going to keel over," John said. He didn't usually indulge in storytelling, but he didn't want Barry going stir crazy. "The waves get really rough on Lake Nicaragua. The perfect waves forming in Playa Amarillo — you know, where we surf?"

Barry burped, then gave a quick nod.

"The winds that make those waves whip right over this lake." John breathed in the air as lake water sprayed up from the boat before him. He was always happy to be out on the water.

Barry didn't seem to be enjoying things quite as much.

Most of the other tourists were heading down into the cabin or to sit in their cars to get away from the chill and the damp air. John decided to make a discreet call to Jorge.

"*Hola*," Jorge's voice came through John's earbud.

"Smiley? It's John."

"*Hola* John! Did you get to Ometepe? Did you see Miguel?" he asked in Spanish.

John wasn't about to give his location away, especially if he didn't know he could trust Jorge. But John had a hunch his former student was clean, and someone else in the pack was the problem.

"No, had to go to Managua. And…I'm sorry Smiley. But Miguel is dead."

"W-what?"

"Check your people. Whoever heard you say to go to the church."

"*Sandinista?*"

John wasn't about to tell Jorge Cuban intelligence was involved. "I don't know. Something like that."

"Okay, okay." Jorge's tone had grown more serious than John could imagine coming from him. There was a pause then some whispering. Like Jorge was ordering someone to do something quickly. "We had suspected an infiltrator at one time but…okay. Thank you John, we'll take care of it."

"Smiley?"

"*¿Sí?*"

"Be careful."

John hung up. If Jorge was the traitor, he'd report that John was off to Managua. If he wasn't, hopefully he could root out the Cuban contact. But John didn't like the odds of student protestors encountering Cuban intelligence. He wondered if he'd just made things worse for them. Nothing to do about it now.

"John?"

John saw what it was a moment before Barry had prompted him. A national guardsman was moving around the deck talking to individuals, asking them questions and checking identification. He climbed the stairs and made his way to the upper deck, beginning with those across from their position.

"What do we do?"

John's expression was impassive. "Nothing."

"What? What do you mean nothing?" Barry asked.

"I'll take care of it."

Barry wanted to reply but the guard was within earshot now.

Barry could feel his nausea rising as the boat swayed and as the guard worked his way across the deck to them. He wore a crisp white uniform with the red and black armband of the *Sandinistas*.

"*¿Entradas?*" the guard asked. *Tickets?*

John was quick to produce them. The guard nodded and ticked something off on a notepad he was carrying.

"*¿Identificación?*"

John shook his head and patted his pockets. "We don't have any."

The guard lifted an eyebrow, wearing a dangerous expression on his face.

"*Carterista,*" John said. *Pickpocket.*

"Your bag," the guard said in English, pointing to John's tac-bag.

Barry glanced nervously at John, but John put the bag on the deck, unzipped it, and pushed the sides open from the bottom. Everything looked fairly regular: some pill bottles, water, flashlight — not much else. The level IV grade armor plate of kevlar and ultra-high density poly-ethylene was hidden in a slip at the back behind the handle; nothing other than a laptop could be kept there, and was of no interest to the guard.

He nodded, and John thought everything was satisfactory until the guard said again:

"*Identificación.*"

Not a question this time.

John looked to Barry, hoping that his partner would confirm the story about getting pickpocketed — which was true — but Barry was whiter than a ghost.

He looked at John, looked at the guard, the ferry gave a lurch, and Barry promptly lost his lunch.

As he vomited he turned to face over the railing and into the sea, but not before bile splashed onto the deck and slopped onto the guard's immaculately shined black shoes.

"¡*Hijo de puta!*" *Son of a bitch!* the guard cried, looking at his shoes then taking on an aggressive stance. He moved to hit Barry. "¡*Puto gringo! ¡Puto gringo!*" *Gringo whore! Gringo whore!*

John grabbed the fist going for the back of Barry's neck in his palm like he were catching a fastball. The guard's eyes widened in surprise but John let go of the fist and raised his hands, deflating an aggressive response before it could happen. He didn't move to hit the guard either. Instead he reached into his money belt and pulled out a thick wad of American dollars.

"Something to clean up this mess," John said in Spanish, pressing the money into the guard's hands. "You can't have *El Presidente* see you like this!" John gave the guard a grin, and when the guard felt the paper in his hands and took a cursory glance at so much money — in American — and he gave a knowing smile back.

One more hour, John thought, as the sound of Barry heaving filled the deck.

CHAPTER 13

Mike had enough to occupy his mind without Barry and Carpenter nearly getting killed by a Cuban intelligence agent. But with John on the ferry and on the way to the Ometepe Island safehouse, this chapter of his problems would be coming to an end. The PAG would get their asset and John could be relocated and reset on standby. Once that was taken care of, Mike could get back to working Sara for information, infiltrating the PAG, and getting down to the dirt of finding out who was pulling the strings behind the Puentes cartel.

When Mike entered the code and opened the door to the command room, half the keyboard jockeys in their seats spun around to give him their attention. Light spilled in from the hallway, making some of them squint. They lived most of their lives plugged into the framework of top secret intelligence gathering and execution. Experts at their craft, Mike couldn't imagine doing half the work they could conjure up. But he was Chief Operations Officer. His job was to direct them. They may be a sharp sword, but only as accurate as he could swing.

"Sir," Barker said, approaching Mike as he removed his jacket.

"Prep for extraction," Mike said, sending his staff back to hammering at their keys and establishing communicative lines for relevant monitoring. The wall in the front of the room boasted massive high-resolution monitors and viewing screens, always making Mike feel like he was in a small movie theater, although the rows of jockeys at their desks clicking and clacking away took apart the illusion. The main screen brought up a strategic map of Nicaragua, highlighted with small moving shapes. They were all color-coded to represent allied assets and any other known items of interest. It always surprised Mike how many different ships and planes from different nations traveled far from their home countries, for seemingly innocent purposes. If the average person only knew...

No use getting distracted on the irrelevant, he thought to himself. "Barker."

"Yes sir."

"What assets do we have in the area?" Mike asked, accepting a cup of coffee made to his liking from his assistant. He looked to the screen and it refreshed its data. This was completed every fifteen seconds, globally.

Barker pointed and an agent following his silent direction zoomed in on the map of Nicaragua, isolating an area and tossing it up on a secondary screen. The colors and shapes of their assets grew larger, and the nuances of their directional paths increased.

"The *USS Ronald Reagan* is just off the coast of Nicaragua, a hundred and fifty nautical miles in the North Pacific," Barker said with a smug little smile as the map highlighted a large moving square in the water. A hovering label '*USS RONALD REAGAN*' followed its movements with the refresh. "Cruising by on hurricane watch. She's a hefty aircraft carrier suitable to our purposes and the Navy has given permission to the SOG to utilize its assets and resources."

"Alright we've got the red tape covered. Let's notify her that we want to borrow a few things."

"Already done sir," a young computer jockey piped up. "Would you like me to place a call?"

"Please," Mike said, nodding his approval at the progress taken in his absence. "Let's make sure everything's as it should be," he said under his breath, just loud enough for Barker to give a ghastly grin.

Mike's headset crackled. "*Reagan* here."

Mike cleared his throat. "*USS Ronald Reagan*, this is an undisclosed division of the SOG requesting assets. Callsign BlackTree."

"Uh…" there was an uncomfortable pause and shuffling on the other end of the call. Barker gave a giggle as he sensed the surprise that must be occurring to the ship's communications. Poor squids.

"Yes sir, BlackTree understood," the voice came back, somewhat out of breath. "Uh…okay ready for sequence protocol-"

Mike glanced at the code on the clipboard Barker held in front of him. The code corresponded to the Special Operations Group's acquisitions number and changed out every week. It was basically a high access master password.

"One-Echo-Niner-Tango-Eight, over," Mike read.

"Received…sending for approval…"

Mike nodded for Barker to get back to managing the team while he waited for the shock to wear off enough of the rust on the communications officer's procedural duties. It was rare if ever that someone in the SOG called to requisition assets, let alone a secret division that had authorization to keep its true project name invisible.

"Captain approves," the communications officer said, again a little out of breath. "What can we do for you BlackTree?"

"I need a chopper for extraction in Nicaragua. Approximately two hundred nautical miles from your position. Sending coordinates now," Mike said, getting a nod from a computer jockey.

"Ometepe," the communications officer said as the coordinates were sent. "Received. What's our timeline looking like here boss?"

"Now."

The communications officer cleared his throat uncomfortably. "Okay…MEDEVAC?"

"Combat."

"Whew, alright. We have a pair of Seahawks on board that can be prepped in fifteen."

"Perfect. We only need one."

"Understood. Is this cleared with Nicaraguan airspace?"

Mike didn't have time for stupid questions. "We have two assets trapped in a zone that may be going hot. Can you get this done?"

"Yes sir. Understood. Sending all necessary data to you now…" the sound of a keyboard came through the headset, "and giving you a live feed. Anything else we can do for you?"

Mike felt like he was on the line with customer service. "No. Thanks. Good hunting."

"Out."

The line dropped. One of the secondary screens now overlooked the deck of the aircraft carrier *USS Ronald Reagan,* via live video provided from the Seahawk. Crew in bright jumpsuits ran across the deck, prepping the helicopter for its launch. Mike was glad to see the hustle. Nothing like a call from black ops to get things moving.

"What's our team comprisal," Mike asked no one in particular.

"Two pilots, three SEALs sir," an agent answered, barely looking up from their terminal.

Mike nodded his approval. They needed to be quick, quiet, in and out. These people had trained a hundred times for missions just like this one.

Hang in there John. We're going to get you home.

* * *

The island of Ometepe crawled closer to them, bobbing as the ferry dipped and teetered amidst the waves. John gazed at the island, allowing himself a small moment of reprieve from his constant alertness, and acknowledging the fatigue that had started to slip in on him. He recalled the words of Mark Twain, who had described the island of Ometepe in his writing:

Two magnificent pyramids, clad in the softest and richest green, all flecked with shadow and sunshine, whose summits pierce the billowy clouds.

There was a surreal quality to the two volcanic mountains sprouting from the water in front of them, like a primal call to times before man.

They were down on the main deck, sitting in waiting chairs to escape the chill air of the upper deck. Barry had enthusiastically explained his app developments to John before he'd decided a quick nap was in order. Now the man was snoring softly, leaning on John's shoulder. John frowned when he noticed the drip of drool slowly making its way onto his sleeve. He shook Barry awake.

"Huh?"

"We're almost there. Stay close. We'll be moving fast."

Barry struggled awake and hadn't quite heard what John had said or what he'd meant. But he found out soon enough.

As the boat was docking, John led Barry out of the cabin and beside the gangplank even before it had rolled out. Other passengers were getting into cars and the crew were trying to herd tourists while completing their docking tasks at the same time.

They had docked in the village of San José del Sur. John texted Esteban that they'd arrived and wasted no time to disembark. He and Barry were the first off and moving for the road. John waved down a taxi and gave the driver an address. He wouldn't give the address of the safehouse as a precaution, but gave a nearby address instead.

Barry gaped at the volcanoes out his window, staring up at them like a child seeing a skyscraper for the first time. John pointed out directions to the driver with his bag on his lap, and other hand resting comfortably on his leg, ready to draw his gun if needed. He'd had incidents in cabs before.

But it seemed that the action of their adventure was coming to an end. They made their way up a sloping road at the base of one of the volcanoes. Houses arose on the terrain like a set of stairs, staggered on the land rising up from the lake. No one stormed the car when they reached their destination, and no one was waiting outside the small nondescript house that would shelter them, and it hadn't been torched like John's own home had. He scowled at the memory, and let any thoughts about that escape his mind. He hadn't slept on the ferry, and he knew fatigue was getting the better of him. He popped a caffeine pill and led Barry to the front door. A number lock kept them from proceeding inside.

"What's the code?" Barry asked.

John pulled out his phone and dialed the rotating general-function code that changed every week. Once entered, he punched in the number for 'safehouse,' 'Nicaragua region,' and the address. An automated female voice read out a small string of numbers, and he entered the code on the keypad.

"Whoa," Barry said, and John gave him a look that Barry took as a wink.

Once inside, John did a cursory check to make sure there were no security breaches: any indication of tampering, break-ins, or even anything left from previous use that could pose a problem. The safehouse had a small and simple layout similar to John's house in El Gigante. Barry flopped on the couch and leaned his head back against the cushion. He looked ready to fall back asleep again. John couldn't blame him. He felt the same way.

But the caffeine pill was kicking in and John hadn't found any issues with the safehouse. He made sure the blinds were drawn on any windows, then began to feel around the walls until a panel pushed in. He popped the thin wooden panel off the wall, revealing a hidden set of shelves and a safe on the floor.

John turned around, expecting Barry to say something in excitement, but the man was out cold, softly snoring away, just as he had on the ferry.

The shelves held various pieces of tactical and survival gear; flares, MRE's, flak jackets, blankets, water, gasoline cans — even a scoped hunting rifle. John grabbed two water bottles and a smoke grenade that was stored on one of the lower shelves and sealed the hidden wall back in place.

He allowed himself a moment to sit on the couch next to Barry and breathe and drink some water. They managed to eat on the ferry but that had been the last of their food and water. Their supplies didn't matter much now though. John checked his phone. Extraction would be inbound and arriving any minute.

John decided not to wake Barry until he had a visual. He peered out the curtains behind them and scanned the sky. It was a bright afternoon sky, and the volcanoes looked as if they were kissing the blue expanse on canvas. It was beautiful. John wished he could appreciate more things like that.

* * *

Mike downed his coffee and folded his hands behind his back, watching the main screen display the helicopter's progress over the lake. They'd watched the takeoff from the *Reagan* and its swift flight over the Pacific through the live feed from the cockpit.

"Sir?"

One of Mike's staff was calling on him, holding a concerned expression that didn't instill any comfort.

Mike wanted to say *"What now?"* but instead simply arched an eyebrow. It had the same effect.

"It's the *Reagan*."

Mike wanted to make a retort but that wouldn't do any good. And an instant later he grew more concerned than exasperated. "Send it to me."

His headset received the call. "BlackTree?"

"This is him. What's the issue?"

"We've got something in the water…sending imagery your way."

Mike snapped his fingers at Barker and his assistant stopped hovering over a computer jockey's screen and looked up at a secondary screen.

"Move it to the main," Barker said, when he saw what they were looking at.

The main screen took on the imagery from the *Reagan*. It was a capture from a sonar still frame.

Their aircraft carrier had found something under the water that shouldn't be there.

The shape wasn't distinct enough to be certain of what it could be, but the size indicated something big. And there were only a few things able to creep around the depths with that kind of mass.

Mike smoothed his expression before anyone noticed his stern demeanor falling. He had to appear in charge at all times. Even in moments of insurmountable surprise.

Mike cleared his throat as the main screen switched out again for their real-time map. A marker appeared in the image's location, beside the indicator for the carrier. It held the shape of an hourglass and displayed in purple, meaning it held an 'unknown' status.

"Is that a sub?" Mike asked the communications officer on the other end of the line.

"We believe so sir. At first we thought it was a whale because of size but, well, metal reads a little different than biomass…"

"Have you hailed it?"

"Twice. Our captain wasn't as concerned about spooking it as much as he wanted to know what it was and what it's doing there."

Mike wasn't sure if that was the right call, but he was thankful that it wasn't his hard decision to make.

"Any word?"

"We're getting identification numbers now…it's confirmed as a submarine."

Mike did the equivalent of twiddling his thumbs by folding his arms and staring at the screen, doing his best to ignore the jockeys ogling the unknown blip.

"BlackTree we have nationality confirmation. It's Russian."

The words rung in his head, reverberating as if a gong had been rung loud enough to stun him. He blinked the feeling away.

"What's a Russian sub doing off the coast of Nicaragua?"

"Sitting in front of our aircraft carrier," Barker said, grinning back at Mike as the purple icon changed to orange, indicating a potentially hostile unit.

Mike scowled back at him and focused on the information he needed from the situation developing.

"Standard reconnaissance vessel," the crewman said. "At least that's what they're saying."

"And they just happened to end up in our way?"

"They're claiming an unplanned pathing maneuver, and unforeseen interception issues."

"I bet."

"It's not as if they could've known we'd suddenly be moving

toward the coast," Barker said.

Mike gave him a scowl that said *nobody asked you for your opinion*. Barker shrugged and yelled at someone to get more real-time data on the sub. Then Mike had a dangerous thought that sent ice down his spine.

"What's the status on that Seahawk?"

Some of the computer jockeys turned to answer him but Barker waved them off as he crept closer to his boss. Barker began to mouth a silent question but Mike gave him a sharp look and held up a finger, telling him to wait.

"On approach now...we're almost clear of the lake," the communications officer answered over the line.

Mike stroked his chin and let his instincts take control. "Call it back."

"Sir?" both Barker and the officer asked, surprised.

"I said call it back! Now!"

"Sir!" The communications officer began to hail the chopper to relay Mike's order.

"What is it sir?" Barker asked.

Agents glanced nervously at Mike until he realized they were looking at him, and glared long enough to send them back to their keyboards. Mike looked at Barker and they shared a stern look.

"That sub would've seen us send in our chopper. It's compromised."

"We don't know that..." Barker said. He didn't sound convinced.

The Russian Navy would have witnessed an American aircraft carrier launching a military chopper into a foreign country's airspace, without permission, on a blackops mission. Unwittingly, Mike had given Russia a front-row seat to watch a secret mission unfold before their eyes, giving them ammunition the next time they needed to tarnish America in the international community. Linda would not be impressed.

Barker squinted as he considered the implications. "What do you think they'll do? Confront the US Navy? Make a show?"

That would force the Navy into an awkward position, all thanks to Mike. But the worst of Mike's worries was yet to come.

He had just previously participated in a clandestine meeting with a shrewd Russian intelligence officer. Mike hadn't been particularly cooperative, and while that could hold its own form of leverage, Mike had a growing gut feeling that they'd find a way to punish Mike's tactics before they'd negotiate further.

"It has to turn around," Mike whispered.

He frowned at the screen as it shifted back to the feed of the Seahawk.

* * *

A black dot formed and grew amidst the clouds, like a small bug on the window. When it formed to the size of a bottle cap, John nudged Barry.

"Time to go," John said, handing him a bottle of water and strapping his bag on his back.

"I hate waking up to you everytime I try to sleep," Barry muttered.

"It's the last time. Come on."

John grabbed the smoke grenade and pushed Barry out the door. He did a quick look-around the safehouse to make sure they hadn't left anything awry, then closed the door. It locked automatically with an electronic whine and click, turning the bolt in place and giving a beep alerting them that the door's alarm was set once again.

"Stand back," John said.

He pulled the tab on the grenade and tossed it a few feet in front of him. Red smoke spewed out of its end, pulled by the wind and spread upward like a spray of bloody seawater. It would give away their position to any enemies, true, but it would also save the pilot the trouble of pinpointing their location through radio or GPS transmission — both of which could be picked up from farther away. Locating personnel for extraction by air was a much harder task than most people assumed, especially in a location with plenty of buildings and varied terrain.

Barry coughed even though he wasn't near the smoke. John kept the tab and shoved it in a pocket. It was always a good idea to keep any leavings from curious eyes, even if he'd be long gone. Putting the tab in his pocket reminded him of throwing his first grenade in basic training a lifetime ago. All recruits had to chuck and duck, and they kept the tabs as a souvenir of pride. If someone asked you to show it, you had to pull it out of your pocket or you owed the other squaddie a beer. But the tradition had soured after one of John's fellow recruits failed a chuck and duck. The pin of his grenade had gotten caught on his shirt and pulled prematurely. The drill sergeant managed to save the kid's fumble and get the grenade in the air, and luckily the shrapnel scattered over their heads as the sergeant pulled the trainee down. But no one felt much like showing a tab at the bar for a while after that.

"Where are they coming from?" Barry asked.

John blinked. They were much closer to the Pacific than Atlantic, and he assumed they'd be sending in a bird off an aircraft carrier. He pointed to the sky for Barry's benefit.

Even though John saw what was coming, he could hardly make out the sound.

Muffled rotor blades whipped in the sky as they watched the helicopter cruise toward them. Stealth rotors masked the loud blades most would expect to hear from a regular craft, especially for how low it flew. She had almost cleared the lake and would be able to take a near-direct line of flight for John and Barry.

"Whoa, is that a Blackhawk?" Barry asked.

John gave him a sharp look. "You know your military choppers by sight five miles out?"

Barry wilted under John's question. "No, no, I mean, it's the only helicopter name I know. I was guessing."

That almost made John smile. "Good guess. In the same family of Sikorsky S-70's, but that there, is a Seahawk."

"So *you* can tell military choppers by sight five miles out?"

"Yeah. It's a different color."

Barry grinned. They were both tired and a little giddy to be getting out of harm's way and each into a shower.

The Seahawk continued toward them, a big grey-blue mass spinning its four rotors and blending into the sky.

John figured there might be SEALs aboard. He always liked running into SEALs. They were his people. He couldn't talk to them about any of his covert work, of course, but they knew that and they couldn't talk about their own. That didn't matter. It was a bond. They could talk about anything else or share comfortable silence, because they all knew the hell they all had to go through to get their rank or sport the frog-and-trident tattoo they all had. John gave his shoulder an affectionate slap.

The sound of rocket exhaust lit the air.

John ducked out of instinct and pulled Barry to the ground. He collapsed, prone, getting used to this kind of treatment and not even complaining about it this time. John squinted at the Seahawk to see what it was firing upon. It had Hellfires at its disposal but no plume of smoke spouted from the aircraft. Instead, John heard the sound of machine gun fire in the air, and just managed to spot the cabin-door-mounted machine gun pointing at a target down below.

A split second later, John saw what was happening. The missile streaking through the air wasn't coming from the Seahawk.

It was surging *toward* the Seahawk.

Like a giant arrow in the sky, the missile moved in a smart arc for the helicopter. The Seahawk's missile approach warning system kicked in and triggered the aircraft's countermeasures. Flares popped off from the aircraft as it banked for emergency maneuvers, but both actions came far too late. The Seahawk was flying low to the surface and the missile was guided.

It smashed into the cockpit and exploded into fire, turning the Seahawk into a wreck of molten metal and flesh as what remained fell from the air. The shrapnel crashed into the water, tossing up a geyser reaching for the sky. The image burned into John's vision before he ripped his eyes away and pulled Barry off the ground.

CHAPTER 14

———

The control room erupted into chaos, echoing the explosion of the chopper.

Initial shock began to wear off and the air was suddenly filled with a frantic energy that was underpinned by a razor taut wire of tension. Like bees in a hive, everyone leaped to their stations and headsets at once, reacting to the emergency with heightened efficiency.

"We need another bird in the air!"

"Get me the *Reagan*. I'll take it on line two."

"Skies are clear twenty miles out…scratch that — two birds inbound! Nikki choppers, identifying now…"

Mike watched the main screen with folded arms and a look of extreme concern on his face. His brow was folded so tightly it was beginning to cover his eyes. He didn't notice. His mind was whirling with contingency plans, counter-strategies, and a string of orders prioritized as fast as they rose to the surface.

Barker snatched the headset off an agent who had made contact with the *USS Ronald Reagan*. He paced while he gave a sharp report, and ground his teeth while he listened to the response.

A series of images taken from the Seahawk on its approach were pulled onto adjoining screens, giving them still imagery or short video clips for a visual of the area. They were remnant clips from before the chopper went down; haunted images captured in time before tragedy.

Mike dialed Carpenter.

* * *

"We're getting out of here," John yelled, not liking the uncontrolled waver entering his voice.

Barry hopped to his feet and looked around at the air, keeping his head ducked as if a bomb would drop on him at any second.

John pointed to the road where masses of people were running and screaming in terror. They'd have to join the stampede and blend in again. It was their only chance.

He thought his ears were ringing as they took off down the escarpment and toward the road when he realized it was his phone. He picked it up.

It was Esteban. "John? Status report."

"The Seahawk was blown by a missile. The source is too far to identify."

"We know this, we're working on it, how is the package?"

John gave Barry a side-glance as he stumbled down the hill. "Alive, unhurt."

By the time John was about to hit the road, he did a full pivot and caught Barry by the arm, reversing his direction and dragging Barry up with him. Soldiers were emerging from both sides of the street, controlling the flow of foot traffic like shepherds with sheep.

"They have *Sandinistas* everywhere," John said, half to Barry and half to Esteban. "They're identifying everyone."

"Shit," Esteban said. "Get back to the safe house."

John fought the urge to ask what the hell had happened. "Understood," John said through gritted teeth, pulling up short and spinning on Barry as he collided into him. He grabbed Barry's arms, spun him

138

around, and pointed back the way they'd come.

"Safehouse," John said. He looked over his shoulder and saw patrol boats speeding over the lake, and a pair of national guards directing panicked civilians on the road toward a checkpoint that was being hastily set up.

It didn't matter much. There was only one way off the island, and the ferry wasn't going anywhere now. It was a containment dream-scenario. And John had brought the target right to the enemy.

Barry was frantically trying to open the safehouse door. "John, the password-"

John pushed past Barry, punched in the code, and slammed the door shut as soon as the man was inside. The familiar lock, click, and beep met the sound of their panting in the room.

"Esteban? Secondary extraction?"

"Working on it," Esteban said. The calm demeanor John was used to hearing was grating against a panic. Or fury. He couldn't tell, but it was unsettling either way.

"John," Barry said, searching his face for some answer to what was happening. Some expression of certainty to alleviate the hell that was unfolding around them.

John went to the removable wall, ripped it off its holdings, and stared intently at the contents on the shelves. He had already clocked its inventory. He knew what he had to work with. There was no point in looking at it further.

"Are you supplied?" Esteban asked.

John bit back a retort. "We can keep them distracted. I give it twenty minutes on enemy arrival, unless they hold."

John wasn't going to ask about air support. An American chopper had just been blasted out of the air. There wouldn't be any other friendly birds in the sky. Who knew how much more anti-air capability the enemy had?

Esteban grunted. "Shit. Okay. Do your best."

"Yes sir."

The line dropped.

"John?" Barry asked, fear creeping into his voice.

John snapped his head around to look at Barry. Barry flinched.

"Get your gun out," John said, pointing to Barry's waistband.

Barry slowly reached for the gun that had been taken from the impostor priest.

"Do you know how to use it?" John asked. "Have you ever fired a gun?"

Barry gave a timid nod. John arched an eyebrow, uncertain if Barry understood the importance of his question. But then Barry released the pistol's mag, glanced at its bullets, and pushed it back in place. It wasn't a fluid gesture by any means and was slow as hell, but the man knew how to do it and made sure to check the safety.

"Once or twice," Barry's voice wavered. "Shooting range with friends."

Barry bit his lip as he watched John scoop up the hunting rifle and look through its scope. Then he began to finger individual rounds into a detached magazine, as calm as if he were prepping bait for a fishing trip.

"John?"

John looked up as he fitted the magazine. "Get ready. You're on the door," he said.

Barry's eyes grew wide. John's eyes bore into him. He was a killer. Not a casual murderer, but a true predator, without passion or remorse.

"Oh my God," Barry whispered. "What have I gotten myself into?"

John pulled the bolt handle back, found it satisfactory, and rammed it home.

* * *

The shock of the helicopter attack had worn off for Mike quicker than anyone else in the room. Part of his job was allowing disasters and mistakes to pass over him like water off a duck. If anything were to be pulled together, it would be up to him. He had his work cut out for him.

"What do we have in the area?" he barked out, snapping agents out of their glazed expressions staring at the viewing screens.

There was an uncomfortable pause while aides scrambled and keyboard jockeys flew through their sieve of information, trying to find something.

"Assets, contacts, something — anything!" Mike called. "Eyes people, I need eyes on this situation ten minutes ago!"

"Sir, the *Reagan* is offering a second Seahawk," said Barker, holding a phone to his shoulder.

Mike read Barker's unamused expression. His assistant was reporting the offer so he had the information more than he was endorsing the idea. Mike agreed with the silent assessment.

"I'm not putting more birds into that theater — not until we can clear the skies," Mike said, letting Barker take care of soothing the Navy for now. "What else?" Nobody answered. The only sound was the rush of people running about and the clacking of frantic computer keys. "Come on, our asset is down there!"

"I've got a drone sir," a petite woman said, raising her hand while holding a phone in the other.

"We had one in the area?"

"I uh, borrowed it from the Nicaraguan army sir. Eyes and ears only, but-"

"They had a drone?"

"Russian import, unarmed. I hope that's…okay."

Mike grinned at the flat-affect of this young woman. She had located and hacked the feed of an active drone owned by the enemy and she spoke about it like she wasn't sure what to wear to a party.

"Proximity?" Mike asked.

"Five miles from asset's location."

"Good work. Everyone else, keep cooking." Mike nodded to the jockey who had found the drone. "Pull that up for me. Main screen." The jockey shrugged off her previous hesitancy and danced over her keys. The main screen brought up a new visual.

A blur of bluish-grey smeared the screen, reminding Mike of a windshield in a rainstorm.

"What am I looking at?"

"It's patrolling the water in *Lago Nicaragua*. It's redeploying toward asset's position."

"Get in touch with *Reagan's* tactical."

"Already on it sir."

That one deserves a promotion, Mike thought.

"Sir?" another agent asked.

"What?" Mike snapped.

"Call coming through."

Mike already knew who that would be. "Patch her through."

Mike's earpiece beeped as Linda's voice entered his skull.

"What the fuck happened?" she asked. Her voice was ice.

"Getting to the bottom of it ma'am, we're assuming it was a MANPAD. But you're not going to like the interference."

There was a brief pause. Mike clenched his teeth. "Tell me," Linda said.

"Russian submarine next to our carrier. Caught it after we sent the Seahawk. They would've seen us penetrating airspace."

"You think they shot down our chopper?"

"I don't know."

Linda made an ugly sound of frustration. "This is going to be a nightmare. I'm already getting frantic messages from our ambassadors. I don't need more leaking through. This is getting more and more public, Mike."

"Understood ma'am."

"Where is our asset now?"

"Holing up in a safehouse with our agent."

"A good one I hope."

"The best. Agent, that is, not the safehouse...but neither are prepared to go up against a nation's army head-on."

"Give me some good news."

"We have a drone feed."

"And?"

"And...it gives us an eye in the sky. Live-action aerial of the battlefield for tactical. We could deploy-"

Linda's low humorless chuckle interrupted him. "You're not actually hoping to send a team in?"

Mike choked on surprise. "What do you — of course I am! The carrier is at our disposal."

"Unfortunately, *we're* at the disposal of international scrutiny."

"We're just going to abandon them?"

There was a pause. "Jesus, Mike, you know I don't want to say it."

For the first time in a long time, Mike felt fear. He'd forgotten what that was like. Cold, chilling, undeniable...a raw truth that cut like a knife. He felt his footsteps landing heavy as he walked toward his private office away from the clattering of keys and whispering of nervous aides. He resisted the urge to look to them for comfort or strength. He was sure some had noticed his posturing. They were perceptive like that. He had to keep up the charade.

"Linda, please...the ambassadors."

"What, ask them to hand over our guys? I'm just trying to get them to forget they were there in the first place!"

"There must be-"

"If they don't end up shot to pieces and your agent manages to protect that Californian money, then yeah, I might have a case to get the civilian home. But you can forget about your agent. You know Latin America isn't generous with cats caught in the cream. I can't blame them."

"You're siding with them now?"

"Mike," Linda snapped with a finality that gave him whiplash. "You failed the mission. You lost."

"This is scummy. We both know it. Forget the Russians — Linda we have Cuban intelligence crawling all over this! We're missing something here!"

"No. *You* missed it Mike. Now clean it up."

Mike took in a slow, deep breath, and let hot fury burn in his lungs. "Yes ma'am," he said.

The connection dropped and he let out his breath so hard that it hurt.

The Nicaraguans steered the drone toward John's position, but a groan from the jockeys rose up when they lost access to the feed. Barker took direction of the room before Mike could pull his senses together and clear the anger that was impairing his decision making. His mouth felt like sandpaper. Even so, the wheels were spinning in his mind. He didn't like where they were leading.

"Barker?"

"Sir?" Barker asked, neck twitching as if it had a separate life of its own.

Mike handed him the business card the Russian spy had given him. "Where's the next meeting?"

CHAPTER 15

"Shouldn't you be watching the door?" Barry asked. "Aren't they more likely to come through the door?"

"I have to pick off as many as I can as they make their way up the slope," John said, leaning his rifle next to the window, and placing his Glock on the floor next to it. He started laying out individual rifle bullets, standing upright on their ends. He had other supplies — more smoke grenades, a couple frag grenades, and flak vests. He tossed one of the vests to Barry and the man pulled at the straps and Velcro, struggling to get the thing on.

"There are two entrances," John was saying as Barry managed to get a head through the wrong hole. "The door and the window. They're going to climb in the window and attempt to bust in through the door. The window is easier to get through but they'll have to force me off it first. The only thing we're trying to do is buy time."

"For what?"

"Secondary extraction. If we cause enough damage, they'll hold back and call for reinforcements."

"Giving our guys time to pick us up."

John nodded. "We're stuck on an island. The enemy can afford to take their time. That's what we're counting on."

Barry looked around the few adjoined rooms that made up the safehouse, looked down at his body armor, felt the sweaty and unreliable grip on the gun he barely knew how to use.

"Do we have any string?" Barry asked, an idea flashing in his mind.

"No. Fishing wire."

Barry grinned. "If we tied one end to the couch here, and string it along the floor in front of the door…"

"You want to set a trap?" John asked. His expression betrayed nothing.

"Uh…yeah. Make them trip and then we…we shoot them."

"Something better." John picked up the two gas cans and put one in front of Barry. "Water the grass outside the door."

Barry was stunned, but proceeded. John took the other and opened the window. He drained the can and observed Barry's work.

It would have to do. John shut the door again and readied their next defense.

They moved the couch in front of the door and dragged the safe out of the bottom shelf of the hidden wall. It was too heavy to lift but they managed to push it against the couch, pinning the door.

"Do we have matches," Barry asked nervously, eyeing the door and thinking about the gasoline he'd dumped outside.

"I'll take care of it."

Barry let out a breath. "Anything else?"

John spied two patrol boats skimming the water, investigating the area of fallen helicopter wreckage. National guards were pulling people off the road and waving others away from the ferry.

John glanced at the coffee table in the room. "Barry, help me move the table to the-"

His thoughts were cut off as a canvas-covered army truck sped down the road, nearly bulldozing over civilians as they jumped out of the way. Thick diesel smoke belched from its engine.

"Move what?" Barry asked.

"Nothing. They're here. Lie down. Stay low. Watch the door."

John lifted his rifle and hugged the wall to the side of the window. He peered out, eyes fixed on the transport truck.

"I'm scared John."

"That's alright."

"What about you?"

The truck stopped at the base of the slope on the road. A dozen national guardsmen were piling out, dressed in camouflage and full tactical gear.

"John?"

"Pardon?"

"I asked if you're scared."

John took a breath, held it, then let it out slowly. He had been in a lot of bad situations. He'd been shot at plenty of times, been pinned in a room under fire before, and had narrowly made it out alive in hot extractions. But he couldn't remember a mission culminating in a situation quite as bleak as the one at hand.

"I'm fucking tired," John said.

The men fanned out, rear-guard taking up positions behind neighboring houses, others kicking in doors. They'd sweep through the neighborhood and establish an urban perimeter. Then they'd close the noose.

John watched it all, focused eyes darting back and forth around the men's positioning, reading through their tactics and painting a picture of their plan. They were giving John time. That was good. But he didn't know how much Esteban needed.

A second truck pulled up, dropping another dozen soldiers. John wouldn't be surprised if that was the small island's full garrison activated.

Two-dozen men against two. Two-dozen well-armed and trained

men against one civilian and one special-trained agent, both armed poorly.

The vanguard pressed up the slope. John spotted Kalashnikovs of various kinds — there was no getting away from the Russians. Their assault rifles were everywhere, and it was little surprise to see them as the dominant weapon in a socialist cousin of the country. He saw a few Uzis on the newcomers too. Massed personnel with automatic weapons fire was not the kind of thing a single Blackthorne agent was supposed to go up against.

It didn't matter how they were armed. It mattered how they used it to get what they needed.

And, John reminded himself, he didn't need two dozen corpses. He only needed time.

Barry was beginning to shake. John risked a glance across the room to where his VIP was hugging the ground. Barry saw John eyeing him with concern, shook his head and gave John a thumbs up. John nodded back. He readied himself and slid down into a crouch, pushing the rifle barrel through the open window, letting it slide over the window sill, and pocketing the corner. He'd have some time while the enemy searched for him. A gun barrel coming from the corner was more difficult to find than one sticking straight out from the middle.

John inhaled and exhaled slowly, controlling his breathing so his gun wouldn't waver. He slid a finger onto the trigger, making sure to press in the middle of the top of his digit; not the tip and not too far back. He needed all the control he could get. He'd only get one chance with the element of surprise. After that, things would get more complicated.

He looked through the scope. It was dusty and unkempt and nothing like the proper military scopes he had trained with. He wasn't a sniper specialist, but it bothered him nonetheless.

He centered his sight on one of the vanguard moving up the slope, dead center. The soldier signaled for two other men to break off from their advance. Flankers off on either side moved onto more houses, moving up the hill, pushing forward a perimeter of held territory. John's smoke signal had dispersed long ago (smoke grenades spewed color for a minute or a minute and a half) so the soldiers weren't able to pinpoint this particular house as the one with hidden insurgents.

More soldiers crept up the hill while others behind took up cautionary defensive positions. John traced his aim as the point-man continued forward. He held the stern and focused expression of a combatant entering action, waiting for it to come from anywhere, at any time.

Inhale.

John pulled the trigger.

The rifle bucked backward but John was prepared for it, catching the recoil in the pit of his shoulder. A hundred and fifty-odd feet from the rifle's muzzle, a hole ripped through the lead soldier's chest and he fell backward like a stiff board.

Exhale.

At the crack of the rifle sounding off, the hill exploded in a flurry of activity. Men dove for ground and cover on deep-trained instinct, scanning frantically for the immediate threat, sweeping to locate and eliminate the source of danger. Every man on the hill wanted John dead.

But John had only taken one shot.

He moved immediately onto a soldier who'd dropped to the ground, prone like so many of his compatriots, but too far up the hill to hide under its slope. John could make out the man's head and shoulders, and the gun being pointed in front of him. The soldier began to army crawl backward.

John's shot took him straight through his helmet and down the center of his skull.

He picked up movement from two buildings down off to his left; a soldier hugging the wall and peeking out at the action.

John moved a hair too fast on the trigger, letting speed get the best of his aim. The shot took a small chunk out of the building's concrete edge and the soldier disappeared into hiding once more.

The briefest of pauses held tense and steady as the soldiers mustered their response.

John had had his surprise attack. Now it was their turn.

Their response was standard and difficult to counter, signaling that John had his work cut out for him. Flankers hidden against building corners like the man he'd just taken a shot at peeked out and swept covering fire, rapid shots that drove John under cover of the window, bullets whizzing across the hill's horizon in a wide arc. That told John they still didn't know his exact position. But they'd be getting close.

By the time he was able to get a sliver of vision, John saw soldiers zigzagging through buildings and slope-cover with urban expertise. There was a reason they had brought Uzis; they were for close quarter room-sweeps.

With a reprise in enemy fire near his location, John picked off a third man with a shot that managed to connect as he had started his attack run. But that also left John out of rounds.

The hunting rifle was just that — meant for hunting. Four rounds were more than enough to take down a buck. The safehouse wasn't about to pack an assault rifle for a full-on attack by the Nicaraguan army but the flicker of a wish still crossed John's mind. He unclipped the mag and held his hands steady as he loaded four more bullets one atop the other, sliding them into place and ignoring the soreness starting to bloom in his shoulder.

Another sweep of submachine gun fire. This time it came close enough that bullets tore into the wall in front of him, narrowly missing the window. John thanked his luck — the window would be shattered soon, he knew — and locked his mag back in place, giving the bolt a good pull and slamming it forward once again.

Peering out, flashes of weapons poked from second-floor buildings closest to the safehouse. He wasn't about to try and make those shots. Distance and enemy cover notwithstanding, he had more pressing problems.

Fifty feet away on either flank, John's enemies ascended the hill, pouring onto him. They may not know his exact position but they knew his field of fire well enough. The angle would soon have him cut off. There was only so far he could point his gun before the window became a hindrance.

John's next shot connected with a runner who crumpled in the street, but in the time it had taken to line up the shot, two more had slipped past his right flank. He swung the barrel around in an attempt to catch another man going for the opening his first shot had created. A third man crossed his sights and John squeezed the trigger. The ground behind the man exploded in a cloud of dust. The soldier had changed direction unexpectedly out of the line of fire. John grunted in frustration. The haste of his second shot revealed how desperate his position was.

The flankers posed the largest and most immediate threat. Again, John swung the rifle back to the front of the property, looking for an opening. His counter-assault had forced most of the attacking force into cover behind the neighboring buildings, their covering fire still harmlessly pockmarking the walls of the safehouse. Another soldier dashed out amidst the covering fire, but not quickly enough to make it behind a low wall. John's shot caught him in the leg mid-step. The soldier yelped as he tumbled to the ground and began to drag himself into cover. John's teeth clenched painfully as the stress of the fire fight started to take its toll. He honed in on the man pulling himself across the ground and fired, finishing him off.

He dropped the mag, reloading again. His training made the action effortless as he kept watch on the attacking force. More men took the opening and flowed toward the safehouse under covering fire. It was only a matter of time until they pinpointed their location.

"Getting close Barry, be ready for it," he found himself saying.

The words were out, rifle reloaded, and trigger finger itching before he could recall doing anything at all in those fifteen seconds.

They would be pressing onto the safehouse now. Men on the flanks would be crashing into neighboring houses on either side, knowing that only one of these few buildings could house enemies according to shot trajectories and casualties. John shifted his view off the scope, counting himself lucky the protruding rifle barrel or reflecting glass hadn't already revealed his position at the window. Another decimating sweep of submachine gun fire poured onto the building, this time shattering the window and bringing sharp chunks of glass tumbling down. John tucked his arms and ducked, sheltering himself from the worst of it, more concerned about the gunfire that had zipped above his head by mere inches.

"John!" Barry screamed.

John didn't answer, having no time to spare for his VIP. He inched out of the bottom corner of the window and was rewarded by the near-instant hammering of return fire. He ducked back down again, hunkering against the wall. Not for the first time in his career, John was thankful that concrete was the material of choice in Latin America for building infrastructure.

"John! They're here!"

John blinked as he took in the meaning of Barry's words. He snatched up his Glock in one hand and clutched the rifle in the other, loping past the window and into the safety of the wall.

"Back up," John said. "You're too close."

Barry shuffled backward on his stomach, reminding John of the man he'd shot while prone on the slope. Barry flinched as more offensive fire came pouring through the window. They were making sure to keep John from countering.

He laid down his rifle and tucked his Glock away, flicking a glance at the door, not sure if he could hear anything outside there over the roaring staccato of bullets hammering concrete. He leaned down and picked up the two grenades he had put aside when they set up their safehouse. They weren't anything fancy and he didn't plan to use them for their damage capability. He needed to scare the soldiers off. Keep them guessing and reassessing the situation. Anything to buy more time. If they'd only decide to back off and wait on specialized reinforcements...

Down the left side of the building, John spotted two soldiers slinking along the wall and moving toward the window. Their eyes flicked to the right side that John couldn't see.

Other soldiers coming that way too...

They'd be making a cross-sweep, a strategic three-man tactic that covered the most amount of area in a small period of time when entering a narrow space, like a door or window. One man would enter on a diagonal, another the opposite angle, and the third covered anything missed.

John wouldn't let them get a chance.

"Cover your ears Barry," John said.

He didn't know if Barry did what he said or even if he could hear him. It didn't matter.

John pulled the pin on a frag grenade, waited half a second while staring at the sliver of window he could safely stare down, then lunged forward and tossed the grenade through the broken window-frame in an underhanded move that would've made a perfect scoop for Bocce.

His hand snapped back as soon as the grenade was free, acutely aware that his arm was exposed to multiple lines of fire. As expected, a stream of bullets pattered off the window's edges and into the building. But John was already hugging the corner, plugging his ears.

The explosion came as a heavy boom reverberating in John's chest. Soldiers cried through a plume of dirt and rock that spewed up like a geyser. Orange flames burst through the smoke and a man began to scream. John didn't have time to assess the casualties or the damage to the wall. John drew the extra smoke grenade, cracked it, and rolled it forward on the floor to the base of the window.

Anything to keep the enemy guessing. Make them hesitate. Maybe even make them back off.

Most trained combatants John knew wouldn't move on a position if an unknown explosion went off followed by concealing smoke. That usually signaled a hard counterattack — a stream of soldiers could descend upon the confused and battered enemy, all while they'd be blind.

Heat and the smell of burning flesh poured into the window as the gasoline continued to burn. But John had another front to worry about.

The door cracked open and Barry cried out, but it slammed back closed after bouncing off the couch pinned tight by the metal safe.

"Smoke!" Barry cried.

"It's ours," John said, trying to calm him while the room slowly filled with a red cloud. He popped a couple rounds off near the window to make any risk-takers think twice before braving through the concealment, then headed to the door. He still had one frag grenade, but the enemy would be close at hand, and there were still too many of them. They had plenty of men to clear a building. Even more so against two pinned-down fighters, desperate in their tactics.

The door slammed open again, buckling back and forth as the soldiers forced it open and pushed against the weight of the safe.

John was on them in an instant, squeezing off rounds from a crouch next to Barry, sending rounds to bite through the door's gap anytime it opened.

"Yeah! Eat shit!" Barry screamed, following John's lead and firing off his own gun when the door struggled to open. His aim was atrocious but John thought he saw a shot slip past the door's edge. He frowned when he heard the constant rapid hammer of Barry's trigger.

"Controlled fire!" John called, doubting that Barry would know what that meant.

Barry yelled that he was out of ammo, which didn't come as a surprise.

The door slammed forward again, but when John fired he saw a riot-shield blocking the gap, repelling his attack. There was a heavy snap once, twice, as John realized the hinges of the door had completely given way. His mind was too much of a flurry and his body was sucking up all his focus for him to realize what the enemy had planned.

They *removed* the door altogether.

Well, shit.

With the space open and blocked by nothing but the back of a couch, John pulled the pin on his final grenade before he even knew he had it in his hand. He cooked it for a second, two, while the enemy struggled to push through. They were squeezing behind the riot shield, which seemed to be their only one. They could have hugged the door frame and blind-fired in with more effectiveness. But John was convinced now they were after a prize instead of two worthless dead bodies.

One last defense.

He tossed the grenade over their heads and behind the shield.

The explosion went off in an instant, rocking the couch off its legs and blowing smoke in a fury around the open doorway. A second later came a burning woosh of fire as ground outside the door sprouted a hungry mass of flame. The man with the riot shield was down with his feet on fire, and John caught a glimpse of blood from another body, and the cry of someone in pain. He grabbed Barry by the ankles and dragged him backward into the corner, making sure the man hadn't sustained any serious injuries. He was screaming and shaking furiously. John didn't have the heart to tell him that it would hardly matter what they did next. Even so, John raised his gun to pop off the last of his rounds.

He didn't see the flashbang, but he heard it clunk on the ground.

"Eyes!" was all John was able to yell as he hunched over Barry to protect him as best he could. He clapped his hands over Barry's ears.

The flashbang exploded, popping loud enough that John couldn't hear anything after the boom. He was lucky enough to get his eyes closed, but the light was so bright he saw veins bulge through his vision before subsiding.

John knew the enemy would be on them then. He retrieved his phone, broke it under his heel, and felt a heavy blow against his temple before falling into unconsciousness.

CHAPTER 16

"I'm about to do something either very smart, or very stupid," Mike said.

"Sir?" Barker's eyes were wide. His boss didn't make stupid decisions.

"Get me a clean line to Juan Puentes," Mike said.

"Juan…Puentes? As in, Guatemalan cartel Puentes?"

"You heard me. I'll take it in my office"

Barker opened his mouth to say something else but the expression on Mike's face made him close it. Satellite imagery on the main screen had come online just after the battle unfolded. If he could only get a team in there…

Mike cursed Linda as he opened the door to his private office, but he understood her reasoning. That didn't mean he had to like it. The same thought went with this plan involving Juan.

As I said. Very smart, or very stupid.

* * *

Juan Puentes, *don* of the Puentes cartel was hurrying down the hall of the luxury family compound when his cellphone started ringing. He saw that it was an unknown number and declined the call. He snatched up a duffle bag with some essentials for his business trip, slipped on an expensive suit jacket, and dashed out the door.

Antigua was sunny today, but that didn't mean it was hot. A brisk wind blew up dust and Juan turned away, back against the wind, shielding his eyes. When the assault ended, he took a moment to look around the immaculate courtyard gardens leading up to the front gate. A lot of men had died when he had wrested power from his corrupt bastard of an uncle, Pablo Puentes. Blood had watered the plants here, making them strong. He walked past the chiseled stone porch, where he had huddled with other men against its small lip as shotgun fire flew over their heads. Before they had made their final push, killing Pablo's old guard, and forging a new force of Puentes loyalists.

He felt a mix of pride and sadness at these thoughts. He knew he had grown since then. But so often, he still felt like a boy. The wind picked up again and he pushed through it, jacket ends curling up his back like a sneer.

His phone rang again. He looked at it against the wind, blinking away the dust. It was the same unknown number. Frustrated, he was about to decline the call, but hesitated. This was a work phone, not a general number that might pick up telemarketers and other scam calls.

Against better judgement, he picked it up.

"¿*Qué*?"

A deep man's voice came through, speaking Spanish. "Hello is this Juan Puentes?" His accent wasn't native Spanish. Probably American.

Juan narrowed his eyes. "Who is this?"

"I have something that might interest you. Does the name John Carpenter mean anything to you?"

Juan didn't overlook the fact that the man hadn't answered his question. Nonetheless, Juan thought of the name. It was the name of the man who had come to tutor Pablito, Pablo's son, before all hell had broken loose in the redistribution of Puentes power. The death of his mother in an explosion downtown...he shut his eyes and pinched the bridge of his nose, shutting away the memories. It was no use dwelling on them, even if they still hurt.

"What about him would interest me?"

"Maybe that he is an undercover DEA officer."

Juan stopped walking toward the gate as his eyebrows shot up. He found himself unable to speak.

"And he is...a guest of mine. Permanently. I thought you might want him more than I would."

Juan had thought about the tutor shortly after he had seized control. Most of his guards said John had fled the estate when the fighting broke out, but one said he had been seen with Pablo downtown. Yet another thought he saw John taking Pablito away on a motorcycle. But Juan couldn't be certain of any of these things, and Marcela — his loyal lover — had worked out more convincing conclusions. Juan would have liked the opportunity to track down the man and put any suspicions he held to rest, but it had been a low priority — he was still rooting out secret Pablo sympathizers amongst his men.

"DEA?" Juan found himself asking.

"*Sí*. Interested?"

"Where?"

"Nicaragua. I can send you an address. But you have to come soon."

Juan frowned. Nicaragua wasn't far in terms of countries, but it wasn't exactly the quick drive into the city he was expecting. "Bring him to me," Juan said. "I will pay for the flight."

"I can't get him out. Local DEA are already looking for him. I'll sell him to the next bidder if you're not interested. You aren't the only interested party in Latin America."

Juan cursed silently. He couldn't let this opportunity pass. But there were too many unknowns attached. He didn't want to turn down a gift, and he never turned down an opportunity.

His doubts washed away a second later as a series of pictures came through on his phone. He scrolled through them, seeing the tutor, John Carpenter, but dressed in various military fatigues and armoured jackets, firing at a range. The man was DEA alright.

"Who are you? Tell me."

The man chuckled. "Ex-DEA if you really want to know. Let's just say John and I aren't exactly friends anymore. Bastard fucked my wife."

Juan grinned. Now *that* was a story he could believe. Besides, perhaps he needed a trip like this to ease some tensions among the men. This would be a victory for everyone. He could even bring Marcela along to entertain him on the flight, and to show off his prize.

The man hung up before Juan could say anything more.

Juan placed a new phone call to his assistant as he backtracked and moved toward his helicopter.

"¿*Si*?" his assistant asked, picking up after the first ring.

"Cancel my meeting with Antonio's people," Juan said. "I have a more urgent matter to attend."

A minute after Juan had hung up the phone, Marcela's hidden phone received a new message:

Agent captured. Rescue op assignment. Priority one. Go with Juan.

It was lucky Marcela had started carrying her Firm phone on her person instead of hidden in her room as she used to. She wouldn't have been able to get away with something like that with Pablo. But Juan had a trust and affection for her that made her job easy.

When she read the message her eyebrows raised and she frowned. The message would delete within a minute. She sighed. An agent getting captured? She hadn't heard of that happening before. Perhaps it had happened and she wasn't informed, but Firm agents weren't exactly prone to making mistakes — and definitely not one of this size. Agents sometimes became compromised, but that was hardly the same thing.

Whoever had gotten captured was an idiot. There was only one agent she wouldn't mind going out of her way for, but she doubted John Carpenter could find himself in a cell. If it were any other agent, well, that'd just put her in a bad mood.

* * *

"Okay, new op," Mike said to the agents before him, some managing to turn their chairs around to look at him fully if they weren't in the middle of a call or situation requiring their immediate attention. Most of them had faces pale with shock and the strained look of someone doing what they could against a hopeless outcome. "Operation Mule is in effect as of this moment."

Some of the agents blinked in surprise at the announcement of a completely new op. But they were trained well enough not to ask stupid questions.

"Barker, pull up the profile of Juan Puentes on a secondary screen," Mike pointed. He watched the main screen's visual provided by a sat feed they'd eventually managed to get into place, in order to follow John and Barry's capture and transportation. "This is an emergency, folks. Just like anything else we do. I won't be losing our asset. And I won't be losing our agent."

He took a deep breath, an unintentional theatrical pause. Mike needed the air because he had a lot to say.

"We can't go in hot. And we can't send in our own. So here's what we're going to do…"

CHAPTER 17

When John regained consciousness he was someplace unknown. It took less than a second for him to move from confusion and to assess what had happened and where he was. He took in his surroundings and gathered as much information as possible.

His head was on fire. A concussive headache by the feel of it, but that wasn't the primary problem. His right arm had lost circulation, and when he craned his sore neck up to see why, he found his hand had been handcuffed to a pipe-beam on the ceiling. He struggled against weak knees to push himself standing upright on the ground, tugging on the handcuff, knowing there would be no chance of breaking out of its hold.

Barry was next to him, weeping.

The man didn't bother to stand, just bent his knees and kept upright by his own cuffed hands up above. A nasty shiner had overtaken Barry's face, and other bloody cuts poked out from his arms and ripped shirt.

The room was dark and industrial, as if in a warehouse, but less airy and more compact. There was nothing in the room. No windows. Only a stark metal door, sealed shut in front of them near the left corner across the room.

Barry continued to cry. John couldn't blame him.

"Barry," John said.

The other man didn't respond.

John had never been captured before. He'd rarely failed a mission, and when he had it was usually due to uncontrollable variables. This was, in all imagined scenarios, the worst situation he could ever find himself in.

Stale air was blowing in through an air duct and fan, the only noise penetrating the room other than Barry's sobs. John tried to mentally feel out how long he'd been unconscious but there was little information to go off of. It seemed like a few hours. Minor concussion, but probably no permanent damage. He pushed past the brutal headache that split his brain in half. His ears still felt raw from the flashbang and he was experiencing a faint constant whine squeezing past his ear canals. The rest of his body started to reveal the cost of the punishment he'd pushed his body through over the last day, without attention or rest. He was acutely aware he was exhausted. His mind and body were reacting harshly to fatigue.

John felt a small thread of panic growing in his core, but his training allowed him to rationalize it away in moments. No good would come from worrying about the situation. He closed his eyes, worked his legs by bending up and down methodically, and breathed in and out, allowing calm, cold, and calculated focus to take over any other instinct that might be trying to pry loose from his control.

"We're going to die…" Barry cried softly, in between his tears.

John opened his eyes. His mission was still to protect and escort Barry. Even while imprisoned, his mission hadn't changed. Barry was still his VIP.

"If they were going to kill us, we'd be dead already," John said.

That just brought on more tears. John managed to refrain from scowling.

"But who *are* they?"

John opened his mouth to speak his thoughts on that but decided it would be safer not to. Their guards would be listening, and John didn't need to be feeding into Barry's fears. He was sure the Nicaraguan government and Cuban intelligence were interested in Barry for some reason, but he couldn't say what for. They needed him alive. Which begged the question — why was *John* still alive?

"It doesn't matter who they are," John said, trying to keep Barry focused and calm. "Are you hurt?"

"No…yeah…I don't know," Barry said, hanging his head and examining himself for the first time.

"Okay. That's good. What about your head?"

"What about it?"

"Does your head hurt? From when they knocked you out?"

"They didn't knock me out," Barry said.

John narrowed his eyes. Information. Finally.

"What did you see?" John asked.

Barry looked up at John, realizing he had something helpful to give to his protector, and he managed to put aside some of his self-pity.

"I…nothing, I'm sorry John. They had a black bag over my head. It was just like back in Playa Amarillo…" tears started to well in his eyes from the memory.

"That's fine. What did you hear? Feel?"

"I…I don't think I was conscious the whole time…I remember being sick, God I puked inside the bag!" Barry looked over John's head, as if seeing his memories play out as he tried to recall them.

"A boat," John said.

"Yes! Yes that's right, because I was seasick again! The waves rocking…" he swallowed at the memory, "better not to think about it."

"How long?"

"I don't know…again I was in and out…we were on the road though at one point. Near the end. I remember the slamming of vehicle doors, the thrum of the road…I'm sorry, I don't know."

A rough map of Nicaragua formed in John's mind. He began to draw a radius around an imaginary map, with Ometepe at its center.

They've moved us off the island. Maybe taken us as far as Managua. That's just over an hour on the ferry, three with the road.

But there was no way to tell for sure. For all John knew, they had crossed the border and were in a different country. Or in a covert anonymous cell somewhere away from the city.

It wasn't a situation John was going to be able to break out of anyway. No, this information could be minutely helpful, but the next test would be to see what their jailers wanted.

That's what everything would come down to.

"I am going to tell you some things," John said in as reassuring a tone as possible. He wasn't sure how long it would be until their captors returned. He kept an eye on the door in the corner. "I need you to listen. Not to panic. Just listen."

"Okay," Barry's voice wavered.

John nodded. "They want something from us. They will torture us if they have to."

"I'll never break!" Barry screamed.

John took a breath. The man was bordering on hysterics.

"Barry, look at me and listen. Just listen." The man did after struggling with his handcuff, rattling madly on the pipe-beam. His eyes were wild and furious, like a rabbit caught in a trap.

"We're being tortured right now," John said calmly. When Barry gave him a look of confusion, John pointed upward to where each of their hands hung, trapped.

"This isn't torture," Barry said.

"After three days it will be."

165

Barry looked up and felt the numbness down his arm with new horror.

"Don't think about it," John said, closing his eyes again.

"How can I not think about it? You just told me we're going to get tortured! How can I not think of torture?"

"You need to be aware of what our captors might do to you."

Barry was about to protest again but quickly realized there was no point. He looked at John, hanging by his arm, eyes closed, breathing steadily in and out.

"Okay. What…what should I expect? Am I going to get my fingers cut off?"

John opened his eyes and eyed the door. "They'll leave the lights on. Loud music. Sleep deprivation."

"That doesn't sound so bad. I was thinking about water-boarding."

"Then water-boarding."

"Fuck."

"They'll only torture you to get what they want. Torture is meant to break resistance."

"So what are we supposed to do?"

"Don't resist," John said, his eyes drifting, as if he were seeing something off in the distance. "Give them what they want."

"What? But that's…we're Americans! Well I am. We don't give terrorists anything."

"We do it all the time."

"I don't! I won't!"

"Then you'll be tortured until you do."

Barry didn't have anything to say to that. There was a long uncomfortable pause. Barry could see the gears in John's head spinning. He wondered what the man was thinking about.

"Why are you okay with me talking?" Barry asked.

"I'm not under orders to kill you on capture. My orders are to get you out of the country. It makes no difference to me if you talk or not."

"What? Wait — you...you'd kill me if-"

"We'll see what they want. But your best option will be to talk. Don't resist."

Barry opened his mouth to object, but at the same instant, the sound of clattering came from outside the door. It grew louder and louder, until Barry realized it was music.

¡Himno de la Unidad Sandinista! ¡Himno de la Unidad Sandinista! ¡Himno de la Unidad Sandinista!

Anthem of the Sandinista Unity!

Voices joined the clattering — cymbals, he realized — and then voices began to cry out, with drum, strings, and flute in tow. It was celebratory music, like he'd expect from a marching band.

Barry looked over to John. His eyes were closed, face calm.

After a few minutes the song came to a close. Barry breathed relief from how loud it had been, and how much it had scattered his thoughts. He tried to stretch his arm out, and felt nothing but pins and needles.

Then the song looped, playing again.

CHAPTER 18

⎯⎯⎯

"Why are they doing this?" Barry asked, in the methodical silent reprieve between song loops. "Why?"

The song started again and anything else he might've said was lost in another three minutes of *Sandinista* anthem. When it stopped for that brief moment after it was finished, John could answer.

"Because they can."

The music took off again, instilling a memorized pattern in John and Barry's minds against all desire to keep the noise out. Barry could hardly hear his thoughts.

"How long have we been here?" Barry asked when it finished again. "How many days?"

John didn't have time to answer. The music had started up.

More blaring triumphant music. A choir belted out its victory song amidst the roar of instruments that tore at Barry's ears and a drum that ripped at his chest. He never wanted to listen to music again. And he was Californian.

"Three hours," John said when the music stopped.

"Three? Only three? How-"

Music.

Barry screamed, but even John standing beside him couldn't hear it. That might still be from the after-effects of the flashbang. He only saw Barry open his mouth and swallow the sounds coming from their torturers.

"The song is two minutes and forty-three seconds," John said on another pause. "It's played seventy-four times. Three hours."

Cymbals crashed, signifying the start of the endless song. Barry imagined it would fill his nightmares if he were able to sleep.

John had been right. Dangling from the pipe-beam, him and John were being exhausted, barely holding onto their senses or their right minds. The lights stayed on, the music played, and one arm stayed painfully cuffed above them, forcing them to stay upright.

Barry didn't know how much longer this continued. He considered how impressive it was that John had been able to keep time by the music. Barry considered John's true job description, and quickly decided not to think about it — not for the first time.

He tried to count with John from his last report, but he felt like he got lost somewhere between twenty-five and thirty more songs. He wasn't quite sure how many hours that was. It was hard to do mental math when his brain was warring against him and he couldn't hear his thoughts.

The music stopped again.

It stayed stopped.

Barry's ears impulsively started creating the music in his head. The pattern took shape without there being any actual sound. His mind couldn't fathom not hearing anything in this extra space.

John opened his eyes and looked at the door.

There was a rusty screech of metal-on-metal, and the door to their room opened. Barry blinked. He could hardly believe his eyes. Nothing had changed in the room since they'd been hung here. The only disruption in their pattern were the words they managed to say in between songs. And it wasn't as if they were having a particularly riveting conversation.

A man walked in through the door. He didn't have a uniform on, but he wore military gear and a balaclava.

Barry stared at him. On the one hand, he was absolutely terrified of this man — who he might be, and what he might be doing in the room. The next phase in torture that must inevitably be coming. On the other hand, the man was blissfully interesting to watch. Finally, something different was taking place.

The man held up a cellphone. The phone's light flashed, the man looked at the screen, then walked on toward the door.

"Hey!" Barry called.

The man didn't even turn his head to regard Barry. He walked out the door, and slammed it behind him, that ugly screech of metal signaling his final exit.

"Well," Barry said, abnormal silence beginning to plague him. His mind was still singing the memorized tune of the anthem, sung in words he didn't even understand but managed to phonetically pronounce. "At least the music has stopped."

John looked at him, gave a grim smile, then closed his eyes.

A cymbal crashed.

The anthem returned.

CHAPTER 19

———

Washington was experiencing a heavy downpour by the time Mike pulled up to the curb outside the art museum, 'The Phillips Collection.' While Barker had taken all of two minutes to figure out where the Russian spy would be waiting for Mike the next day, it had hardly been a puzzle. The name on the card said 'Phillip' and the occupation was an art curator.

Real creative there, thought Mike, as he fished for change for the parking meter. He'd already inserted a dollar before he realized it was free parking in the evening. He rushed off down the street, ignoring his better senses to walk slow and casual with the standard covert gait. A Russian sub was sitting off the coast of their operations, he had an exploded chopper, people captured, and it had taken over fifteen minutes to find parking.

On a goddamn Thursday evening.

As Mike hurried up the stairs to the art gallery's doors, he found himself without an answer when he asked himself when he'd last been happy.

As always, best not to think about that. There was never time to think about that.

The Phillips Collection was supposed to be impressive by artist's and tourist's standards, but it was smaller than he'd thought. Off to the left from the entryway hall a large square room boasted thirty-odd people, speaking in hushed tones as if they were at the theater. One third of the people were staff, serving hors d'oeuvres and champagne as others mingled and gazed upon paintings resting on the lighted walls. It was a good thing he'd left Barker behind this time around. He would've enjoyed himself far too much.

A quick scan of the room told Mike the Russian wasn't there. He considered the Russian wasn't present at all. Or Barker had been wrong. Perhaps the clue had indeed been too easy. Then again, Barker was never wrong.

Mike found his man two rooms down the left side of the gallery.

The Russian was sitting on a padded backless bench in the middle of the room meant for art spectators. He wore a nicer suit than the one he had at the park. It was a silky navy blue and was coupled with a Rolex on his left wrist. There was no humble boasting here. Between that and the product in the man's hair, Mike could've placed the man's age twenty years younger and four times richer than the crusty man playing chess he had met before.

It appeared Mike's Russian spy was no stranger to spycraft's subtle ways of disguise. Age ambiguity could be difficult to achieve even for seasoned spies.

Mike wasn't about to give any compliments. He stood over the Russian, arms folded, stern expression bordering on outright fury. The Russian took his time to finish appreciating some detail in the painting he gazed upon across from the bench. He smiled, nodded to himself, then looked up at Mike. His face held innocence, bashfulness, and a gentle honesty that could fool the devil himself. The loathing Mike held for the man in this moment couldn't be compared.

The Russian reached for a flute of champagne beside his foot and raised it to Mike. "They are having a special celebration event tonight. Recently acquired their third Cézanne. Very impressive."

Mike knew the artist's name but wouldn't be able to tell a Cézanne from a Van Gogh. Nor did he care to.

"Did you blow up my chopper?"

The Russian's eyebrows raised. "Why don't you get yourself a drink. It'll clear your head." The Russian took a delicate sip from his flute of champagne.

This time Mike controlled his fury. Being angry was one thing. Rising to the bait was another.

"I'm fine."

The Russian gestured for Mike to sit next to him. Mike looked at the bench like a scorpion sat waiting there. There may as well have. The Russian's eyes twinkled.

Play the game, Mike reminded himself. He wouldn't be able to get anything if he wasn't able to play. Their previous chess game had taught him that much.

He sat down and folded his hands together, looking at the painting across from them.

"Do you like art?" the Russian asked.

Mike scowled. "No."

"Ah. A shame. You don't like art, you don't like chess…it makes me wonder what you do like."

You and me both.

Mike kept his composure. "What am I looking at?"

The Russian was back to sipping his champagne but stopped at the question. He glanced from Mike to the painting on the wall.

"*The Mediterranean*, by Gustave Courbet. Oil on canvas, nineteenth century."

Mike grunted. The canvas on the wall was a mess of mottled greens and blues. He thought it was some sort of artsy-fartsy abstract thing, but now he could make out the rocks, waves and sky. It was unimpressive even for his tasteless standards.

"You don't like it?" the Russian asked, reading his mind.

"I've seen better."

The Russian smiled. "It's not Courbet's best, unfortunately. *The Desperate Man,* his famous self portrait is the real prize. I saw it ten years ago in Frankfurt. I found such…solace in that work. It has a visceral companionship with the viewer."

"Okay."

"Courbet drifted from the Romantics into Realism. Tired of what people wanted to see and started painting what he actually saw. I find it no coincidence he was a socialist too."

"Good to hear."

"What a strange relationship between Realism and Impressionism, hm?" The Russian let the words hang in the air while he took a leisurely sip from his flute once again.

Mike waited a few beats of silence, then figured he'd put in enough time for the game. "A Russian submarine was spotted off the coast of Nicaragua earlier today."

"And an American military helicopter was spotted flying into Nicaragua."

"I have American casualties and thirty million dollars worth of damages. I'm not in the mood."

The Russian pursed his lips, deciding to spend more time appreciating the painting before them.

"You may think you have leverage Ivan, but you forget that Americans will break before they bend. I'm very inclined to go straight to the Cubans and let them know your agents-"

"I don't break things, I fix them," the Russian interrupted. "You forget, but that is my job. *I* didn't bring down your chopper."

Mike rubbed the side of his nose, irritated by an itch. "Here's what

I think. You Russians didn't shoot that thing down. But you sent a high-priority message over to Nicaragua and they scrambled to get some air defense weaponry into place. Probably a portable piece on a trooper. And if that's the case, yes, you brought down my chopper and killed five American lives with it." Mike licked his lips as the Russian turned to look at him, expression even and unimpressed. Mike pushed on. "We still have a bead on that submarine. The Navy wants revenge. It'd be a shame for a hundred Russian sailors to die in an iron tomb crumpling up like a ball of paper within the fist of deep water pressure."

"That is not-"

"You should see some of the toys we have these days. Oh, I'm sure you're familiar with the Mk. 54 torpedo — 40 knot takedown with countermeasure penetration, and the RUM-139 isn't bad either. But who'd have thought we'd have the budget to get the F21 heavyweights over from France? Those things are silent as a shark in the water and twice as fast."

The Russian raised a hand for Mike to stop, indicating that he had scored a point. But the Russian knew how to play the game, even with Mike's blunt, brute force way of playing.

"Yes. It would be a shame for two large nations to be at war. We both know a broken helicopter is not a war. Do not turn it into one."

Mike stared hard into the man's eyes, not bothering to hide his fury. The Russian's gaze was just as hard, steady.

Mike broke eye contact. If nothing else, he was a pragmatist. He had let the Russian know he tread on thin ice. The ball was in the other's court, both their opening hands played.

"I cannot say for certain. But yes, I assume we shared the information," the Russian conceded. "I doubt we gave the recommendation to stop a bird from flying. But I also do not know why you act so surprised by this. You are America. I am Russia."

"Nothing surprises me anymore. I'm just disappointed."

The Russian laughed, but grew serious once more. "We are not allies. We have never been allies — even when we were."

"You said you wanted to work together."

"Yes. On this." The Russian looked down the hall toward the other guests at the exhibition before patting his breast pocket. Then his hand cut through the air in a sharp motion. "On nothing else. Nothing else changes."

Mike wondered what the Russian had in his pocket. He found himself staring at the painting. He didn't have a good answer. He'd let the Russian continue. Then he'd figure out what response was needed. Or Linda would.

"Have you heard of the Christmas truce during World War I?" the Russian asked.

Mike cocked his head at that. "Of course I have. Germans and British in no man's land. Shaking hands and playing soccer."

"Yes. That is what I'm asking you for."

Mike rolled his eyes. "A day of peace. Then back to killing each other the next day?"

"Exactly. We had manners back then," the Russian sighed. "Please. Let us stop fencing. There is more important work."

"The secret information in your pocket you want me to act on, because you guys screwed up. Then shot down a chopper."

"I don't want more downed choppers. Or ships sunk. Or Russian and American lives lost."

"Or Cubans finding out about Russian trespassers. Just Americans passing through."

"What more token of goodwill can I offer?"

There!

Mike froze. Chips were on the table. Chips for the taking. He'd have to maneuver this trade carefully.

"The listening station across from our embassy in Nicaragua, shut it down."

"That…won't happen," the Russian frowned. "I know I can't get that."

Mike feigned disappointment. He expected that answer. "The submarine?"

"No guarantee but I don't imagine it stays there long. It had a different destination originally."

"We have a pair of Americans in Nicaragua mixed up with the authorities. Could you get them out?"

It was the Russian's turn to freeze. He looked up at the ceiling, thinking about the prospect.

"I have an agent-"

"Dimitri."

Mike broke out in a smile as the Russian frowned. "Yes…Dimitri. But I don't see how I could exfiltrate these prisoners for you."

"Then I don't see how we can have a deal."

There was a long pause after that. Mike glanced sideways at the Russian.

"I'm sure there's a way," the Russian said. "What do you need?"

Mike furrowed his brow. "Transportation. That's all."

"Fine."

Which was as good as it was going to get. No guarantees. If the Russian ghosted him, Mike could easily send their report off to Cuba.

"Give me the file," Mike said, hand open like a kid ready for candy.

The Russian hesitated again. He glanced down the hall at the exhibition room, with its quiet murmur of staff and patrons, clinking glasses and subdued laughter.

Mike was about to open his mouth and give a retort — two meetups with nothing to show for it, when the Russian's hand ducked into his inside suit jacket pocket, and pulled out a square of folded blue paper, covered in clear plastic wrap.

Mike took it wordlessly, as if accepting a cigarette from a friendly stranger. He moved to put it in his pocket, but the Russian's hand shot out and gripped his forearm. The grip was stronger than Mike would've thought coming from this man and it was painful, like a vice.

"You read it here."

Mike's eyebrows dipped downward. "Now?"

"Now."

The vice released and Mike leaned back, giving the Russian a sideways glance, expecting the intensity of his grip reflected in his eyes. But the Russian was gazing at the painting again, apparently finding more meaning in those colors than Mike could find in a lifetime.

He tucked the flimsy package between his legs and tore open the wrap. When he pulled out the blue paper, he found it thin like tissue paper, and sticky where his fingers lingered.

Sugar paper.

The stuff had to be handled carefully because excessive touch or heat made it dissolve. It was some of the better quality sugar paper because it didn't stick to itself, but Mike still had to pick at corners and let it rest on the tips of his fingers in an open flat palm to avoid massive dark blotches appearing over everything. He hadn't seen sugar paper in a while. But it did what it needed to do, and was reliable. Placed over top of a standard piece of paper with print or writing, the sugar paper picked up an impression if applied with a light but firm pressure, like a printing press. Of course this couldn't be done with your hand, because then the sugar paper would melt into a sticky mess, but another piece of paper or plastic wrap on top, smoothed out a few times over with a forearm, and you had yourself a portable photocopier, evidence destroyed in a pinch. Spycraft could ask for little more.

The print appeared in dark blue type over the lighter blue page. It was a single page, and appeared to be from a report or the similar equivalent of bureaucratic business. It had that sharp typewriter-like font that Mike had seen a thousand times in his department as standard. And it was clear this was the first page of a dense file, headers and indicators lining the top of the page. He scanned it quickly to see what he was dealing with here.

The words *Clasificada* stuck out immediately in bold, and Mike caught the words *Dirección de Inteligencia* right after.

Cuban intelligence.

Subject: Analysis and Assessment of Twenty-First Century CIA Infiltration...

Mike's eyes grew wide. He turned his entire body as he swung his incredulous expression on the Russian. And what he saw in the Russian's face haunted him. A dark acceptance of dangerous knowledge. Mike didn't say anything. He could feel his brow furrowing so hard it was becoming painful. The Russian gestured for Mike to continue reading. He'd done little more than glance at the headers.

Mike read the document from top to bottom. Then he read it a second time. He skimmed over parts to ascertain keywords and the descriptions he could hardly believe. He read it a third time. It was only the first page of a larger document. The information trailed off, making him feel as if he'd only scratched the surface.

"Impossible," he finally said.

There was no way the thing was real.

A long-standing infiltration program. Penetrating the CIA. By Cuban intelligence.

Mike cleared his throat and spoke again, mostly just to hear his own voice give him certainty in something. "There's no way."

The Russian gave a sad smile and looked down at his hands. "It is happening. You need to take care of it."

Mike coughed out an ugly laugh. "You're insane. Dropping it in my lap like this." It was like cleaning fingerprints off a murder weapon before handing it off.

"I have already done what I can on my end."

"On your end? What, you managed to get page one of a questionable report?"

"It is not questionable. Don't you see? Our agent died for this."

"The Cubans think it's *our* agent! They already think we're onto them!"

"Not necessarily. Our agent passed this on before he was killed. Otherwise we wouldn't have it now. But this is all the more reason to move quickly."

"Are you saying we have a mole?"

"I am saying what this," the Russian pointed to the delicate page sitting in Mike's hands, "is saying. A Cuban program exists to infiltrate your intelligence agency, and it appears it's passed the first phase."

"How did your agent get this information?" Mike was still suspicious of the credibility of the whole thing.

"Please. Let a rival keep some secrets."

Mike pinched the bridge of his nose. This was all too much. His heart rate had risen and he felt the thrill of chasing something bigger than himself. He had to slow down and break things down as best he could now. He wouldn't get another chance like this. And a fearful realization was growing within him. This would be on his shoulders — his alone — to solve. The potential breach of the CIA, all its assets, information, and future plans…there was no way to know how bad things were.

The whole thing also seemed too far-fetched. The Cubans allegedly had a sophisticated infiltration program targeting the CIA. That didn't mean they actually had a mole. Let alone the ability to get one in there.

Allegedly was the key word here. Caution was king in intelligence. "And what if I don't believe you?" Mike asked.

"It is you who has more to lose. *Much* more. The only thing I can do is give you the information. Speaking of which," the Russian reached over and snatched up the sheet of sugar paper. He placed it on a handkerchief which had been laid across his lap, then he folded the whole thing up into a ball, squeezing it tight and kneading it with his fingers.

Mike rolled up the plastic wrap into a ball and placed it on the bench between them. "How many people know about this?"

The Russian blinked and his eyebrows bobbed, an approximation of a shrug.

"No, Jesus, I'm serious," Mike said, struggling to keep his voice low and he forced himself to slow down. "Who the fuck knows about this? Just you and me?"

The Russian pursed his lips. "I think you are catching onto why I am so reluctant to show you in the first place. There is no way to know."

"Take a guess."

"I can only speak to my circle. I would have no way of knowing who else has stumbled upon this. I doubt this as probable. But if anyone had, they would be few and far between. I can't imagine too many Cuban agents know either"

"Your circle then. How many?"

"Five."

"Already too many."

"Agreed. It will be more soon."

"Why? Who else do you have a meeting with?"

The Russian shook his head. "No, not me. You. Americans have their confidants. But I accept this risk. As long as this stays low. Do not tell your superiors."

Mike scoffed at that and the Russian threw him a sharp look. He remembered that condition being emphasized the last time they had spoken. Was this Russian simply testing the gullibility of American's agents? Attempting to tie up a nation's resources in a wild goose chase to open up a front elsewhere? There was no way to know. And unfortunately, Mike was grudgingly coming to the conclusion that it didn't matter. He'd be forced to look into this. There was a brilliance of security behind the Russian's play coming to light. He was forcing Mike's hand.

Cat and mouse.

The best time to accept a truce was when you were at a disadvantage. Mike wasn't so brash that he couldn't see the value in that. But he had gotten enough information now that he could put this Russian in his place. Show him he wasn't asleep at the wheel. He'd connected some dots.

"Why do you want it kept low? Why not send this up the chain? Let the big boys handle this."

The Russian looked clenched his teeth but resumed his calm demeanor. "I would prefer to keep those who would make this… political, out of it."

Mike gave a slow nod and didn't say anything for some time. "You speak as if you have American interests at heart."

"I have world stability at heart. Mother Russia doesn't like to see other nations falter. This causes world instability. Russia is a part of the international community, as much as NATO doesn't accept it."

Mike had to stop himself from laughing out loud. "Convincing, really. Some of that's true. But there's more to it than that."

"Hm?" The Russian seemed genuinely confused, with surprise on his face for the first time that evening.

"Russian intelligence doesn't give a rat's ass about the safety of the CIA. The real question is, who helped Cuba put this together?"

The Russian furrowed his brow and shook his head. "You think-"

"This document reminds me of another one I've read. Archived material of the Soviet's program to infiltrate the CIA fifty years ago. The wording is remarkably similar." Mike waited a moment before continuing, letting his words sink in. "It was supposed to be decommissioned along with all the U.S. and Soviet spies mutually retracted from each other's nations, via the Malta Summit. I bet your spooks included the Cubans in your program, which is how they got involved. You probably didn't ask for their opinion on pulling the plug, just like missiles getting pulled by Khrushchev. So they decided to stick it to Russia by continuing the program. It still damaged America, so it wasn't hard for Russians to brush it under the rug."

The Russian narrowed his eyes. It may as well have been an open admission.

"Your agent died running an op against Cuba without Cuba knowing their own ally is trying to keep them on a leash. America finds out about the agent from Cuba. As soon as we tell Cuba he's not ours, they start digging."

The Russian raised a hand to interrupt but Mike continued. "Hold on, I'm almost done. I'm betting there's more. I'm betting you tried to reason with Cuba first and get a piece of the pie, but they denied sharing their intel with you. Having little Cuba appropriate Soviet plans *and* keeping you out is quite the snub. Not to mention…I mean, I can't imagine some of the damage they could do if they manage to burrow deep enough in the CIA. They'd have access to everything we have on Russia — and I know for a fact some of it would piss Cuba off. The CIA knows more about Russian affairs than Russians do. Maybe some of those revelations don't exactly encourage the socialists in Latin America to fight the good fight. Latin America. That's your desk, and that's mine. And as dramatic as all this predicting bullshit is, it's America who wins Latin America in this scenario. That probably hurts your budget. I don't need to keep breaking this down, do I?"

There was a long pause. Mike pretended to enjoy the ugly painting until the Russian could be brought to reply.

"Good thing neither of us can afford to be losers."

"Good thing," Mike agreed. He relaxed his posture now that his riposte was finished. "Help us in Nicaragua. Stay in touch about this. And maybe we can both dig ourselves out of a hole."

The Russian nodded, satisfied. It was the equivalent of shaken hands. And perhaps a little more — the mutual recognition between equals.

The next few days would determine if anything good could come of this.

Was it risky to let John and Barry fall into less than friendly hands? Certainly. But Mike wagered this against them being trapped in ultimately hostile hands, perhaps lost in Nicaragua forever. He didn't like it — he didn't have to — but giving leverage over to an opponent could still be useful. The Russian would try and play him. He counted on it.

Not all wrapped boxes are gifts. Barker had told him that once, after giving him salted nuts that turned out to be a spring-loaded gag gift. But the sentiment was powerful. One of the paradoxes of working in intelligence was that at any time, information could be misinformation, any boon a bust. That's why trust was so expensive.

Mike's thinking was interrupted before he could figure out his next move.

"It does not seem as if you've come alone as you suggested, Mike Morrandon."

The words were like electricity in the air. Mike's eyes widened, suppressing his impulses to look around. "Where?"

"3:00. Main foyer. Don't look."

Mike made it look like he was stretching and cracking his back, giving him two seconds to peek down the halls. Someone was hurrying out the exit, checking a phone and sliding it into their pocket.

"Shit. They snapped a picture?"

"I believe so, yes. Our mutual appreciation for art has come to an end."

Mike looked at the Russian. A man of similar rank, intelligence, but most importantly, a sense of obligation for justice. Mike couldn't forgive the man if he'd had anything to do with United States SEALs and pilots being killed in the air and jeopardizing his mission, but grudgingly he accepted that he'd been on the other side before. They were all bastards doing what bastards did.

The Russian nodded. Mike frowned but nodded back. They'd already been spotted, so they couldn't risk talking details or specifics any longer.

Two tall, muscled men were walking down the halls toward them.

Mike began to reach for his gun when the Russian stood and walked toward the men. One scouted out toward the exit where their photographer had taken off, while the other eyed Mike suspiciously. He reminded Mike of a bulldog who hadn't been fed in a while.

"You didn't come alone," Mike said. "You bastard."

"Aren't we all? Have a pleasant evening, Mike Morrandon" the Russian said, turning to face Mike. The man gave a weak smile, letting his age slip through his mask. "I hope one day you will be able to appreciate things like chess and art."

"I hope we never meet again."

The Russian laughed then turned with his men and was off.

Mike knew he had to wait for the Russian and his bodyguards to leave before he could leave himself. Spies never left together, even when spotted and tagged. Mike waited impatiently for ten minutes that felt like a hundred before getting up himself and making his own departure.

I don't give a damn about art, Mike thought, passing by the paintings on either side of him. *I can hardly appreciate reality.*

CHAPTER 20

It had been almost twelve hours of the same continuous anthem over and over before John dipped in and out of consciousness and lost track. The fluorescent lights stayed on overhead, sometimes flickering from power failure — a common problem in Nicaragua. Occasionally their captors stopped the music in long breaks, only for it to start again unpredictably. No one else had entered the room since the one masked man had broken their monotony to snap a picture. Barry and John's arms had gone permanently numb long ago. John had managed to float in and out of a meditative sleep, earning a small bit of desperately needed rest. His headache had thankfully dulled to a distant throb and his hearing had resumed to normal although his ears were still raw. Barry couldn't sleep a wink or allow his mind to drift into pleasant distraction like John had; his eyes were bloodshot and he was sure he was going insane.

So when the music stopped, and stayed stopped for longer than its ten seconds, or even its longer few-minute breaks, Barry hardly registered the change. John opened his tired eyes and watched the door.

As he suspected, it opened. The man with the balaclava carried a long metal table into the room, close to where John and Barry were hung like drying sausages.

The man left. John and Barry stared at the table. A pair of chairs were next, followed by a third, the same masked man setting them two on one side, one on the other. Everything was made of metal, giving off a crude industrial feel.

John was intimately familiar with this setup. It took Barry a moment to clue in but even he could read the room. His eyes filled with fear.

Interrogation.

John didn't share the same feeling. He was curious, contemplating how this would go. He was used to being on the other end, after all.

While it did instill a natural anxiety tucked far away in the recesses of his consciousness, he also knew the risks involved with interrogative tactics. No victim would consider the difficulty of the task at hand for an interrogator, but John knew how hard it could be. During a period of capture, interrogation provided the most fragile balance of power, with the most exploitable opportunities creeping through. If someone was being interrogated, they assumed they were up against an inevitable force. In reality, it was an exchange. It may just be an instance of pain delivered for information. But even that held a certain amount of risk. Squealers tended to embellish facts. Or lacked the calm needed for a coherent answer.

No, John saw things very differently than others in similar situations to this. The setup in front of him was a bargaining table. If an answer was wanted, a question had to be asked. That vulnerable moment could tip the balance in either side's favor.

It was also the tipping point in other ways. This moment could easily end their lives if played poorly. John mustered his faculties. He had to be on. If only he weren't so drained.

He almost didn't notice the door hadn't closed. There was a brief murmuring of men's voices — Spanish, John couldn't make out any words — and a new man entered the room.

He wasn't wearing a mask. He was shorter than average and didn't appear particularly intimidating. In fact, he came across as a kind-faced, youthful spirit. The only betrayal was a cunning intelligence John could read in the man's expression as he examined John and Barry. No malice rested there, but a strange and twisted humor rested behind the eyes. John wondered what the man might see in his own.

While they were sizing one another up, the masked man entered with a pair of keys dangling in his hands, and moved to unlock the cuffs that kept them to the ceiling. While the man approached, John considered his options. He looked to their interrogator, calmly taking a seat, and appearing a little too self-assured.

They were out of time.

Barry slumped forward as he fell to the ground, the weight of his body on his weakened legs too much to bear. He panted, tears welling in his eyes from the mix of pain and relief experienced from the extended period of time spent in one position.

The guard hadn't even bothered to remove the cuff locked on Barry's hand. He'd simply undone the lock attached to the bar overhead. Barry was still stuck with the discomfort of the cuff rubbing against his raw wrist — not that that was the most pressing concern for him. But John noticed the subtlety of the gesture. No deal had been made for their release — otherwise they would have removed the cuffs entirely for courtesy's sake — yet they still wanted information. Perhaps that information wasn't required so quickly that they couldn't toy with their prey.

John considered his options as the guard moved to uncuff him. He still had control of one arm and his legs even if he were cuffed in place. He could spring up on his toes and pull himself up into the air thanks to the pipe he was attached to, and get his legs around the guard. Then he could use the guard as a shield against enemy fire and take the man's pistol…

The problem was Barry.

John could take that sort of risk if it were just him in captivity, but he had a mission and a civilian to protect. He couldn't afford putting Barry in that sort of danger. John would have to go along with this interrogation and hope a plan for their release was still taking place in the background. He'd keep his eyes out for a more promising opportunity in the meantime.

The guard gave John a threatening look through his balaclava as he undid his cuffs.

"Please," the Cuban said in a soft voice to match his gentle face and stature. "Sit."

John stretched his limbs and made his way over to the metal table and chairs. Barry followed soon after, looking like a stray lamb, rubbing at his wrist.

The Cuban sent the guard out of the room. John raised an eyebrow at that. It sent a powerful message to allow John and Barry free of their bonds and under no further restraint.

The chairs were cold and uncomfortable, but being given the ability to sit after hours of forced standing brought immense relief to both of their bodies. Barry made an audible sigh of pleasure.

The Cuban smiled. "Let's talk."

The feeling of relief left Barry as quickly as it had come. He mustered his courage as best as he could. "We'll never talk. Americans don't negotiate with terrorists."

The Cuban laughed. John grimaced. Barry folded his arms, determined to stand by his words. Wordlessly the Cuban reached below the table and produced what looked to be a well maintained Makarov. He turned it over gently in his hands before placing it down on the table between them, his easy smile never wavering.

"You will talk."

The gun was right in the middle of the table, less than an arm's length away. Barry stared at it. His eyes flicked to the Cuban, who leaned back, looking smug with his implied threat laying in the middle of the table.

Barry was never one to turn down an opportunity. Especially when it capitalized on someone else's mistake.

"Don't," John said, but Barry lunged for the gun across the table before John could stop him.

The Cuban reached for it a second too late, and Barry had it in his hands. He fumbled with it, but only for a moment, and then had the safety off, finger on the trigger and cocked.

"Freeze, motherfucker! That's right!"

The Cuban's eyes were wide with surprise. John kept his mask neutral.

"Barry in the house! Yeah! Barry's got a gun!"

"Barry," John said, reaching out a hand.

"No John, I've got this." He turned back onto their interrogator. "Alright dude, you're going to stand up real slowly and open the door for us."

The Cuban didn't move.

"Barry-" John said again.

"Hands up! Hands where I can see 'em!" Barry screamed.

The Cuban didn't move. There was a silence, and Barry began to get agitated with the lack of response from the Cuban. Or from John, for that matter.

"John, get up and get him moving."

The Cuban's wide-eyed surprise had dropped. Instead, his gentle, smug smile returned.

"The gun isn't loaded," John said, sighing.

"What?" Barry asked. Fear crept into his face. He pointed off to the side and pulled the trigger. There was only a faint click. He tried to fire a few more times with no response from the gun.

The Cuban held out his hand to Barry, like a patronizing parent taking back a child's toy that they weren't responsible enough to have. Barry loosed the magazine and looked inside, still trying to look for bullets and blinking in confusion when the lights above them flickered, straining for power. The Cuban lost some of his patience and raised his other hand above the table. It held another pistol, and John was sure this one was loaded. Barry didn't notice the action at first and John cleared his throat. Barry looked to John, looked to the Cuban, saw the gun in his hands pointing at them, and then put the gun he had stolen on the table, slowly sliding it across the surface.

"Thank you," the Cuban said, picking the gun up from the table and placing it off to the side. He lowered the other gun in his hand back under the table — it would still be pointing at them, just in case of any more sudden, stupid moves. But everyone sitting at the table knew that that wasn't going to happen again.

Barry looked pained. John felt a mild sense of embarrassment. It was an old, stupid trick. He had hoped Barry was smarter than that.

Let's get this over with, John thought.

"I'm assuming you know how this works," The Cuban said, speaking to John.

John nodded. "I know how this works."

If they gave up what their captors wanted, there was a chance they'd be set free. It was a small chance, and it depended on what was happening behind the scenes, but the time for waiting was finished. If they resisted, their captors would resort to torture without a second thought. John and Barry could choose how they wanted to proceed.

John had extensive training in how to resist multiple torture methods. Officially, he wasn't supposed to give up any information in any instance of torture or death. But Barry complicated things. John was still tasked to be protecting a U.S. civilian and had to minimize the threat to his life. He might have to trade information to do so.

But more to the point, their captors probably knew most of what they needed to know anyway. John didn't have any interesting information to provide. If they started digging into safehouse locations and weapon caches then he'd shut up like a clam. But he'd see where this went first.

Barry pounded both fists on the metal table, wincing even as he tried to make a show of force. "We'll never-"

"Let's begin," John said, putting a firm hand on Barry's shoulder and pulling him back.

"What are your names?" their interrogator asked.

"Barry Bridges," John said, jerking a thumb beside him, "I'm John Carpenter."

"Nationality."

"American."

"Who do you work for?" The man looked to John.

"American interests."

"What organization?"

"I don't know."

"What organization?"

"I don't know. They don't tell me."

"What do you do?"

"Whatever they tell me."

The Cuban narrowed his eyes, trying to decide if John was toying with him. But John was talking, and that was usually the first hurdle to overcome. The Cuban decided to press on this track.

"Who is 'they'?"

"I have a single contact. A handler."

"How do they contact you?"

"A phone."

"Where is this phone?"

"Destroyed. In the house we were captured. I'm sure you have the remains."

The Cuban smiled, a tight line across his mouth that held no satisfaction. That confirmed for John that he was doing something right.

"What are you doing in Nicaragua?"

"I live here."

"What are you doing with this," the Cuban pointed to Barry, "Barry Bridges."

"Trying to leave the country."

"Why?"

"I was told he might be in danger. My handler was correct. I am trying to get him safely out of the country."

The Cuban blinked. John suspected he hadn't gotten any useful answers. John decided to push back, just a little.

"I haven't done a very good job, have I?" John said, rubbing the back of his head and doing his best impression of a young sheepish boy asking a girl to prom.

The corners of the Cuban's mouth twitched.

Unfortunately, if John didn't prove useful enough, the Cuban might just eliminate him. He'd have to see if he could bait the man with something to peak his interest.

Just wait, John reminded himself, *give it time. We only need time.*

He doubted there was much movement on his behalf, but the U.S. wouldn't be happy about a private citizen like Barry stuck in a foreign country under duress. John had to admit, he had that much to thank Barry for.

"You," the Cuban turned to Barry.

Barry gulped. "Me?"

"You. What are you doing in Nicaragua? What were you doing in El Gigante ?"

The specificity of the question threw Barry off guard. "Just…a think-retreat."

194

"Think-retreat?" The Cuban frowned.

"Yeah like…you know-"

The Cuban's frown deepened. "No I don't. What were you doing in El Gi -"

"Vacation!" Barry cried. "I was stressed with work and shit so decided to take off for a few days! Is that a crime? Jesus!"

"No crime," the Cuban said, calm as ever. "But troubling for us. Very troubling."

"I don't know who you are, man. I…don't know who you are." Barry slumped in his seat. The adrenaline of reaching for the gun and being threatened was wearing off, and the exhaustion and pain was creeping back in, reminding him of what his body really thought of all this treatment. "I don't know why my think-retreat should bother you. Or be any of your business, for that matter."

The Cuban took that in and nodded. "Does the name Antonio Romero mean anything to you?"

"Oh shit, what?"

"Does it?"

"Of course it does!"

John didn't know the name. The Cuban didn't appear to expect him to recognize it. This was all Barry's turf.

"What the fuck does he want?" Barry asked.

"I — and he — want to know what you are doing here. In Nicaragua. It's a long way away from the United States."

"I told you! Think-retreat!" Barry paused then spoke up again when he saw that answer wasn't satisfying enough for his interrogator. "Vacation!"

The Cuban shook his head. "Try again."

"I'm not lying!"

"Were you trying to hide from us? This seems a stupid place to hide. It is closer to us than not."

"I'm not trying to hide from him!"

John knew this interrogation tact. The Cuban wasn't really interested in Barry being in Nicaragua. He was testing Barry and putting him on the defensive for the real question. But John couldn't do anything to prevent him from taking the bait.

"Very well. Let us say you are here for your short and mysterious vacation."

"I am!"

"What do you think the outcome of the upcoming Senate hearing will be?"

"What?"

"Do I need to repeat the question?"

"No, I..." Barry looked confused, looking off to the side to consider the question. "Are you talking about *my* Senate hearing?"

"Is there another Senate hearing I might be referring to?"

"Uh, no. No. Okay. I mean...yeah I have that next week. I just had to get away from it all. Surf some waves. Enjoy the heat. Then come back with a clear head."

"Of course, of course, understandable." The Cuban's next words held more bite. "Is the discretionary committee going to get what they want?"

"Wait, *that's* what this is about?" Barry looked incredulous. He looked at John, then the Cuban, and laughed. "All of this? Getting kidnapped and shot at and imprisoned? Oh man, you had me scared. You still have me scared! But come on man, that's nothing to worry about."

John was out to lunch. He had no idea what was happening. But this information could be important for his mission. If he were alive long enough to continue it.

The Cuban didn't seem swayed by the good-natured assurances from Barry. This was still deadly serious to him, for all his calm and gentle manner. "Mr. Bridges, you were called to a major hearing, then took pains to make a quiet exit from the country. That doesn't exactly look like nothing to worry about."

Barry was still unphased. "Oh, right, right. Yeah I guess I could see how that would look suspicious. I was just trying to keep a low profile! I don't think you know how big I am back in the U.S. People love me! I don't blame them!" He gave a wink. The Cuban didn't react. "Anyway…no yeah, I go to the meeting with my pitbull lawyers, I slip a couple bribes in the right corners, and I go under the grill. All according to plan. I don't have to give them shit. There's no way I'm giving up the anonymity that makes my platform work. That's its whole point."

"Even to the U.S. government?"

"Well, yeah. It doesn't matter who they are, they're not getting it."

"Even if Antonio wanted it?"

Barry froze. "What? Why would Anton want that? I thought your whole point was making sure it didn't happen."

"No, if you were to give access to Antonio, instead of the U.S. government. The anonymous features would still remain in place for everyone else."

"Oh." Barry furrowed his eyebrows. "I…I can't do that."

"Can't? Or won't?"

"I…" Barry felt sweat starting to break out on the ridge of his hairline. "He doesn't own the app. I own the app."

"Yes. You may keep owning the app. He's not taking that away. He would like you to keep running it."

"I might be able to work out something with limited or partial access for extenuating circumstances but-"

"I think you can see this is not a negotiation." Barry grew silent as the Cuban continued. "There are two simple options, and two following outcomes. Give Antonio the overrides, and you may go freely — assuming you don't allow the committee to get what they want."

"What's the other option?" Barry asked, already having an idea forming in his head. He and his big mouth just had to ask anyway.

"We kill you to make sure no one gets access."

Barry swallowed against a hard lump forming in the back of his throat.

The Cuban shrugged. "I am actually of the mind to follow the latter option. Much simpler. Safer. But Antonio insisted we try this instead."

"I thought Antonio was a business partner," Barry said, anger overtaking his fear. "And I don't even know who the fuck you are!"

A heavy bang penetrated the air, making Barry cover his ears, and John ducked and reached for the non-existent gun that would usually be on his person.

A thin stream of smoke curled away from the gun the Cuban had shot at the wall. John slowly brought himself back up in his chair. The Cuban's gentle facade had faded. Cold intensity lay there now. The seriousness and legitimacy of his threats could not be questioned.

"What is your decision?"

Barry was on the verge of tears. Emotionally, he felt like a yo-yo. Anytime he was scared, John assured him not to be. Anytime he was brash, it was the wrong choice. He felt utterly useless. And this last encounter was the nail in his coffin.

"I…I'll…give access."

The Cuban smiled, and the gentleness returned to his face. "Excellent. We will bring you a computer."

"That's it?" Barry could hardly believe it. He felt relieved. And he remembered what John had said earlier. All they had to do was give them what they wanted. He couldn't say for certain what would happen next, but there was a chance they'd get out of here.

"For you," the Cuban said with a sly grin, turning to John. "You are going to tell me what is on this."

John's eyes locked on the narrow rectangle held between the man's fingers. It looked like a USB, but it wasn't one. It was a 'wig — a useful bit of hardware that allowed the user to copy and download an entire computer's data in thirty seconds or less.

The 'wig that had been in his possession. The one with the Puentes cartel data he'd been sifting through each and every night since that last mission. Kept on him at all times.

John met the Cuban's eyes, feeling them match the penetrating cold of his own. "You are going to give me access to this," the man repeated.

CHAPTER 21

When it became clear that Barry and John would cooperate, even if begrudgingly, the Cuban's entire demeanor changed and his two prisoners were treated much better. It was like new air had been pumped into the room. Coffee, water, and sandwiches were brought in by guards who took up lazy posts in chairs, guns resting next to them as they ate and drank with the others. Barry snatched up a bottle of water and drank it fast against John's insistence to pace himself. The man coughed and gagged while John took a few sips of water before tasting the coffee. He frowned when he discovered it was instant — as he'd expected — but he didn't suppose he could put in an order for a latte.

Although circumstances had grown more comfortable and Barry had grown much less panicked, John wasn't put any more at ease. He wouldn't be lulled into a safe sense of security. The Cuban still wanted what he had come for.

Two laptops were placed on the table in front of Barry and John.

"You will grant access to Antonio for your app, Mr. Bridges," the Cuban said to Barry, finishing a sandwich and licking his fingers. He pointed at John. "You will show me what is being protected by password on this USB." He laid the 'wig on the table and slid it slowly across to John, daring him to try to make a move.

John accepted the 'wig without comment and turned on the laptop provided.

There was silence for a few minutes as Barry and John waited for things to load. The computers were basic and beat up. John suspected the computers were rounded up quickly as the mission to capture the two *gringos* unfolded.

John was the first to produce results. He plugged in the 'wig, entered the password, and opened the massive file. He had considered lying about a rotating weekly password and that he was unable to access the file, but he couldn't risk the Cuban calling his bluff. A tech-savvy spy of middling grade would be able to identify that the 'wig was an independent component that wasn't integrated into a larger network, even if they didn't know exactly how the thing worked.

"What am I looking at?" the Cuban asked, strolling around the corner of the table. He didn't seem worried about getting close to John. John was sure the man would be difficult to take down, and the other two guards in the room would have him and Barry dead before he could try anyway.

John shuffled his chair back, inviting the Cuban into his space to look at the screen. "The entire data content of a laptop copied from a previous op."

The Cuban's eyes grew focused and betrayed a hint of confusion as he stared at the data. He probably hadn't expected such a mess of information. John had considered the dangers of giving over this information, but the more he thought about it, the less critical the whole business seemed. Even if the Cuban shipped the 'wig off to a bunch of computer wizards to hunt and isolate the data, he figured there would be little use or interest in the laptop of a drug cartel from Antigua. The only thing John considered they'd be intrigued by was any contact information that would connect U.S. personnel to the cartel — the very thing John was hunting for. John wanted to hold that information against whichever corrupt bastard had gotten his friend killed. If the Cubans could do that job better than he could, he wasn't about to stop them.

"Drug cartel," John said. "Rich family based in Guatemala. The laptop had information I thought I could use for the op so I swiped it. Unfortunately, well, it's a little less useful than I was hoping. It's all yours."

The Cuban frowned, then rotated onto Barry. His expression didn't improve. John leaned over to peek at Barry's screen, and was caught off guard by what he saw.

Barry was playing solitaire.

The Cuban grew angry. He smacked Barry hard across the cheek, and Barry fell from his chair.

"Ow! What'd you do that for?" he managed, pulling himself back into his seat.

"This is no game," the Cuban rumbled. "I have no time for games."

"No, no! I'm just waiting on the internet!" Barry raised his hands, defending his face.

The Cuban stared at Barry, then looked at the screen displaying Barry's game of solitaire. John noted he wasn't particularly good at the game. That at least, didn't surprise him.

"What's wrong with the internet?" the Cuban asked.

"Man, what isn't wrong with it! Slow as hell. Look!" Barry pulled up his browser and refreshed the page. A loading bar moved at a crawl, inching across the screen to pull up the site Barry was trying to load.

"You can't…do this without internet?"

Barry laughed. "Dude, do you have any idea how this stuff works? I can't just wave my magic wand and poof, backdoor for Anton!"

The Cuban didn't answer.

Barry shrugged. "You guys could have preloaded any of the software I need, but you didn't. Okay, fine, I'm not trying to mess around here. I have to download the programs, then I need to access and fork my codebase through my dev portal so I can do what you need me to do from this laptop. Then I need to actually implement the changes. *Entiendes*?"

The Cuban frowned and narrowed his eyes at Barry.

One of the guards leaned forward in his chair from the corner. "*¿Hay algún problema?*"

The Cuban shook his head to the guard then turned back to Barry. "How do we make this go faster?"

Barry tentatively took control of the trackpad again, watching for the Cuban to react. "Get a higher speed from your provider." When he assessed the coast was clear, Barry moved one of the solitaire cards on the screen to a new stack.

* * *

It took a good half hour before the Cuban had figured out he could establish a hotspot with his phone to provide better internet than what Nicaraguan infrastructure could provide. The man was flustered, especially after exercising other options before realizing this more efficient solution. Barry's download had begun, but the delay was still provoking frustration from their captors.

"It's a big file," Barry had said, turning the laptop to show the Cuban he wasn't lying.

In the meantime, the Cuban had taken to having John help poke through the data on his 'wig. John admitted he hadn't got very far or discovered much of anything useful, but was able to navigate enough to parse certain sections for the Cuban, who was overwhelmed by the amount of raw information. He was just beginning to show signs of dropping the whole affair when he spotted something amidst the files.

"What is this? Go here," the Cuban said, pointing at the screen.

John was in a smattering of data containing numbers and locations. He had previously combed through this data, reading through any finance streams he could find. But he had been looking for money moving back and forth from the United States. He wasn't a tech specialist but he was competent enough to sift through data. The Cuban pointed out something amidst a mess he'd already skimmed through before. It made him perk up, though he didn't say anything, and tried to obey the Cuban's direction.

His captor lost patience and took over the trackpad on the laptop, shooing John to the side as he leaned back to make room. But he watched closely to see what the Cuban was highlighting.

Isla de Anticipación.

A region listed with a series of others. John figured these were locations of contacts, supply yards, private airports, or manufacturers for cocaine production. Valuable information for someone in the DEA perhaps, but of little use to him. Even less use to Cuban intelligence… so why was the Cuban so interested in this?

It could be nothing, but John filed away the information. Anything that could be used as a bargaining chip had to be gathered.

The lights flickered.

"Okay, I finished downloading," Barry said, interrupting John's thoughts. The Cuban seemed locked in thought too, taking a moment to turn away from John's laptop and switch over to Barry's.

"This is the program?" the Cuban asked.

"Yeah, this is my baby. Let me just log in." Barry looked over his shoulder. "Um, can you not hover like that-"

The Cuban snarled, grabbed Barry by the top of his head, and shoved him, as if he were disciplining a puppy.

"Ow!"

The door opened and everyone looked up. A guard John hadn't seen before entered. He looked at John, then Barry, and then the

Cuban's angry face and hesitated, deciding it was better not to enter as far as he'd originally been intending.

"*¿Qué?*" the Cuban shouted at him.

"*Lo siento. Hay hombres en la puerta.*" *Sorry. There are men at the door.*

The Cuban gripped his pistol and the guards in their chairs took attention. One sat up in his chair and picked up his AK-47, while the other stood and looked to the Cuban for direction. The Cuban gestured for him to be calm with his pistol, as he examined the mag and slid it home.

It was a catalyst. Which meant it was an opportunity.

John unplugged the 'wig from his laptop and palmed it with the expertise of a magician performing a card trick. Barry was nervously looking at the guard approaching them and didn't notice John plug it into his own laptop.

"*¿Hombres?*" the Cuban was saying. "*¿Los hombres del Presidente? ¿O tenemos un problema mayor?*" *Men? The President's men? Or do we have a bigger problem?*

"I don't know," replied the man who had barged in. "…not *gringos*. They say they're from Antigua."

"Antigua?"

"Guatemala."

"I know where Antigua…" the Cuban composed himself. His eyes flicked over to John then back to the guard. "What did they say?"

"What are they saying?" Barry whispered to John.

John had his attention split between the 'wig downloading Barry's laptop and the interaction. "People at the door," he whispered.

"Who?"

"That's what they're trying to figure out," John said, dropping his voice as the guard in the corner moved closer to them. The man nudged Barry in the back with the barrel of his AK-47. John kept the 'wig covered with a casual hand.

"Man, why do you guys keep hitting me instead of him?" Barry moaned.

John frowned.

The guard was about to push Barry harder but the Cuban gestured for his men. They walked over and listened as the Cuban spoke to them so John and Barry couldn't hear. The guard that had prodded Barry looked over his shoulder and glared at him suspiciously.

"If you have to go do something, this is going to take a little while," Barry said, shaking his head at how long the laptop was taking to load.

The guard scowled and turned back toward their huddle.

John could hear chatter and a pounding on a door coming from far down the hall. The 'wig would be finished. He unplugged it, inserted it back in his laptop, and tensed up. He was lucky to get away with that. He had to be ready for anything now.

Unfortunately, that was when the Cuban had finished giving his orders, and the same guard retrieved the handcuffs that had been removed earlier, and approached the prisoners to re-cuff them. The guard looked warily at John, sensing what he might be capable of. The Cuban had already turned to leave, but the other guard held his pistol out with both hands, pointing at John.

John eyed up the guards. The man with the pistol returned his gaze, daring John to try something. When John didn't react, the man switched his aim onto Barry.

Barry put his hands up immediately, gulping.

John held his hands out. It wasn't time. Not yet. He'd have to let this play out.

The Cuban shouted for the guards to hurry up, and John was cuffed behind his back, then Barry. The guard that had cuffed them nodded to his colleague as he left the room with the Cuban and the messenger. The door was shut, and the guard with the pistol remained behind, leaning against the shut door. His gun was held in both hands, pointed down but ready.

There probably wouldn't be a better opportunity to get out. If John's handler or the parties interested in Barry had made progress, John would've expected more development or cooperation on the side of his captors. Instead, the two of them were giving up their final bargaining chips with disclosing their intel. Sure, John had encouraged Barry to do so because there was really no way around it. But the situation had changed.

Hands cuffed behind his back. One guard. One gun.

Good odds.

John scrunched up his face and twisted in his chair, making it look like he was stretching his back and working out a kink. He saw the guard jerk slightly out of the corner of his eye in reaction, but then relaxed seeing that John wasn't trying anything. The guard may have seen John twisting his back, but hadn't paid too much attention to both his hands stretched out. John grabbed the armrest of his chair from behind his back — risked a glance at the guard who had looked down at his gun — planted his feet firmly on the ground, and spun — flinging the metal chair across the room with all his might.

It was a calculated risk. If the guard shot Barry, hopefully it would be a flesh wound. If it wasn't, well, in a roundabout way John was stopping Cuban intelligence from gaining access to whatever app they were so obsessed about. And if John were shot well…he was getting tired of being cooped up in this room. But when a large metal object comes careening toward an opponent, the last thing they usually think of is standing firm and firing back.

The man's gun discharged as John slid to the floor, a hand flying out to pull Barry from his seat even while Barry jumped a foot in the air at the shock of the blast. They fell to cover under the table while the guard's shot went wide, as expected.

But the guard had gotten his arms up and turned away from the chair, stopping most of the blow when it collided. John had to move fast.

He pulled into a crouch and slammed his shoulders against the bottom of the table, then stood and threw the whole thing with another enormous effort. The table flipped long-ways, tumbling toward the guard, who was just beginning to get his bearings and line up a proper shot. The guard pulled back to cover himself from a second incoming object, and, while the table was flipping, John took two strides and lunged for the guard over the whole mess.

He tackled the guard against the wall with his shoulder and body weight, looking like a fish out of water with his hands pinned behind his back. They slid to the ground, John's shins striking against the edge of the table that had slammed to the floor. The guard had it worse. His back came down hard on the metal chair haphazardly scattered nearby, its feet raised in the air like a rocket battery. He cried out in pain when he collided but realized the seriousness of the situation and shrugged off the pain quicker than John would've liked. The guard tried to find room to use his gun and pushed John back with a hand, preventing his opponent from getting a clean blow or grab in on the gun-hand.

With half a second before the inevitable trigger pull, John twisted and body slammed against the protective arm, turning and getting his hands onto the man's gun-hand. He fought with both hands against one until the guard redoubled his efforts with both to grapple over the weapon. But for John, that was a distraction.

Now that John's back was to the man, he bucked, whipping his head and feet back, kicking the man's legs and slamming the back of his skull into the man's face. The guard screamed like a banshee. Pain rattled through John's skull, but he was able to take advantage of the man's reflex to hold his battered face.

"Gun!" John yelled to Barry.

Barry was up and running now, shaking off the surprise of the attack but knowing his part. He kicked at the man's hands and the gun fell out of his grasp. Barry swept a leg and slid the gun across the room, then chased after it, bending down and grabbing it awkwardly off the floor with his hands behind his back.

With the gun out of play, John pulled himself away like a caterpillar, bringing himself to his knees, then working to stand. The man was doing the same but John was stable first. He didn't know if Barry had the gun yet. He wasn't about to wait to find out.

John kicked the guard in the crotch, waited a second for him to double over, then followed through with a second kick to the face when he bent down in pain for maximum impact. The man crumpled onto his side, and fell to the floor, arm stretched out and grasping for his gun that wasn't there.

"On the door," John said to Barry, and Barry, wide-eyed as always in crisis, moved toward the door and turned around, aiming the gun at the door while facing backward.

"Step over your cuffs first," John said, bewildered that Barry actually considered firing backwards with hands cuffed. John stepped over his own cuffs, one foot at a time, moving quickly. Being caught halfway between that maneuver would mean the end for them.

With Barry paying attention to this task and the door, John brought his hands under his feet and stepped over the cuffs, shook out his arms, then took a deep breath and raised a boot. He brought it down against the guard's neck. There was a snap, and John let out his breath.

He looked over his shoulder and saw Barry staring at him.

"The door," John said.

Barry gave a short nod. His hands were trembling.

John searched the guard for keys to their cuffs but came up empty handed. The other guard or the Cuban must have them.

"Shit," John whispered.

That made things more complicated.

But there was no time to dwell on the circumstance — there was only time to better their slim odds. He propped up the table on it's edge, giving them a short barricade of cover. John brought Barry down into a crouch, hunkering against the edge, and took the gun from him. He checked the magazine and chamber to make sure the thing would work. As a rule, agents never used someone else's gun if they could help it, because one never knew what someone else's equipment was like. But this wasn't exactly the time or situation where John could afford to be choosy.

"What now?" Barry rasped. "They'll be back any second."

John handed back the gun. "Aim it at the door. Be ready to fire if we have to."

Barry swallowed. The man's discomfort was growing but John couldn't do much about that right now.

"I can…I can shoot the first person but then…there'll be too many."

John stood and hobbled over to the side of the door. "I'll catch us someone. That gives us two."

Barry managed a smile. "The prisoners become the captors."

John didn't have time to answer. The sound of voices could be heard coming down the hall.

The door opened.

Barry opened fire.

CHAPTER 22

———

Barry fired off as many rounds as fast as he could pull the trigger. As John feared, he fired too soon and the first two shots pinged off the metal door as it opened, but the guard opening up the door didn't react in time to close it again. Three more rounds went wide but Barry managed a leg and gut hit with the last two. The guard staggered back into the shocked expressions of the other people behind him.

John pounced to snatch up a victim, bringing his cuffs around their neck and pulling them into the room before they could shut the door to safety. With the first guard taken care of, John blindly hooked the second person and pulled them close to the sound of a surprised scream.

He hadn't caught a guard or the Cuban. He'd caught a woman.

It took John a long moment to recognize who was in his arms.

Marcela elbowed John in the ribs by instinct and whirled around to knee him in the crotch when she came face to face with him, no more than an inch between noses and nothing more than the chain of his handcuffs behind her neck keeping her there.

John's eyes went wide with surprise even while he struggled to contain his reflexive doubling-over from the elbow. He hadn't even noticed one hand balled in a fist and ready for an awkward jab, the other grabbing Marcela's leg by the knee to block her incoming blow to his crotch.

The door slammed shut to the sound of yelling from the men on the other side.

They stared at one another, both in shock.

"Marcela?"

Marcela was less surprised. "What the fuck John? Why did you grab me?"

"I was trying to-" John was utterly stunned. "What are you-"

"Obviously trying to rescue you," she said, ducking under the cuffs. "Let go of my leg."

John quickly removed his hand and defensive posture. Over Marcela's shoulder he saw Barry aiming the gun at her.

"Barry, she's with us."

"What?' Barry asked, squinting at Marcela as if to look for some sort of good-guy insignia.

There wasn't much time. And too many new variables. John had to figure out a plan and-

Marcela spun around at the sound of the door. "Shit, they're opening the-"

The door burst open.

"Barry! Cover!"

The distinct rattle of AK-47 fire blew in from the hallway as small holes appeared in the opposite wall. Barry was laying prone, fully covered by the table. That was one thing John didn't have to worry about right now at least. He half-expected the man to stand and return fire.

John pulled Marcela back in around the waist with his cuffs. She began to duck and spin by instinct but realized what John was doing in time to override her training, allowing him to pull her back in close and away from the line of fire.

"Stop! Stop shooting, he has me!" Marcela cried, waving her arms.

The gunfire continued, oblivious to Marcela's screams. Luckily it was spraying in a narrow arc, mostly focused on keeping Barry pinned down, unsure of where John and his hostage were. If they wanted to find out, they'd have to make a push into the room. John figured that would be their next course of action. He knew Marcela must have a gun hiding under her dress, but she couldn't use it or their hostage charade would be blown. Not to mention her cover.

"Gun!" John shouted over the gunfire at Marcela.

"I can hear you, you're right in my ear!"

"Which leg?" John asked, quieter this time.

"Left," she said over her shoulder. Then she turned back to the door. "Stop shooting you idiot, you're going to get me killed!"

The gunfire finally abated, and John heard the plastic clatter of an empty magazine. Marcela heard it too, reaching down to help John retrieve her hidden gun, guiding his hand amidst lifting her dress.

"Always with the legs John."

John decided not to acknowledge her words as he felt his cheeks growing hot. "I've got it-"

Marcela's hands shot back up as they heard the guard scramble for a new magazine and the shuffle of feet ready to charge into the room. They had to nip this in the bud.

This time John dragged Marcela in front of Barry and the doorway, stopping the three men in their tracks, the guard holding the magazine in one hand, unloaded gun in the other. Juan and the Cuban both had pistols out and trained on John and Marcela, squeezed together in the narrow hallway. They nearly opened fire when John entered their line of sight.

"Please!" Marcela cried. Her feigned distress would've put a telenovela actress to shame.

John had her in a chokehold against the crook of his elbow, hiding the gun he'd retrieved behind her head. The others should think John and Barry only had one gun between them. Every edge they could manage mattered.

The guard started to slowly reload the AK-47 while eyeing John, but John jerked Marcela who acted limp for him.

"I'll snap her spine like a toothpick," John said with a snarl. "Put your guns down."

The guard's eyes flicked between Juan and the Cuban as he began to lower the Kalashnikov.

The Cuban slapped the back of the guard's head. "Reload!"

"That's my woman!" Juan protested as John shook Marcela again as a warning.

Out of the corner of his eye, John saw Marcela tap her fingers and thumb together. A signal for his eyes and understanding alone. John flexed his arm lightly on her throat, twice, to let her know he'd received it.

"I don't know who you are!" the Cuban yelled at Juan, keeping his gun trained on John. "You show up and demand my prisoner, and now expect me to stand down because you can't control your woman?"

Juan flushed, growing angry, a flood of thoughts invading his mind. This whole thing may have been a trap. A set up by one of his rivals…some Cuban cartel, or even the DEA itself for all he knew. And what did he really plan to do with John? Soon after John had showed up at the estate, so many things had gone wrong. If the rumors of him kidnapping Pablito were true, John had meddled in matters far more than he'd suspected…it would be best to clean this whole mess up. Clean slate. Juan was a new man — his own man.

He turned his gun on the Cuban. The Cuban blanched, then composed himself, growing stiff with a vicious smile taking over his expression.

"Oh that's how it is?" the Cuban asked.

Juan bared his teeth.

The guard craned his neck and awkwardly began to spin his weapon on Juan, then looked back at John, hesitating and undecided if he should turn back to cover the room. He was still fumbling with the magazine.

The sound of boots warned John of more men rushing through the hallway. Juan's men or the Cuban's, he didn't know, and that didn't matter. He lifted the gun held hidden behind Marcela's head, pointing it upward and inching it over her shoulder to point at the doorway. The sound of approaching men grew louder. Juan and the Cuban both strained to look down the hall at who's men were coming, not willing to fully take their eyes off one another or lower their weapons. A bead of sweat formed at the ridge of the guard's hairline and began a slow drip down, lingering on his eyebrow. He twitched at the itch and slammed the magazine home. The sound pierced the tense air as the stamping of boots continued.

Barry poked his head up from the cover of the metal table, swinging his pistol over the edge and aiming at the doorway, attracting the attention of everyone. The guard's hand slowly crept up the AK-47 to ready his position...

The lights flickered and everyone looked up.

Then darkness enveloped them, not a patch of light to be seen anywhere. The power had gone out.

John fired first.

CHAPTER 23

The light from muzzle flashes pocked the dark like a symphony of fireworks. John and Marcela retreated from the line of fire and onto the wall just before the reloaded AK-47 blasted away where they had stood the moment before. Light blossomed from each rapid shot.

"Why did you shoot?" Marcela hissed, pressed up against the wall, inches from John. "You're going to get us killed!"

His arms were still around her, and he lifted them to give her breathing room. "You gave the signal," John said, leaning out from the wall and popping a shot off into the darkness of the door and hallway. "Fingers and thumb, rapid tap. Lights flickering."

The sound of more AK-47 fire rang out, but it was coming from down the hallway. The guard had stopped firing into the room, or was dead.

"Barry?" John called. He had seen two flashes from the further side of the room but nothing since.

"Yeah?" the voice came, an octave higher than usual.

"Stay put!" John said, raising his voice as gunfire erupted again. It sounded like there was a firefight growing behind their opponents in the hall, which would mean Juan and the Cuban and guard might be pinned, if they weren't dead already.

"The signal for lights flickering?" Marcela said. "Are you a dumbfuck? That's the signal for talking! Chatter. Let the enemy talk and then-"

The guard had turned back to spraying into the room, probably providing cover fire for the Cuban, or to make sure John and Barry didn't advance on them. Which meant that was what they should probably do.

John edged closer to the doorway, fired once at the door to ward off the guard, hoping he'd dip back. But just as John began to pull from the wall to advance, the lights flickered and came back on. He was caught out in the open.

"Oh, fuck this," Marcela said while the others blinked. She reached under her dress and pulled a gun off her right leg, firing at the guard kneeling in the doorway. He managed to fire off two panicked rounds before he went down with the single shot penetrating his chest.

John nodded his thanks and peered into the hallway. Not ten feet away was the Cuban, blood pouring from a wound in the shoulder and another in the gut. He coughed up blood and tried to turn over.

"Barry! Check this guy for keys!" John yelled, gesturing to the dead guard at his feet with his gun, not taking his eyes off the hall. Juan was nowhere to be found.

"What? Oh!"

"Get the keys!"

"I am!" Barry scrambled up over the table and moved to rummage through pockets on the body at John's feet.

John held his pistol firm and made small sweeping motions as he moved into the hallway. He made sure things were clear before kneeling down next to the Cuban. John grabbed the man's shirt by the chest, lifting him up. But there was no time to ask questions or get information. The man's eyes looked at John's, then glazed over as his head lolled to the side.

Frustrated, John dropped the man back to the ground, and searched his body. The only thing he found was a phone.

"Where did they go?" Barry asked. "Is…everyone dead?"

"We're going to have to find out," John said.

Marcela came up behind him, pushing a metal filing cabinet on wheels.

"What's this?" John asked.

"Filing cabinet."

"I know it's a filing cabinet, what-"

"Stay behind me, you're not in fighting shape," she said, wheeling the filing cabinet in front of them. Marcela had hastily packed the drawers with paper until they burst. The filing cabinet would act as a shield as they pressed down the hallway against any attackers.

John was about to argue but Marcela pushed past him, with Barry arriving just behind John in the hall, shaking a pair of keys.

"What now?" Barry asked.

"Follow her," John said, taking the keys and unlocking Barry's cuffs. He unlocked his own then ran back to the room they'd been held in. He winced against a stitch in his side as he bent over to snatch up the AK-47 that had been dropped on the way. It might not have a full mag — the thing looked standard, that made fifteen rounds at half a mag — but a short spray was enough covering fire to move. 'Three feet for every bullet' was the philosophy his drill sergeant back in the day swore by. That is, if you were doing it right.

John found the laptop he'd been using and the 'wig still stuck in its USB port. He bent down to retrieve it and gasped against pain again as he stood back up. He realized he was breathing more heavily than he should for this much exertion, even considering their treatment in captivity. He put a hand to his side, fearing the worst and proved himself right.

Blood stained his fingers.

He moved back down the hallway, shouldering the AK by the strap and keeping his pistol ready, but he lifted his shirt and glanced at the wound. There was a steady bleed; not a flow. That gave him half an hour until serious blood loss started causing him issues, instead of the mere minutes something more serious would leave him with. At the touch of his back (wincing at pain there as well), John knew the bullet had gone clean through. He hoped there weren't any broken bits left behind, but at the close-range he'd been skewered he doubted that. He could only hope the shot hadn't hit his liver.

"John are you taking a nap or did you forget a sandwich back there?" Marcela called.

John caught up with the others, finding Barry had been assigned the duty of pushing the filing cabinet out front. That made sense to John; him and Marcela could shoot while Barry couldn't, he'd be safer, and they played to their strengths.

"You had another gun," John said.

Marcela didn't look back as she moved. "A lot of secrets under the dress John. Not all of them are for you."

"John, who is she?" Barry asked.

"A friend," John said.

"Right," Barry said, giving John a knowing glance before eyeing Marcela.

John scowled. "Focus," and he pointed ahead.

None too soon. The rattle of gunfire came from down the hall, getting louder as they approached.

"Barry, no matter what happens, just keep moving forward," John said, already not liking his words as they came out of his mouth. "We'll have you covered."

"Seems to me like I'm covering you," Barry said.

"*Gringos,*" Marcela muttered.

"Here we go," John said. "Go!"

Barry picked up the pace and John and Marcela followed. John glanced down at the wound he knew bled under his shirt, noting the small trickle and stain running onto his pants.

As soon as they saw figures ahead, John and Marcela opened fire.

Barry screamed at the sound but John prodded him forward and was thankful the man didn't slow down. The sound of gunfire was heavy and loud in such a narrow space, and rang right beside Barry's ears.

John only spotted three men, but someone fell to the ground as he made the assessment, making it three out of four. He trained his sights on one man who was playing too far in the center of the hallway, squeezed off two rounds as Marcela did the same. John knew he couldn't afford to double up on shots like that. He had been running on one mag since their captivity room, keeping a mental count of shots fired. Marcela would've given him extra ammo if she'd had any.

"Keep to the right, I'm on left," John said, corresponding to which side they stood next to Barry.

"¡*Mierda*!" Marcela growled.

Two men turned to face the new threat, firing tentative shots down the hallway, then moving to full auto as they saw their shots stopped by the shield. Barry screamed as metallic pings bounced off the metal cabinet, bullets stopped inches from his face. He broke into a run, continuing to yell, his fear becoming battle-fury.

"Barry, slow down!" John ran to keep up, struggling to aim as his line of fire shrank with Barry in the way. The hole in his side wasn't blocked by adrenaline anymore, allowing a scorching lance of white-hot pain to fill the area.

"*Mierda. Gringos. Mierda.*"

Marcela was able to keep up at least, dashing forward and downing both men before either could unload much of anything. The start of their rapid fire was cut off, drowning the sound of gunfire in silence.

The loudest thing in John's ear was a ringing sound and his labored breathing.

"Do you have a car outside?" John asked through breaths.

"No," Marcela said, sweeping while Barry slowed down, panting.

A light opened up at the end of the hallway as someone opened the door. John and Marcela both fired, and the man stumbled back. They couldn't tell if they'd hit him or he'd simply retreated.

"No...car...?" John asked, breathing between words.

"Do I look like a cargo container? Two guns were hard enough!" Marcela checked her magazine and slammed it back home. "Juan has a helicopter." She risked a look back and saw the sweat coming off John's forehead. "What the fuck is the matter with you?"

John lifted his elbow and glanced at his wound again, seeing Marcela do the same.

"What the...*mierda, mierda, mierda*. How bad?"

"We'll have to...find out," John said, struggling to keep up with the other two. "Twenty...minutes...blackout."

"Okay. Bert, ditch the cabinet."

"What?"

"The cabinet! No more filing cabinet!"

"My name is Barry!"

"I don't give a fuck, take this gun now!" She forced her gun into his hand and spun the filing cabinet down the hall behind them, revealing two bullet holes that had penetrated the metal as it turned.

John unshouldered the AK-47 and she took it gingerly from him, nodding.

"Juan's helicopter is off to the left. In a field," Marcela said.

"Then we go right," John said, managing more steady breaths. "Away from him and his men."

"I thought you knew this guy you came with," Barry said to Marcela.

"I know he'll pull out your fingernails for fun if he catches you," she replied. "Fine, we go right. Try to catch a car on the road."

"Maybe loop around and take the chopper."

"He brought a lot of men."

"Doesn't sound like much of a rescue plan," Barry said. Self-pity was starting to grip him past fear.

John was glad Marcela was here to deal with that. "Sounds like you're a coward. Guess it's just you and me, huh John?"

"Wait! What? No!" Barry squealed.

"It's okay, three is too many," Marcela said, unclipping the AK's magazine and frowning at the half-spent load. She slammed it back in place and slapped Barry hard on the back to show she was joking, then brought the AK-47 up tight against her shoulder and close to her face. "Here we go *señoritas*."

"Right," John said once more to emphasize where they were going.

They came up to the door without resistance. John fell against the left side of the wall a little harder than he'd meant to, peering out.

"Clear."

He nodded to Marcela who crossed over the doorway and outside, using the cover of the door hinged open to look out the left. They heard the sounds of gunfire and men yelling.

"Firefight, fifty metres. Go now."

John took point and dashed outside, Barry thankfully quick on his heels.

"I don't know how far a meter is," Barry mumbled, pointing his gun off to the side as they ran.

"Covering fire!" Marcela screamed.

Her AK roared as John and Barry took off as fast they could, feet spitting up gravel as they ran. More gunfire erupted from the field ahead of her. Juan and two of his men were squatting next to their helicopter, firing at a Cuban guard taking desperate cover behind two rusted oil drums.

It felt surreal to be outside again, with fresh humid air washing around them.

"Where are we going?" Barry yelled.

No enemies were in front of them, but John still wasn't sure what to do. He glanced back at Marcela, seeing her pop a few more rounds as she backed away, stopped and fired again, then gave up the effort and moved to join them. John took in his surroundings. There was a small field behind them and a forest next to it — good hiding, but too far to make. They had emerged from a small industrial building located in a dip in the ground reminding him of a shallow crater covered in gravel. A road led off over the short lip.

"Road," John said, gesturing with his gun.

Barry ran past him, taking over the hill. John didn't want him advancing without him but his body forced him to swallow, making him unable to call out. He coughed as he pushed himself up the lip.

An empty highway ran away into more fields, no cities in sight. And no vehicles either. He turned over his shoulder to see Juan and some of his men circling the side of the building, gaining on them. They must have killed the pinned Cuban guard. All they had to do was cross the lot and climb the short ridge. Everything past them was flat and wide-open.

"No cars," John whispered.

And like providence, he heard tires scrape against gravel, pulling up behind him.

It was a large army truck, dark green with a canvas top over the back. It rolled to a stop beside the ridge. The truck was too high up off the ground for them to see who was inside. Marcela and Barry both brought their guns up, Marcela turning to spend the rest of what little of her magazine remained in a futile effort against Juan and his men. She spat on the ground beside her.

John expected a squad of Nicaraguan troops to pour out the back of the truck. Instead, a long barrel poked out the driver's side window.

Confused but still wary at the sight of a weapon, John moved to hunker up next to the truck, his gun aimed at the window, having to leave his back open to the truck's reinforcements if it had any. But the sight of the man in the rearview mirror looked oddly familiar.

The sharp bark of a sniper round bit the air. John snapped his head around, fearing that Marcela had been shot and feeling a sharp stab of pain in his gut worse than his wound. He took a quick breath and released it when he saw Marcela also looking up at the truck, standing there as she had before, perfectly safe.

One of Juan's men was down. At this distance, John could barely make out the man's expression, but could hear vague cursing and yelling as him and his one other bodyguard backtracked and retreated behind the building's corner. They were retreating.

The door on the driver's side door opened up, and a lean man with a hawkish face watched their enemies turn tail and run, a slick-looking sniper rifle in his hands. He followed the enemy for a moment before lowering the rifle, then surveyed the three of them below.

"Need a ride?" Dimitri asked.

CHAPTER 24

"What do you get when you put a Russian, a Mayan, an American, and a Canadian together in the back of an army truck?" Barry asked.

No one answered. Marcela was rooting through a first aid kit Dimitri had found under the passenger seat but was otherwise focused on the road. The truck was moving fast, and there wasn't any traffic to speak of — there didn't seem to be any large cities nearby either — but there was no telling if Juan would give chase, or if any of the other factions in Nicaragua would pull them over.

"Nobody?"

"Berty, shut up," Marcela said, pulling out two thick gauze pads. "Focus."

Barry had his hands on either side of John's wound, trying to stop the blood flow as Marcela had instructed. He nearly threw up when he saw the wound. They'd pulled John onto his side as he lay on the flat of the truck. The rubber gloves Marcela had given Barry had been of little comfort.

"I am focused."

"Then put pressure on it!"

"I am putting-"

"You're holding this like you're putting together a sandwich.

Pressure!" Marcela gripped him by the forearms and pushed them down.

John yelled in pain.

"Ah!" Barry cried. "Too much pressure!" he eased off but Marcela gave him a light slap on the cheek.

"He's not supposed to like it. You're supposed to stop the blood." She pulled out a bottle of antiseptic solution and put it next to her while continuing to dig through the kit. "No tape! What kind of first aid kit…*mierda*…okay, Berty, get ready to lift your hands."

"My name's Barry," he muttered, if for no one else than to remind himself who he was while escaping Cuban intelligence, torture, and treating a gunshot wound on a man he'd met a couple days ago.

The truck hit a bump and John grimaced as Barry's hands lifted and pressed again as they all bounced. The bottle Marcela had put aside fell over and rolled down the truck's floor. She scrambled to grab it.

"I said lift!"

Barry eased his hands off the wound and blood ran like he'd uncorked a barrel. John moaned then sucked in a breath as Marcela snatched up the antiseptic solution and returned to John. She poured the liquid onto the wound, one side after the other, then slapped the bandages in place. John had his teeth bared, but remained conscious. Barry didn't know if that was a good thing or a bad thing.

"What are you doing?" Marcela snapped her fingers in front of his face. "Pressure!"

"But you said-" Barry sighed. He decided it was best to stop talking, and put his hands back on the wounds, now covered by the pads. His bloody gloves stained the bandages.

Marcela lifted John's shirt up further and pivoted on her knees as she unspooled a roll of gauze behind John's back and around the bandaids, repeating around and around his lower torso, tying the bandages on tight. She bit the gauze off and twisted it into the bands she'd created, tying a small knot.

"That will have to do," she murmured before lowering John's shirt and looking at him. "You still alive?"

"Yes," John said, breathing heavily.

"Good."

"Where are we?" Barry asked, gingerly slipping off the gloves, careful not to stain his clothing or fingers as he took them off.

Marcela pulled out her phone and accessed a map of Nicaragua, zooming in. Neither John or Barry had their cellphones anymore, and neither of them knew where they had been being held.

"East of Las Palomas."

"Is that good?"

"Depends where we're going," Marcela said. "Hey! Russian man, where are you driving to?"

"Airport. Las Salinas," Dimitri said, making a hard turn that made Barry slide across the floor.

Las Salinas was just past El Gigante. John struggled to sit up, leaning against a long army truck seat along the wall while his legs splayed on the floor. "No. They'll intercept us back at Rivas."

"If Juan doesn't catch us by helicopter first," Marcela said, putting away the first aid materials and pulling herself into a seat across from John.

"I thought we were done with that guy," Barry said.

Marcela grimaced. "We can hope."

"What's he doing here?" John asked.

"Juan?" Marcela asked and John nodded. "Got a mysterious phone call and said he was going to Nicaragua to receive a gift. Undercover DEA agent John Carpenter. Esteban said for me to follow."

John scoffed before he realized how much it would hurt him. "Esteban used me as bait. Blew my cover."

"He used Juan as a mule to get me inside. And blew *my* cover."

Barry deposited his bloody gloves in a corner of the truck and sat on a bench across from Marcela, gathering himself. "Why go back to Rivas? That's away from El Gigante."

Marcela and John both interrupted each other as they tried to explain, but John gestured for Marcela to continue. He should try to limit his speaking.

"Students control the N-220, and we'd need that to get onto the…" she moved the map on her phone around with her finger, "62. Otherwise we're forced onto the 72 back to Rivas."

"We're not going back to Rivas," Dimitri called into the back.

"Then where?" Barry asked. He felt like he'd asked a smart question for the first time in days.

"I said, we're going to Las Salinas," Dimitri said, keeping his eyes on the road.

He moved the shift-stick and a rumble in the truck took hold of the floor, vibrating their feet and John's whole body. Then they took a sharp turn and a series of heavy bumps began.

John gritted his teeth as he held his wound with a hand, trying to hold it tight against the bumps. He exchanged a glance with Marcela.

They were going off-road.

Dimitri tore through two fields before finding smaller backroads that would eventually wind their way up to the 62. John was concerned the truck would be more noticeable from air moving off the roads so he was thankful they managed to get back onto pavement — or dirt — with no sound of a chopper above them. John knew they were making good progress once they hit the Rio Brito.

"How much longer?" Barry asked, wringing his hands.

"Half hour?" Marcela guessed.

"Twenty minutes," Dimitri said.

"Close the window," John said, gesturing to the sliding glass between the driver's cab and the back truck. It was similar to the one found in some taxis.

Marcela gave John a questioning look but obeyed.

"No offense Dimitri," John said.

"None taken."

Once the window was closed, John sat up a little straighter and looked up at Barry.

"What did the Cuban want from you?"

"What?" Barry laced his fingers together and fidgeted, trying to hide his obvious nervousness at the question. "What do you mean?"

"Exactly what I said," said John. He sat up straighter, and even with a bullethole through his side and in obvious pain, he could still put fear in Barry's mind. "The Cuban wanted you to do something for someone named Antonio."

"Oh, that," Barry said, chuckling as if John had said something impolite at a timid dinner table. "It's nothing, just business stuff."

John didn't lift his cold stare.

"It's private," Barry said.

"You're going to tell me."

Marcela looked to John but only received a quick glance from the corner of his eyes as a reply. This didn't seem like something John had been tasked to find out. If that were the case he would've done it by now, one way or another. It wasn't direct disobedience of orders, but if agents weren't ordered to extract information, and were escorting someone with sensitive information meant for the US government, they weren't supposed to squeeze them. Especially if it didn't pertain to their current situation.

"Hey take it easy," Barry said, putting his hands up defensively. "I can say a few things. I told you about my app right?"

"You're a developer or something?" Marcela asked.

"Yeah, I guess I haven't introduced myself. Barry Bridges; entrepreneur and tech investor, specializing in disruptive innovation."

He held out his hand to Marcela. She looked at it with a raised eyebrow.

"Anyway…our torturer friend back there, he's interested in my app is all."

"Why?" John asked.

"Right, right…well I told you about *Anono* back on the boat."

"An anonymous chat app," John said.

Barry raised a finger. "*Guaranteed* anonymous *interaction* app."

Neither John or Marcela seemed particularly impressed.

"Ah…well I'm pursuing a completely different angle in social media platforms. My app has none of the data collection and location tracking that the government and other businesses get away with slipping into their software. It guarantees anonymity. People are starting to realize that their privacy is a commodity now, and people will pay for it. I'm true to my word. Maybe you heard the big thing that happened last year? Winter?"

John's expression stayed stone cold.

"Okay…well, the app was brought to the world's attention and I was in the headlines. There was this serial killer in Arizona, at least that's what people said, but one of the murders ended up not being by him and two murders don't get you serial killer status, so it was overhyped. But you know, big controversy, great for marketing."

"Were you the killer?" Marcela asked.

"What? No!"

"Okay then just tell us the thing," Marcela said.

Barry looked irked but obliged. "Basically the investigation eventually found out this guy was using my app to talk to women and lure them out into meeting up before killing them. So the investigation came to me to unlock the anonymity on his account. I'd be a real hero."

"So you helped them," John said.

Barry smiled. "No, actually. I didn't."

John narrowed his eyes and Marcela's grew cold. Barry took it in like applause.

Marcela began to interject but Barry spoke over whatever she was about to say. "The police and detectives came to me assuming they could just get me to override my product. In what kind of society do we live when authorities *expect* a business to break its policies with its customers, invade their privacy, and violate the integrity of their product? No way."

"You helped a killer!" Marcela jabbed a finger at Barry.

Barry spoke as if he were the teacher of a young and ignorant student. "I didn't do anything. I refused to violate the strict code and terms that I sell my application under. Someone using my app doesn't make me a killer. And me choosing to let the authorities do their job doesn't make me an accomplice."

"No one would use your app if you had unlocked the account," John said, a statement not a question.

Barry grinned again. "That plus the PR? I fast tracked my way to Silicon Valley stardom."

"And how's that working out for you?" Marcela snapped.

"There were legal challenges after the incident. They tried for charges. Went to court. Fought it, and we won. Largely on the grounds that this was private enterprise, and state influence would be overreaching — true anonymity is the entire purpose of the app. If the good guys can use a backdoor in the app, so can the bad guys. And there's no coming back from that. All the attention I'd been getting also meant more people bought into it and the stock soared, so the pressure didn't help the court. But really, the main thing was the precedent. It would've established something that would ruin a lot of businesses. Not just anonymity, but private enterprise."

"Americans hate regulation," John said, not knowing what to make of what Barry had said. He had a sour taste in his mouth.

"We really do," Barry said. "The problem now is federal regulation is starting to crack down. Most people don't realize that the government hasn't really figured out what to do with social media since it boomed. There aren't any real laws in place."

"Sounds like it needs some," John said.

Barry shrugged. "I'm just an entrepreneur. Actually, I was supposed to appear before a hearing committee this week. A part of me is hoping we don't get back in time."

"Why's that?" Marcela asked.

Barry gave another one of those wry grins John was getting tired of seeing. "Because they want the same thing from me as the bad guys."

John felt that knowledge sink in. He found himself staring off, his pain numbing in his side, but his mind ticking around what Barry had said. Esteban wanted John to get Barry out of the country. Both US and Cuban intelligence wanted the backdoor on Barry's app. Barry probably didn't realize how much of a catalyst this upcoming hearing committee was for international intelligence. The Cubans had to make a play for the backdoor before the Americans got it. Other than their methods, both nations wanted the same thing. The Americans seemed interested in regulation, like Barry had said. But did the Cubans use a high-level operative and call in some favors on Nicaragua to disrupt that regulation? Did they want to undermine a US company and get data on a bunch of its citizens? Or…or were they trying to stop the regulation because they were using it themselves.

John's eyes widened.

Had Cuban intelligence found enough security in Barry's secured anonymous guarantee that they were making use of it for their communications? That seemed a stretch, but not that much of one. Then there was the Cuban interrogator finding a specific region from all the collected data of the Puentes laptop. *Isla de Anticipación*. John would have to follow up on that, assuming they didn't get gunned down before completing the mission. It didn't necessarily mean that region and Barry's backdoor were at all linked either, but intel always started out as a series of stars before becoming a constellation.

Marcela asked Barry the question John needed before he had thought of it.

"Is that it? This one app?"

Barry folded his arms and leaned back, realizing for the first time how good it felt to have a semblance of safety and not have to worry about being tortured at any given moment. "Nah. I really made my success off a previous thing — crypto."

"Ah. Bitcoin," Marcela nodded. "I made money off that too."

"Right, but no," Barry said. "I developed my own cryptocurrency platform called *E-Buck*. It-"

"Sounds dumb."

"- did fairly well, still does to some extent but isn't as wide as some of the others. But when I saw the success of it and crypto it got me thinking about how it can be used to curtail governments through, well, its anonymity kind of — and that's how I came up with *Anono*. I wanted a crypto concept for social media."

"Clever," Marcela conceded.

"A lot of criminals use cryptocurrency," John said. "As you said. Curtails governments."

"Sure, but-"

"And sounds like criminals are using *Anono*, too."

Barry began to form a petulant scowl. "Inventors can't control what people do with their products."

John didn't answer. He knew Oppenheimer wasn't comparable to Barry but it was who he was thinking about. It was also the same rationalization he had for the missions he was sent on. But at a certain point he couldn't blame a target's death on the gun in his hands or the orders sent from the top.

"Who's Antonio?" John asked suddenly.

That made Barry perk up. "Uh…business partner. Again, this is kind of private stuff…"

John was about to push harder when Dimitri knocked on the window, making them all turn their heads at once. Marcela slid the glass open.

"What?" she asked.

Dimitri pointed forward at the windshield. "Our friends are back."

John craned his head to look out the windshield. In the distance, not far away, was a helicopter.

CHAPTER 25

The whipping blades of the helicopter rotor were deafening, but even they couldn't drown out Juan's fury.

He had been lured into a trap. John Carpenter, unsuspecting tutor for his uncle's son Pablito was a fearsome DEA agent. The rumours his men had told him were true. He had lost two loyal soldiers in the fight that followed John's escape today. John had taken his uncle, his mother, Pablito, but worst and most shocking of all, he had taken his woman. Marcela. Juan had loved her, and she had betrayed him. All this time, that DEA bitch had been playing him like a fool...

"There!" he yelled, standing from his seat and pointing to the army transport truck racing on the stretch of road in front of them. "Stay on them no matter what!"

The pilot grimaced but nodded, and Juan slapped the man's helmet. He turned to his remaining soldier who had helped cover Juan's retreat to the chopper.

"Are you ready?" Juan asked, holding the man by the shoulders.

"*Sí.*" The man tilted his head to the side and gave his neck a crack. Then he hefted the FN MAG, a general-purpose machine gun that mounted out the window. It was a Chinese model but it did the trick. "*Muerte desde arriba,*" he grinned. *Death from above.*

Juan didn't smile. Like his uncle, he took no pleasure in delivering justice.

* * *

"Shit," John said, struggling to stand. Dimitri had picked up speed and hit an unfortunate bump that sent John staggering. He held a hand against the wall while holding his bandages. He rasped, struggling not to cry out in pain.

"John, you are weak as a lamb," Marcela said, standing up and peering at the helicopter through the front. It was closing fast. "Let me handle this."

She pulled the sliding glass open wide, kicked off her shoes, then hoisted herself through the gap. Barry's eyes rose when her dress flared but John caught him with eyes that could've frozen a volcano and he looked away quickly.

Marcela shook her hair out and reached for the sniper rifle leaning against the door once she righted herself in the front passenger seat.

"I'd prefer to be the one shooting my gun," Dimitri said through thin lips. He had one eye on the road and the other on the helicopter closing in.

Marcela followed his gaze. "You want to switch?"

He exchanged a glance with her, looked at the steering wheel and eyed the helicopter.

"Just don't miss," he said.

Marcela winked and began to look over the rifle.

"It's ready," Dimitri said.

The man wasn't wrong but Marcela acted out of habit, checking the chamber and scope.

"It's a Dragunov SVD."

"Oh yes I can see that." Marcela chuckled silently. It was Cold War-era weaponry.

Dimitri read her mind. "Sorry I couldn't get you a Chukavin. I'll put in an order next time."

"That would be nice," Marcela said as she looked through the scope. Her view blurred past the helicopter and she pulled her eye away, twisting the distance to something manageable.

"It's set for eight hundred meters. I eyeballed the one back there," Dimitri said, referring to when he'd rolled up in the truck and shot one of Juan's men.

Marcela dialed it back by half, then trained the rifle back on the helicopter.

It wouldn't be easy. The helicopter was a fast moving target, had air-advantage, she had nothing to stabilize the rifle, and the wind blew hard at her as Dimitri gathered more and more speed. Her hair danced around her face, and growing frustrated after half a minute, she tied it back with an elastic.

"Let's go *devushka*, or you take the wheel," Dimitri said.

Marcela licked her lips. She pushed her head and the gun out the window, trying to edge into a good firing position. She trained her sights on the helicopter, which was closing into six hundred meter range. She brought her knee up to stabilize the sniper as best she could, and let her finger fall to rest on the trigger. Through the scope she could make out the figures inside the helicopter. She trailed its flight path for three seconds before jumping ahead so she could lead it at the same pace. One...two...

"*Vniz!*" Dimitri yelled as he floored the gas pedal. *Down!*

Marcela fired off her shot, kicking the butt of the sniper hard into her shoulder, and she followed the momentum to duck her head before knowing why Dimitri had called out.

The truck made a series of dangerous popping sounds, metal on metal like a cluster of ball bearings had been tossed in a metal bowl. Distant gunfire erupted from above and chained together a series of rapid-fire ticks like a low motor groaning for control.

Juan was shooting back at them.

The windshield shattered and glass spilled over Marcela and onto her seat. She slid onto the ground in an awkward sitting position and looked up just in time to see her seat grow pock-marks — one… two…three — in a second before the strafing fire must have moved on.

She was panting hard, and she knew she must look like a ghost from brushing death so closely.

"*Devushka?*" Dimitri asked. *Lady?* His face was inches from her own; he had his head ducked down low under the dash as his arms stretched up to keep the truck stabilized with its high speed run.

Marcela nodded and glanced upward with her eyes, forming a question.

"Passed over us," Dimitri said, pulling himself back into a normal seating position to drive.

"They'll be back for a second pass," Marcela said, feeling pain in her tailbone as she brushed glass off her seat.

"Marcela?" John called from the back.

"Okay!" Marcela called back. "Almost, but okay!"

She climbed back into her seat and lifted the gun, but Dimitri raised a hand to her.

"Falling back," he said, looking at his rearview mirror.

Marcela narrowed her eyes and looked at her own mirror. The speck of a helicopter in the sky was growing more and more distant.

"Did you hit them?" Dimitri asked.

"I don't know," Marcela frowned. "Maybe."

"Well that's — *blin!*"

"What?" Marcela half-raised the sniper at Dimitri's exclamation, looking for danger before spotting what he'd seen out in front of the road.

"What is it?" John asked, poking his head through the screen between him and the main cab.

"Barricade," Marcela said, pointing for John to see.

He squinted and saw the familiar concrete blocks, flags and people milling about one of the student barricades that was such a common sight in Nicaragua.

"We can fight," Dimitri said, reaching for a sidearm neither Marcela or John had noticed before. "But if we-"

"Stop the truck," John said, standing up and taking a breath through the pain numbing his side. The wound seemed to be reaching a certain plateau of hurt. He could deal with that.

Dimitri put the brakes on heavier than anyone would've liked. John grabbed onto the ledge of the screen while Marcela braced herself against the dash and her door. John heard Barry slide down the seats behind him with a small cry of surprise.

The truck pulled up the road until they were within shouting distance of the barricade. The wheels squeaked to a stop and John made his way to the back.

"What are you going to do?" Marcela asked.

"Talk to them," John said.

He lowered himself down the back of the truck and onto the ground, the vibration of feet hitting the ground sending a shock to his side. He breathed through it, hid the pistol in the back of his waistband by lifting his shirt over it, and walked over to the protestors.

A young man and woman, probably students, were already walking toward him. The girl held a homemade mortar launcher, while the boy had a pistol clipped to his side, his hand resting nervously on it for comfort.

John kept his gait calm and casual, letting his hands be seen freely at his own sides.

The girl put up a hand. "*Se dió la vuelta*," she said. *Turn around.* She didn't sound hostile, but the words weren't friendly either.

"*Simplemente de paso*," John said, lifting his hands to show he meant no harm and had no weapons. "*Sin problema.*" *Just passing through. No trouble.*

The boy shook his head with a frown, not wanting to negotiate. He tapped the pistol on his side, but it was hard for John to take the kid seriously. He had a thin film of hair on his upper lip. John imagined he'd been trying to grow the sparse hairs to that length for quite some time.

"Okay," John said, "Okay. Can we-"

"¿*Profesor*?" someone called from behind the two protestors.

A young man dashed around the stacked cinder blocks and almost tripped over a rusted barrel before John could make him out.

"Smiley?" John asked, a surprised smile beginning to take over him.

Smiley laughed and waved, pushing through the other two students. They protested but he hissed at them and they argued until Smiley sent them away. They both gave John wary glances and the boy tapped his pistol again before backing off and returning to manning the barricade.

"I'm lucky," John said. "I thought you'd still be on the barricade toward Rivas."

"Had to fall back. We got overrun."

John didn't let the grin Smiley gave fool him. He saw the scratches around the student's face more clearly now, and noted him favoring one of his legs.

"Ah," John said, not knowing how else to respond.

"I'm at least glad to see you still alive *Profesor*! After Ometepe and Miguel...I'm sorry to have sent you there. I thought it was a good idea."

John shook his head. "Be more sorry for Miguel."

Smiley gave a solemn nod. "I'd just hate to see you get hurt."

John lifted his shirt to expose his wound. "Little late for that."

Smiley's eyes popped open wide. "John! Holy *mierda*! Do you need-"

"To get through. That's it."

"Fucking *Presidente*," Smiley spat on the ground. "Gunning down teachers now." He turned to his friends manning the barricade. "Let this one through!"

The students were surprised to hear the order but obeyed, moving cinder blocks aside as quickly as they could.

"You should get out of here too, Smiley," John said, shaking the man's hand. He tried not to wince when Smiley brought him into a hug, squeezing his side.

"No way. We'll cover you."

John's face fell. "No, Smiley, you don't understand. There are people after us — not just paramilitary — probably the National Guard too. This barricade is admirable but..."

John looked over at the students and their homemade mortar launchers. The two or three AK-47's they'd managed to procure. A barrel full of fireworks. He spotted half a dozen pistols for those fortunate enough to find one like the boy who had stopped him. He doubted they had enough ammunition to put them to good use. They really were just kids.

Smiley watched John's gaze. "Okay fine. We won't cover you. But we're going to stay and fight against any *Sandinista* trying to get past us."

"Smiley..."

"Revolutions never die John. They're a never-ending cycle."

"I never taught you that."

"Nope. Nicaragua did. Now go, before I tell them to move the barrier back!"

Smiley was staring at the road with intensity. John wanted to say something more, but couldn't think of anything appropriate. He'd already said everything he could, and he knew he had to get moving.

Dimitri started the engine as John hopped back into the truck, passenger side. He picked up the sniper rifle and laid it across his lap, sighing and feeling the steady throb of his side. Marcela was looking at Barry's phone, probing through the *Anono* app.

"Everything okay?" she asked John.

Dimitri pulled the truck through the barricade as John craned his neck to look out the window. A small dot grew on the horizon.

"No," John said. He readied the rifle.

CHAPTER 26

Mike was trying to get through to Linda with a third phone call by the time he pulled into underground parking for his apartment, but she still hadn't picked up. He had to get ahead of this thing. Someone had snapped a photo of him meeting with Russian intelligence, all while he danced a line with Sara and the PAG into spilling its secrets, an operative and asset being captured in their Nicaraguan mission, and unraveling Cuban intelligence infiltration.

I don't have time for this shit.

The list of potentially interested parties spying on him were large, and there was no telling what they'd do with that kind of picture. Blackmail? Explode his career? Just keeping tabs on his activity? CIA? Russians? PAG?

Whoever it was they could do serious damage to both him and Blackthorne. But that's not what concerned him. If someone realized what information had just passed between Mike and his Russian pal, it would be bad news in any scenario. The PAG would have new ammo against him, the Cubans might make a move to bury their assets before he could root them out, and hell, anyone hoping to disrupt American intelligence would find no better opportunity than now.

Mike clenched his teeth as he waited for the elevator which seemed to take longer every day he rode it up and down.

Maybe I should start taking the stairs.

He dialed for one of Linda's aides to ferret her out of whatever meeting was occupying her time as he got inside and rode the elevator up, but slowly lowered the phone from his ear as he opened the door to his apartment.

It was dark, which meant he should've seen the glowing green lights from his alarm system. But there were none.

The alarm system was off.

He hadn't done that. Which meant someone was in his apartment.

Mike hung up and pulled out his gun.

"Drop it."

Mike froze, hearing Sara's voice come from the opposite side of the room. As his night vision began to kick in, he saw her sitting in his easy chair, past the doorway in the adjacent room, a gun pointed directly at him.

"I said-" she began.

Mike tossed the gun on the floor at his feet. "Can a guy take his tie off when he gets home?"

Sara gave him a grim smile. "Sit."

Mike didn't take his eyes off her as he slowly took a step toward her. "You've already taken my seat."

"Not going to ask again."

"Don't feel much like sitting."

"Damnit Mike! Colluding with the Russians? What do you have to say?"

"Huh. So it *was* PAG tailing me. Figures," he muttered.

"I can't hear you. Why were you talking to the Russians?" Her voice was commanding and cold. Punctuated by the hammer of her pistol being pulled back.

"That's Special Operations business. Last I checked, you're on the other team."

"We're all on the same team!" Frustration and anger dripped into her tone.

Mike gave a mirthless laugh. "Yeah I guess we're both American, but only one of us has American interests at heart."

Even in the dim light Mike could see the fury on Sara's face. "Not you, us! American interests! I'm not the one talking to rival powers!"

"You're pulling strings in our own governance. Interfering with Americans. If you count that as American interests, then you're right."

"What are you plotting with Russia? What did they give you?"

"Confirmation."

"On what?" When Mike pursed his lips and kept his eyes level, Sara repeated herself, putting more bark in her tone. "Confirmation on what?"

"That the PAG is more of a threat to American democracy than Russia ever dreamed."

The gunshot blasted its way through the silence of the dark apartment and slammed into Mike's gut. He doubled over then fell backwards in surprise, a flailing arm grabbing for the kitchen table and snatching up the tablecloth as he tumbled. With it came the dishes he hadn't cleaned from last night, smashing onto the floor around him.

"Agh!"

He barely heard the sound of footsteps through the shock of pain in the middle of his stomach.

"I won't watch this country crumble around me." She stood over him and pointed her gun directly at his head. He could see up into the barrel, a dark portal to oblivion.

"Neither will I," Mike managed.

He kicked his leg out at her shin and connected hard with the bone. No one would consider Mike a skilled fighter, but a kick to the shin would make anyone hurt.

Sara didn't have time to react to the pain. Mike swept his feet around and tripped her to the ground. By the time she looked up and aimed her pistol from the ground, Mike had snapped up his own discarded pistol and brought it up to fire back.

His shot went wild, and Sara pulled herself up off the ground and bounded across the room and over the sofa as his second and third shots failed to trace her. Mike threw himself into an awkward log roll. The floor where he had been laying exploded as Sara returned fire from behind the couch. Mike managed to retreat into the hall and press up next to the wall, legs splayed out in front of him. He tried to catch his breath.

"You're a traitor!" Sara yelled.

Mike ripped open his button-up shirt to check his stomach, buttons flying off into the gloom. The Dragon Skin ballistic vest had done its work, although the American military wouldn't say so. Dragon Skin had been thoroughly rejected after several failures to meet ballistics testing, which meant the overstock that hadn't been recalled was easily requisitioned by anyone in the know. Mike touched the hole of ripped fabric and burnt his finger when it found metal. The bullet lodged in the overlapping ceramic plates that gave Dragon Skin its name was still hot with kinetic energy. Mike would deal with a bruise over a mortal wound any day, but he didn't have to like it. He sincerely thought he was more likely to be shot by Russian intelligence than American, which was why he was wearing it in the first place.

Times change, he thought, knowing he had Barker to thank for the armor suggestion.

"Sara," he said through gasping breaths and a dry throat. "Don't do this."

"I never wanted to," she responded, an undeniably shaky quality washing out the confidence in those words.

"Don't you get it? It's the same thing that happened with Locklee," Mike cried.

"Locklee was a traitor!"

"Goddamnit Sara," he said, inching to the edge of the wall, hoping his words would distract her. "Why can't you-"

Shots raced toward him as he poked less than an inch out into the room. He pulled back and glanced at the jagged edge of wall that had exploded above his head. Sara must have had her gun trained on the wall, waiting for him to look out. If he had raised his head a foot higher he'd be dead.

Oh fuck this…

Mike didn't take the time he needed to recover. Instead he decided to press an attack to keep his opponent pressured and guessing. He stuck his gun out around the corner and blind-fired. He thought he heard two shots of return fire but it was hard to tell against the blaring of his own. He felt a heavy *whump* against the wall, but after three pulls of his trigger he was on his feet and grabbing a pot of dried up rice that had fallen off the table, blasting off another round at Sara's sofa as he charged.

Sara had taken cover from his fire. By the time she heard the metal scrape of the pot on the floor and heavy footsteps of Mike bounding through the room at her, she hardly had time to raise her gun.

Mike second guessed himself and whacked the hand that held the gun, not thinking he could raise his own gun in time. Her gun fired off, the shot hitting the ceiling, and she cried out in pain as her arm was bashed out of the way. He pointed his gun to finish the job, but with Sara's gun gone, she'd switched into a close-combat mindset faster than Mike could follow. It had been a long time since he'd practiced hand-to-hand combat. He was about to regret his negligence.

Sara snapped an arm up to stop him pointing his gun, then grabbed his wrist with her other free hand and dug a thumb into the center of his tendons.

He yelled in surprise, the pressure point shooting pain up his arm, and found himself unable to focus on holding onto the gun. It fell from his hands and Sara caught it by the barrel. She flipped it around but not before Mike flailed and smashed the pot into the side of her skull. She screamed and somersaulted over the couch in surprise and pain, clutching her ear where a narrow trickle of blood began to stream down her cheek.

"Bastard!" she hissed at him in primal rage.

He felt the same hot fury taking control of his mind and body, and felt a sadistic laugh bubble up from his belly. "Aren't we all?"

He threw the pot at her, dried rice spraying in the air. But Sara crossed her arms and took the blow on the strength of her forearms, shrugging off the attack. Mike noticed the gun she'd taken off him was nowhere to be found, and must've been lost in the scuffle. Seeing this as an opening, he charged her.

Roaring like a savage bear and acting the same, he tackled her around the waist and pulled her off the ground before slamming her onto her back, pressing his weight into her as they fell.

She kicked with her legs but couldn't find purchase while he pinned her down. But as soon as he lifted himself for his next attack, her hand managed to find something in its desperate scrambling.

A ballpoint pen.

She stabbed at Mike's neck and he just barely grabbed her arm. She doubled-down with her second arm, shoving the sharp end of the pen closer and closer to his throat. Her eyes burned into him as his own flicked back and forth from her eyes and the impending death from the pen.

He bellowed and smacked her in the face with his other hand, then shoved her attack off while she was distracted. But she swung her arms and the pen back around like an elastic band, jamming it into his thigh, two inches deep.

"Agh!"

Mike ripped the pen out of his leg while Sara slithered out from under him, kicked him in the stomach once she was up, and moved into a defensive posture while he struggled to fully stand himself.

They locked eyes.

"The sex wasn't quite this good," Sara said.

Mike grunted; his eyes locked on his gun laying on the floor beside the couch, where Sara must have dropped it. When he looked back at her, she was looking at it just the same — she had followed his eyes.

"Shit…"

They both ran for it, shoving at one another, gripping jaws and jabbing ribcages to throw the other off balance in the effort to retrieve the weapon. Sara managed to rebound off one of Mike's pushes and punch his jaw, snapping his head sideways, but his hands connected with the gun on the floor, even if he couldn't see it.

A foot kicked at his hand, and while it connected, he managed to keep hold of the gun. He hip-checked her while she was off-balance on her one foot, and she raked her fingers across the wall from top to bottom while she fell, trying to find purchase. Her fingertips hit one of Mike's shitty paintings, and it broke her fall as she righted herself. She ripped the painting free of the wall and brought it down over Mike's head. His head burst through the canvas as if he were surfacing from underwater. But, while disoriented, Mike was still able to swing his arm up, even as Sara brought both her fists toward one another to pincer his skull, bashing his ears and muting his hearing.

It muffled the sound of the gunshot that tore through Sara's abdomen.

She staggered, eyes wide looking at Mike, then looking down at the bloody hole just below her chest. Then she collapsed, like a marionette whose strings had been cut.

The room fell silent, except for Mike's heaving lungs. He tore the painting off his neck and tossed it over the sofa. Then he allowed himself a moment to process everything that had just happened. A luxury he didn't usually take.

"Goddamnit…" Mike muttered, hands on thighs and doubled over so he could catch his breath. He tossed the gun back to the ground, clattering with finality. "Goddamn."

The sound of electronic buzzing broke his rest. He jerked upright, looking around for what was making the noise as if it were a bomb. He told himself to calm down, and found that it was his phone buzzing, and it was in his own damn pocket. He pulled it out and froze at the name on the screen.

Linda Kim.

"Shit…"

The first thing he thought was that things couldn't get any worse. Mike had been spotted with a Russian, then killed an American agent inside his apartment. All while he was trying to destroy an infiltration ring from Cuban intelligence that was so closely linked with American intelligence, it looked like he was trying to destroy American intelligence. Oh, and there were photos of his meeting as evidence.

"Hello?" Mike answered the phone.

"Mike? You called. I swear to God this better be important-"

"Yes, Linda…"

"...called a short break with our Nicaraguan ambassador friend just so I could-"

"Sara's dead."

Silence.

Then Linda responded sharply. "What?"

Mike couched his cellphone against his shoulder as he checked himself over for any major wounds his adrenaline might still be covering up. He was still winded, his ears burned and were ringing, and his sternum had a bruise full of popped blood vessels ready to show but that seemed to be the worst of it.

Then he saw the wound in his leg, caking his pants with slowly drying blood.

"Fuck," he said.

"What? Excuse me?"

"Sorry," Mike winced as he walked toward the washroom to see to the wound. He dropped trow and rummaged for hydrogen peroxide. His hands were shaking and he knocked over half a dozen bottles under his sink before he found what he was looking for.

"Sara's dead," Mike repeated, wincing and biting his shoulder from the painful white bubbles forming over the wound as bacteria burned away from the hydrogen peroxide. "You'll find her in my apartment."

"Jesus Christ Mike, what?"

"Yeah. She shot first. I've got cameras in every room. You'll find that in my security footage you're going to recover. Oh, and before I forget: give the Pinnacle Armor folks a second chance with that Dragon Skin body armor contract will you?"

Linda started to say something, then seemed to change her mind and ask something else instead. "What else do I need to know?"

Mike grimaced as he put the bottle of hydrogen peroxide down and broke out the bandaging and gauze he thought he'd never need hiding under the sink. "I've been talking with a Russian handler. PAG knows this. Their photos will confirm it too."

"What the…Mike, you need to come to Langley immediately."

"Of course," Mike nodded while wrapping the bandage. His hands were still shaking and the roll of gauze slipped. He picked it back up and finished tying it off. The leg was going to hurt like hell in the morning. "I'm on my way now."

"Good."

"Just know that no matter how this all looks, I'm not in the wrong here. I think I found out just how bad this PAG corruption is."

"Okay Mike, let's not talk crazy. I can finish my meeting with the ambassador. Tell me everything when we get to Langley," Linda said.

"Take your time," Mike said, limping into his room and opening his closet. He located his go-bag at the bottom under his hanging clothes. "Last thing: you don't have to worry about the asset in our Nicaraguan op."

"Okay Mike, I'm sending over a security detail…and cleanup-"

"I'll wait for them inside."

"Mike I'm heading back into my meeting…is our asset in Nicaragua en route back home?"

"I said not to worry about him," Mike said, a bite he normally never used with Linda starting to slip into his tone. "The PAG won't be able to get to him."

"You didn't answer my — Mike we need to get your ass to-"

"Locklee scratched the surface. He was an asshole. But he was right."

Mike hung up. Fire burned in his leg as he knelt down to access the safe in his closet. He dialed Barker.

"Sir?"

Mike opened his safe and snatched up three passports as well as ten thousand in cash. "Barker. I need you to book me a flight."

"A flight? Sorry sir, one sec, let me step outside…" Mike heard acoustic guitar and mumblings of a crowd in the background fade into the distance. "Open mic night — you remember that cafe we went to?"

"Barker. Get me a flight to Miami. Off the books. This might be the last you're going to hear from me."

Stunned silence came in on the other end of the phone. Mike could picture Barker's gaping expression, the one that always made him seem like a dying fish.

"Sir? What…what's happened? I don't understand."

"That's the idea." Mike placed a heavy hand against the wall and tried to calm his breathing. "You've been a great partner Barker. A good friend too."

Mike heard Barker start to say something else before he hung up the phone. He limped over to Sara's body and searched through her pockets until he came up with her phone. He looked around the trashed apartment — a broken painting lying on the floor beside an old pot of rice, blood splattered in places and smeared in others — and took one quick look at Sara's body. Then he hoisted the go-bag on his shoulder, opened the door to his apartment, and limped away.

By the time the security detail showed up at his door, Mike was long gone.

CHAPTER 27

———

Jorge 'Smiley' Ramirez gathered his people together, preparing them for whatever they were about to face.

"A lot of you had a feeling we'd be fighting today, and it turns out you're right," he said to the nervous faces around him. Most were students from universities, young men and women, and they were scattered across so many barricades that he wasn't able to find as many of his friends in the same place as he had in the earlier days of the protests. Jorge made sure to give particular looks of determined confidence to his lieutenants. The protestors didn't actually have any sort of formal command structure, but Smiley was an undoubted leader, responsible for so much organizing and he knew who he could trust — for the most part.

"Fedé is on his way with help but they spotted trucks along the 62. They'll be here any minute."

Fearful comments broke out among the group.

"What about that *gringo* with the truck, Smiley?" Alejandra asked. She and Narek were two of his lieutenants, and had recently stopped John on the road.

"An old friend. A *trusted* friend," Smiley emphasized.

"We were supposed to do shake-downs today," Narek said, resting a hand on the pistol strapped to his waist. "We already lost two barricades in fights this last week. What is this?"

"We don't get to choose this fight," Smiley said. "It calls us."

"This *maldito* fight," Narek spat. "We still have wounded. They are too strong. We can't fight."

Smiley took a step toward Narek and some of the others looked warily at one another, stepping back themselves. "Give me the gun. Take the wounded to the car and go."

Narek's face fell. "No, I don't-" he looked around, seeing accusing glances of cowardice thrown his way, others refusing to meet his gaze altogether.

"You heard me," Smiley said.

For a moment it seemed as if Narek would thrust out his chin proudly and say he was staying, but Smiley knew as well as he that it wouldn't be a bad idea to try to get the wounded out. Both men were left with a bad taste in their mouth as Narek begrudgingly unclipped his token holster and handed over the gun.

Smiley handed the gun off to one of his other lieutenants, then he turned to Alejandra. "Make sure Palmere and Kadie have AKs. I don't want to hear them complaining they didn't get a turn like last time."

Some of the students chuckled at that.

"Mortars are ready, Jorge," a big chubby boy said. Jorge still hadn't learned his name and he felt bad for it.

"Good — line them up, and make sure the reloaders are actually paying attention — I'm still pissed about what happened at Nandaime."

The chubby boy nodded gravely and set to the task.

"Oh, and everyone, please" Smiley called out as his team began walking away to see to their tasks. "For the love of *María*, actually use cover this time — we didn't stack cinder blocks for fun!"

"Smiley," Alejandra put a hand on his shoulder.

Smiley turned, looking up the road and seeing what she was about to say to him before she said the words.

"They're here."

Not enough time. Not enough weapons. Not enough anything.

Trucks were speeding down the road, waves of dust flying in their wake. Smiley had managed to pull together twenty or so protestors for this barricade but they could hardly compete with a proper group of paramilitary — especially with how well supplied they'd been by the government. Many suspected the Russians had been feeding extra guns and money to help support the enemy as well.

"Get on the radio and tell Fedé to turn around," Smiley said softly.

Alejandra stopped when she heard the second part of his order. "What? But they're our only reinforcements!"

"Yes, and he's too late unfortunately," Smiley said. He rubbed her hair and she swatted away his hand. He grabbed her hand and pulled her into a hug. "Send the message. Tell him it's not his fault. Then come support me in the center. Someone needs to keep an eye on Palmere and Kadie."

Alejandra wiped the tears welling up in her eyes and nodded. She ran to the radio they had in a tent not far down the street to send the message.

Just like the French, Smiley thought with a grin. *¡Viva la Revolución!*

He sprinted up to meet the others at the cinder block barricade, slapping backs and shaking hands before crouching low and pointing his handgun forward with both hands, as he had learned to do for the first time three months ago. As so many of them had learned for the first time months or weeks or days ago.

The trucks came to a stop and a woman wearing all black and a balaclava hopped off from the back of one. Smiley could see their raised weapons but was more concerned about the grenades he thought he spotted in one man's hand before he ducked back against the tailgate.

"¡*Moverse o morir!*" the woman yelled. *Move or die!* She fired her AK into the air, making the students jump. Smiley heard someone let out a sob from down the line.

Smiley tapped the chubby student's shoulder. "Let them have it," he said.

"¡*Disparar!*" the boy roared. *Fire!*

Smiley grinned at how much gusto the kid put into the command. Homemade mortars launched and exploded around the trucks. One connected with a windshield and a man piled out from behind the driver's seat and onto the road, rolling and screaming. Unfortunately, most of the other mortars pocked the road or overshot their targets.

"Reload!" the boy yelled.

But there wasn't any time to reload, and Smiley knew it. He pulled the trigger on his pistol as fast as he could while keeping some semblance of aim, and the few other guns they had popped from behind the barricade. Alejandra appeared from behind him and lit off a firework, the sound whistling and exploding into bright red sparks in front of the trucks.

The *Sandinistas* opened fire in unison, shredding anyone who hadn't taken cover in time and even blasting through some of the cinder blocks. The left side began to crumble and students tripped over one another trying to move toward the center.

Jorge fumbled to reload but by the time he came back up to meet the enemy, two grenades had been tossed, one landing directly in front of the barricade on the right, and the other landing behind, right beside him and Alejandra.

He gave her one last smile. "Revolutions never die."

CHAPTER 28

———

"¡*Vamos!*" Marcela yelled from the back of the truck.

She'd been watching the helicopter close in from behind as they'd sped along the 62. A thin column of smoke rose in the distance from where they'd been stopped by the student barricade.

"You were told to pick us up," John said to Dimitri.

Dimitri made a hard turn as the 62 wound through El Coyol, knuckles growing white on the steering wheel. "Yes."

"To take us where?"

"North Pacific."

Marcela scrambled up behind the cab and pounded on the screen. "Hello? I said *más rápido!*"

Dimitri didn't answer. All his focus was on the road. They were pushing eighty miles an hour, the sort of speed that would be fast for a regular car on the highway but they were in a bulky army truck meant primarily for long transport. As Dimitri pushed their speed he also had to be more careful about taking his turns.

"Give me the SVD," Marcela said, pointing to the rifle beside John. "They're going to strafe from the back."

John handed her the sniper rifle over his shoulder. His wounded side protested as he hefted the weight of the gun "As long as you give it back for when they make their second pass at the front."

Marcela gave him a predatory grin. "Ha! Okay." She scrambled past Barry and back to the rear of the truck, getting a bead on the helicopter before it came into range.

"Where on the coast?" John asked, resuming their conversation. He felt like he didn't have enough information to put a good plan together in his mind. Until he could do that, he couldn't place much confidence in his decisions as their current crisis grew.

"I have coordinates for the North Pacific. Not far out. We're going to *Aeropuerto Internacional de Costa Esmeralda*," Dimitri said. "I have a helicopter waiting for us there."

John thought about that. "We'll have to shake these guys first."

Dimitri grimaced. "Agreed."

The sharp *crack* of the sniper rifle cut through the air like a knife. John had been waiting for the sound so hadn't reacted much, but he knew all this was wearing more and more on a civilian like Barry. John still hadn't finished talking to him. Something felt fishy about this whole thing, and not just because they'd been compromised and captured.

The sniper cracked again and John heard Marcela swear in frustration. He looked out the rearview mirror and saw the helicopter swerving erratically from side to side. Perhaps it'd slow down their approach, but hitting a moving target at range was already difficult. Snipers were meant to lie atop a hill and wait for an order to eliminate a target at long distance; not shoot at dodging air targets at medium range. Which made John wonder why Dimitri had a sniper on hand as his weapon of choice while in Nicaragua. But John knew he didn't have time to think about that.

He twisted in his seat to face Barry, whose face was buried in his hands, elbows resting on legs bouncing up and down. "Barry," John said.

Barry looked up with a tight face and gave John a nervous smile back.

John didn't bother trying to placate the man. "Who's Antonio?"

Barry's face dropped. "Look, John I don't want to-"

Marcela's sniper cracked a third time, making Barry cry out as he jumped with fright. She grunted and readjusted her sights. John saw the helicopter was closing on them but hadn't opened fire yet. He leaned an arm on the ridge of the screen and pulled it closed until it nearly touched his face, blocking out Dimitri from the conversation as best he could. John pulled out his pistol and looked it over, gesturing for Barry to lean in closer so they could talk.

Barry closed the gap so they were inches apart, and John was counting on the gunfire and roar of the engine to help keep their conversation private. Barry was a fast learner. He eyed the gun and gave John a look of submission.

"Antonio," John said, still examining his pistol.

"Yeah," Barry whispered, looking over his shoulder to watch Marcela follow the sound of rotor blades in the sky. "He's this big rich guy, right? Met him through Silicon networking after *E-Buck* got some attention. Turns out he was into crypto and liked what I'd done."

"He gave you the idea for *Anono*?"

Barry blinked, surprised at how quickly John had jumped to that conclusion. "Well…I had the idea in the works, but he said he'd fund it if I could actually create what I described."

"Complete anonymity."

"Right."

"Antonio is a criminal, isn't he?"

Barry began to feel heat on his face as he turned red. He blew what felt like steam out of his mouth. "Depends who's asking…"

"Anticipation Island," John said suddenly.

Barry snapped his head back like he'd been punched in the chin. "What?"

John didn't answer. He just stared down Barry, like he'd do interrogating any other nervous person trying to hide a secret. He didn't need to say anything to get Barry to think John knew more than he did.

"How do you...are you in on it?"

That made John think about how to answer. "No."

"Then-"

"How do I get in on it?"

Barry's eyes went wide. "Um...well it's not that simple."

"I'm the guy that's either going to get you home or not," John said. "It's easy to get lost in Nicaragua."

"Okay, okay," Barry said, a frantic look in his eyes. "So Antonio is rich, right?"

"You said that."

"And because he's rich, naturally he has an island."

"Anticipation Island."

"Yeah. It's sort of the meeting ground for a lot of powerful rich people. And well...you know how powerful rich people are. They have eccentric tastes. And they don't want people knowing about those tastes, but they still have to communicate..."

"*Anono.*"

"Exactly. So...good thing I didn't have to end up giving Antonio access, right?"

"A lot of people would've been exposed."

"Right."

John narrowed his eyes. It reminded him of a certain kill-switch he had to deal with back with Marcela in Antigua. Funds passing from the CIA to a drug cartel, recorded by email. Which he had helped smother, unknowingly at the time.

"You saved a lot of people man," Barry gave the window a playful rap. "Not just me."

John was starting to feel sick and it wasn't from his wound. He wasn't usually so sensitive in this way. His mind was racing against a fever he felt starting to crop up on his forehead.

Was the Puentes family involved in Anticipation Island then? Why else was the location on the laptop? And was the Senate interested in regulating *Anono* because of its criminal activities...or because they were using it too?

"Why are the Cubans involved?" John asked suddenly.

Barry blinked. "Antonio is Cuban."

Marcela's sniper snapped as another shot split the air.

"*Mierda.*" She sat back on the floor of the truck and tossed her hair back, holding the sniper upright so it rested on its butt. "Dimitri *dorogoy*, can you go faster?"

Dimitri didn't answer but John watched as he pressed himself lower into the seat, as if it'd make the truck more aerodynamic.

"Juan?" John asked, happy to get out of his head and back to the task at hand. They weren't out of the woods yet.

Marcela shook her head. "Peeled off."

"If they're looping around for the next pass that means you have to share the sniper," John said.

He was hoping that'd get a smile out of Marcela but she looked at him with a grimace. "New *problema*."

She pointed out the back and John looked down the road. Dust was parting amidst a train of heavy vehicles.

"What's up?" Barry asked, not liking the hard look shared by John and Marcela as they looked down the road behind them. "Who are they?"

"Army?" Marcela shrugged.

"Paramilitary or National Guard," John said.

Dimitri looked back at them through the rearview mirror. "Both. Hold on."

He put more gas into their already dangerous speed and Marcela readied the sniper rifle once more.

CHAPTER 29

"What's the count?" John called over the roar of the engine.

Marcela was looking through the sight of the sniper, trying to figure out how many enemies were chasing them, debating if it was worth popping off a few shots. She wasn't sure how expendable their ammunition was.

"I count…four? Five! Four civilian vehicles and an army truck!"

John did the rough math of how many people there might be chasing them. "I'm guessing around thirty combatants. A third trained, but all armed."

"We are fine. *Aeropuerto Internacional de Costa Esmeralda* and we're off," Dimitri said. A bead of sweat rolled down from his forehead. He took his hat off, wiped his face, and put the hat back on his head, careful with his one hand on the steering wheel now that he was pushing ninety.

"It's too far," John said.

"It's not."

"It is."

Dimitri didn't reply.

"I don't like it, but I'm right," John said.

Dimitri looked out the rearview mirror and turned back to the road, not looking at John.

"I don't have any other secret Russian plans, John."

"Fine. El Gigante."

Dimitri raised an eyebrow.

"Get us to Playa Gigante."

"Why? John, it's the same distance."

"We need to get off the 62."

Dimitri's expression grew tenser by the second. "We need to stay on the 62 if we're going to-"

"We can weave through a town, but we can't lose them at the airport."

Dimitri ground his teeth, looked at the rearview, gripping the steering wheel tighter as the trucks continued to chase. They whipped past Nica Transportation Service and the Pingüino Market on the left as they came out of San Antonio, and the Guacalito de la Isla road grew parallel in front of them.

The sniper rifle cracked as Marcela squeezed off a shot. John watched trucks swerve around one another as one of them drove off the road and crashed into a ditch.

"Turn here," John said.

"*Chyort*," Dimitri swore. He changed his foot off the gas and onto the brake and made the turn.

Everyone in the truck lurched as they were brought from ninety to sixty around the sharp left turn. John thought for a moment they'd career off onto two wheels before falling over but Dimitri gauged the timing well.

"Playa Gigante," John said, sitting up in his seat and readying his pistol.

"As we begin, so we end," Dimitri said.

"What are you doing?" Marcela called. "Why the turn?"

"John has a plan!" Dimitri yelled.

Marcela looked at John. "No you don't!" she moved back into position to watch the trucks trying to make the turn behind them.

John watched trucks fly past Guacalito de la Isla road and one other spin out as it tried to make the turn. That would buy them some time at least.

"Do you have a helicopter hidden somewhere in the village?" Dimitri asked.

"No," John said.

Dimitri frowned.

They picked up speed again as they hit the dirt roadway and jungle began to take over. Tree branches scraped against the top cover of the truck and John saw monkeys scrambling through the trees, angry at the rude interruption of this truck blasting into their jungle. The road became winding, kicking up dust and gravel.

"We have some time!" Marcela called over the roar of the engine and wildlife. She scrambled over to the front sliding window before the cab. "They're still working to catch up, but I won't have a good shot for a while."

"Or many bullets left," Dimitri said.

"That too."

"Hey this looks familiar," Barry said, poking his head into the front. John had thought the man had curled up and left them to figure things out. But Barry was right; they were back on the road they had run to a lifetime ago, when they had taken the motorbike and tried to make it for the border.

"There," John pointed to a small building coming up on the right. Let me off here."

"What?" Marcela and Barry said at once.

"I'm not stopping," Dimitri said.

John expected him to say that. "Fine. Get to the beach."

"Which one?"

"The middle of Playa Gigante."

Marcela looked at him with concern in her eyes. "But John, we're about to-"

"Playa Gigante," John confirmed. He held his gun and popped his door open against a nasty wind that nearly blew it back on him. Leaves and branches rattled against it from the foliage. "If I'm not there in ten minutes, I'm not coming at all."

He hopped out of the truck before anyone could respond, landing hard on the ground and spinning into a roll. His side spiked with pain as he knocked it against the road one, two, three times, then pushed himself up by his hands. He ran over to the small building — the abandoned granary — and trained his gun on the padlock.

He held out a hand to protect his eyes from the potential ricochet, and fired, blowing the lock off the door.

CHAPTER 30

—————

"Where is he?" Marcela asked as Dimitri pulled their truck onto the beach.

The wheels struggled against the sand as onlookers pointed and stared at their army truck tearing past the town, down the ridge and into groups of fishermen. Most of the tourists and surfers had taken to the hills after the *Sandinista* attack, but the rest of the villagers didn't have anywhere to go, and this was their home. The charred remains of trees, stalls, and burnt-out buildings lay scattered amidst those that had escaped the *Sandinista* raid. The townsfolk had simply proceeded to rebuild as best they could.

"I don't know," Dimitri said, deciding he'd reached the approximate location John had told him to go. "But we have to go now."

Marcela muttered under her breath as Dimitri reached back over the screen to take the SVD back from her. He popped his door open and braced himself against a brutal wind that picked up fine sand to attack his eyes.

Marcela frowned and waved to Barry. "Let's go Berty."

"My name is-"

Marcela interrupted him by kicking down the tailgate, its rust squealing painfully at their ears as the hinges gave way. It fell down with a bang. Marcela offered Barry a hand to jump down.

"No helicopter…" Dimitri was saying, walking over to Marcela while scanning the sky.

"That's good. I'm surprised *El Presidente* didn't send a few of his own though," Marcela said. "If we're as important to the Cubans as I think we are."

"They won't send air," Dimitri said.

Marcela pulled out her pistol and leaned up against the truck, looking around for any sign of enemy activity. "Why not?"

Dimitri pointed out over the water.

Marcela caught her breath.

Barry looked out as well. "Holy shit."

Darkness had overtaken the entire horizon. At first glance Marcela thought it was night and she'd gotten her time wrong somehow. It took a few seconds to realize the smear of black against the sky were storm clouds.

"You can see the rain out there too," Barry pointed, mouth agape. "Over the water, that mist."

"It's coming in fast," Marcela said. "And right toward us."

"How are we going to get out?" asked Barry.

"The storm makes this difficult," Dimitri said.

Marcela shook her head. "Not a storm. This is Nicaragua in the fall. It's a hurricane."

Barry was the first to notice a figure down the beach waving their arms at them.

"It's John!" he cried.

In silent agreement, the three of them took off at a run to meet with John. A small crowd of Nicaraguans were gathering nearby as well. Dimitri and Marcela slowed when they saw the weapons in their hands. They were mostly farming tools like pitchforks, pickaxes, and many held machetes.

"Paramilitary?" she asked.

"I don't know," Dimitri said, hesitating. He had his handgun out and ready just as she had.

Barry pulled to a stop much too late, not noticing the weapons. But by the time Marcela and Dimitri had caught up to him, they'd noticed that they were friendly with John.

"Not paramilitary," Marcela said.

"Villagers," Dimitri said, eyes growing wide. "Arming themselves since the attack that happened here. Dimitri looked over the crowd and onto the ridge, where blackened remnants of charred shacks and houses remained.

John pushed through the small crowd as the three of them cautiously picked their way forward.

"I've got our way out," John said. A young but rough looking man stepped forward, brandishing a harpoon and wearing a determined look on his face. "Kervin says we can borrow their fishing boat," John continued.

The others saw that just beyond the crowd lay a small but long wooden boat, looking questionable in its seaworthiness. It was clear the thing had been heavily used.

"It is my cousin's but I'm sure he won't mind," Kervin said, eyeing Marcela and giving her a wink.

He held out a hand and John shook it. "*Gracias amigo,*" John said, putting as much emphasis in those words as he could find. He turned to the others. "Let's get going."

Barry looked warily at the boat but didn't protest when he saw Dimitri climb aboard. Marcela pulled John aside.

"John, a hurricane's coming."

John looked at the dark storm clouds that moved toward them. A wind began to pick up and blow off the water.

"No choice," John said.

"Yes but-"

Marcela's words were interrupted by the squeal of tires and roaring of engines.

The paramilitary and National Guard had arrived.

The trucks that had been chasing them raced down the ridge and onto the beach. The villagers from the crowd raised their weapons, some of them running toward the trucks.

John pulled Marcela away from the unfolding action and she helped him into the boat against his injury. Dimitri sat at the bow, pointing his sniper, watching their pursuers.

"Save your bullets," John said.

Marcela pushed the boat into the water as John stepped over the seats to where Barry was fumbling with the engine. He looked over his shoulder as the boat scraped against the sand and finally released its tension onto the water's surface, watching the enemy stand and ready weapons over the cabs of trucks, others leaning out of windows with their guns.

"Get us out of here," Dimitri muttered.

Marcela finished her last push, turning the boat around and hopped in, while Barry pulled the engine's cord, letting a choking sound rip as the engine got to work.

The paramilitary and national guardsmen were yelling at the villagers on the beach who were standing their ground, covering John's escape with the boat. The trucks roared, inching closer, threatening to run over the villagers. They were all waiting for the inevitable.

"They'll be slaughtered," Marcela said as John moved toward her and Barry.

"Don't be so sure," John said, moving over to take the tiller from Barry.

Just as Marcela thought the trucks would race toward them in a blaze of gunfire, finally ending their escape, she saw a mob of people walking down the ridge. Two of the trucks turned around to face them.

More villagers. With more weaponry. It seemed like every villager held an AK-47. Some even held grenades.

Dimitri pulled back from his position, putting his sniper down and watching the scene unfold with awe. Paramilitary were getting out of their trucks, tossing guns on the ground and holding their hands up as the mob surrounded them on the beach.

"Where did they get all those weapons?" Barry asked. "The barricades hardly had anything like that."

Dimitri eyed up John. "This wouldn't have anything to do with a missing armament shipment a few months back, would it?"

"Not at all," John said.

He turned away to hide his smile, then pointed them in the direction of the nasty storm clouds and raced ahead to meet them head on.

They were on the waves for less than a minute before a helicopter was spotted in the distance.

CHAPTER 31

"I'm not going into that storm!" the pilot cried at Juan. His eyes were panicked. Drops of blood were splattered against the side of his helmet. Juan had blood on his arm and shirt as well. Their machine gunner had been killed by John and Marcela. A lucky shot had pierced the floor of the chopper and through the soldier's seat.

Juan clambered over into the passenger seat and looked out the windshield. Rain peppered against their chopper and peeled back, sliding off the glass as fast as it hit.

"I didn't come all this way to lose my men and my woman so we could turn around," Juan said. "This ends now."

The pilot slowed their advance and shook his head. "*Don* Juan. The storm. We can't-"

Juan pulled out his pistol. "Do not be afraid of the storm," he said, giving the pilot a dark look. "Be afraid of me."

The pilot swallowed, then nodded, pressing forward with the cyclic stick.

Juan tucked his pistol away and returned to the gunner's seat. He pulled open the side door and cursed as he shoved the soldier's body out of the door and into the roiling waves below, before taking control of the FN MAG himself. He gripped the gun tight and stared out the open door into the building hurricane. The wind and rain continued to grow in fury. It whipped at his face and tore at his ruined suit.

But no storm would stop him.

"I *am* the storm," he whispered.

They raced after the boat and into the gale.

* * *

"If you're not going to shoot it, give the gun to me!" Marcela cried over the roar of wind and waves.

"I didn't think they'd follow us into the storm," John said, frowning at Dimitri. "How many rounds left?"

"You don't want to know," Dimitri said. "Drive straight."

John tightened his grip on the tiller as the helicopter raced to meet them. There was nowhere to hide except between the waves as the sea threw their tiny vessel up and down.

Barry raised his head from the side of the boat where he'd been retching. "It's starting," he croaked before throwing up whatever he had left.

The rain spit on them for a heartbeat before torrential downpour began. The raindrops fell hard and painfully, relentless as machine gun fire.

"Fucking shoot!" Marcela yelled.

Dimitri's face bunched up and he did as she asked, the shot nearly drowned out by the sound of crashing waves and rain.

"We're going to need to bail," John said, raising his voice as another wave came in from the side, and he changed their direction to match the swells. He tossed a small metal pail to Marcela before Dimitri could say something rude to her.

"*Mierda,* okay," she said, catching the bucket and moving to the center of the boat where the biggest dip in the hull was. Indents and warping in the wood began to collect water like puddles in a street.

"I can't…John, don't turn!" Dimitri called over his shoulder, trying to line up another shot.

John evened them out as the waves grew bigger, with whitecaps beginning to form at a rapid rate. But just as he'd straightened them, the water around them exploded with quick ferocity and two loud pops rang out somewhere in front of John.

"*Vniz!*" Dimitri called, two seconds too late.

The helicopter had closed the range enough to open fire,

John dove to the meager cover provided by the hull of the fishing boat, searing pain radiating from his wound. It was like a hot poker rammed into his ribs, and his throat opened as he let out an ugly squawk of pain.

"John!" Marcela shoved the pail into Barry's hands and scrambled over to John on all fours, leaving the engine unmanned.

Marcela held his face in her cold hands, the rain's downpour sapping any human warmth from them. She lifted his face and began examining him, trying to find where he'd been shot so she could attend to the new wound.

John raised a hand to stop her, before dropping it back down to support himself. "Not…shot…" he managed to point to the ugly red-brown stain on his shirt where his original wound was. Marcela pushed him back lightly so he could lie down somewhat in the boat. With little enough room, his knees remained raised and his head bounced off the wooden bench painfully, but it was enough for Marcela to lift his shirt and examine the wound she had bandaged earlier.

"How…bad?" John managed, hissing through the new pain that had arisen from the old ache in his side. The numbness was gone, replaced by constant spikes of fire.

"*Mierda.*"

"That…bad, eh?"

They both heard a gunshot snap off and ducked down by instinct before recognizing the sound of the SVD going off in Dimitri's hands. John could make out the helicopter in the air, veering off.

"Leaving?" John wheezed.

"No, coming back around," Marcela said, slicking back her drenched hair that had found its way onto her face. She shook her feet, splashing the water in the bottom of the boat that had tripled in the last minute. "Too much water…Berty, bail!"

"I am!" He didn't bother correcting her on his name.

Dimitri pulled back from the bow, eyeing the helicopter and adjusting one of the dials on the scope. "This is a mess."

John didn't want to know how many rounds the man had left. He felt his mind waver in the face of his pain, and tried to mentally slap himself into focus.

"Farther into the storm," he managed.

Marcela gave him a grim nod, then stepped over him to take on the engine. She opened the throttle and grabbed hold of the tiller, cutting across a seven foot wave. The white cap crashed down behind them.

"Where are we going?" Barry cried, still bailing like a madman.

Dimitri had his phone out, examining an app with a compass and coordinates. "Close. Marcela!"

"What?"

"West, one more kilometer."

She arched an eyebrow at him and he directed which way she should go with an arm.

"Ah, okay!"

She adjusted, bringing them about again, and Barry managed to keep back any lingering bile.

Lying on his back in the bottom of the boat, John saw nothing but swirling darkness, streaks of rain falling in sheets around them, drenching them no differently than if they'd been swimming in the ocean instead of sailing above it. The water in the boat was starting to lap at his legs.

"Leak!" Barry cried.

"What?" Dimitri asked.

"A leak! We have a leak." Barry pointed to a hole near the bottom of the boat, slowly taking on water as they dipped through the waves.

"Maybe from their shooting…" Marcela mused. "How much farther?"

Dimitri left his phone on the bench before him and glanced at it, nodding. "Direction is okay, maybe six hundred? Keep going." But John was following Dimitri's eyes as he prepared his sniper one last time.

The helicopter emerged through the clouds and dipped like a falcon swooping down on its prey. It had its target in its sights and trained forward, not bothering to weave or compensate for buffeting winds.

Dimitri could ask for little more. He fired off a round and nodded. "A hit, but I don't know what good it'll do," said Dimitri. The gun locked the bolt back and confirmed what he already knew. "No more rounds."

A sinking feeling gripped them all as they watched the helicopter continue through the air. There was lingering hope that the storm would press on the helicopter's ability to fly, but even as the wind and rain battered it, it continued on its trajectory.

Dimitri and Marcela pulled out their handguns, and John struggled to reach behind his back for his own, but felt a tear in his side, leaving his arm to fall flat and limp against his stomach.

"What the-" Barry cried, the only person not watching the helicopter in gritty determination. "Watch out!"

Marcela spun her head around to see what Barry was going on about. Ten foot waves had been springing up all around them for a while now, pushing them up and down like a pendulum. But she watched as an unnatural burst of white foam exploded on the surface not one hundred meters away.

"What is-"

Gunfire erupted just out of range from the helicopter, racing across the water toward them as it closed the distance. But from below the bubbling water rose a dark tube with a spark on the end, the thing difficult to make out in the darkness and rain. Slow at first to emerge, then surging with an intensity, the thing sprang into the air.

John watched it fly, trying to calculate size and distances against the sluggishness plaguing his mind and body.

"A missile!" Marcela cried.

Juan must have spotted it too, because the machine gun's growl stopped and the helicopter veered hard off to the left. A gust of wind sprang up at the same moment and tossed the metal bird farther in its turn than expected, spinning it out of control and into the darkness of cloud and sea. The missile disappeared off into the distance silently, the fire at its tail trailing out and smothered.

A dark hulk of shadow remained where the missile had emerged; a long black metal lingering on the surface against the seafoam, bobbing gently in the waves.

A submarine.

"That's our ride," Dimitri said, shouldering his SVD and directing Marcela. "Go, now!"

Marcela nodded and spun their steering, cutting across another wave cresting and crashing onto itself, and getting caught up in a second. She maneuvered and drove the boat along the power of the wave before pushing to the edge, slipping out of its momentum and pulling up to the submarine with a heavy lurch.

There was movement from the submarine's sail, and they watched a hatch open and a man poke his head out. He smiled and waved to them with wild gusto, bringing a smile and relief to their own beleaguered spirits. He climbed out onto the sub and set up a rope ladder dangling toward them.

Dimitri stood and grabbed Barry's arm. "Let's get you home," he said, guiding Barry to grab hold of the ladder leading onboard. He stood carefully, trying not to dip their rickety boat, and Dimitri readied him to pull himself aboard.

Marcela cut the engine and worked to lift John by the shoulders while he pushed his feet against the bottom of the boat to bring his back up against the bench. He took in the sight of the submarine, mind already classifying its type and best-guess at armament.

But something seemed wrong. The ship was probably an American Seawolf class, a small submarine fitting the size and mass in front of him as best he could figure out. But if that were the case, the sail should be taller and narrower, not as flat and wide. He tried to figure out if he couldn't quite see it right amidst the hurricane bearing down upon them.

"That's it," Dimitri said, helping Barry as he climbed up the submarine. He pulled the rope ladder but slipped in the process. His leg fell through the ladder and he slid into a straddle, but managed to pull himself back up. Barry laughed and got to his feet, pulling Dimitri onto the hull to join him after he reached the top.

"Come on John," Marcela whispered into John's ear against the pattering of rain, falling fast enough to hurt where the drops landed. "Let's go."

John grunted and managed to pull himself into a sitting position onto the bench. He did a quick look-around out of habit to see if they had everything they needed from their sinking vessel even though the boat held nothing but water, then climbed to his feet, pulling himself into the rain and wind battering his face.

He moved to the edge of the boat and was about to take hold of the rope ladder, when he looked up to see Barry disappearing down the submarine's hatch and the sailor that had waved to them helping him down. The sailor ducked out of sight and Dimitri followed him up the sail instead of helping the others aboard.

"Not a Seawolf," John said.

Marcela turned to him. "What?"

"It's a Kilo-class. Russian."

Marcela spun her head back around to look at the vessel with the same eye John had.

"No hard feelings my *mysh*," Dimitri called, smiling as he reached up to close the hatch.

Marcela screamed in frustration and anger as she realized what was happening. John and her both pulled out their pistols and fired as the hatch slammed shut. John lost his balance and managed to break his fall into a slide as he collapsed back into the boat. He tossed his handgun into the pooling water that had filled nearly a third of their vessel.

Marcela was still standing, watching in stunned silence, gun still held in front of her, smoke from its barrel twisting away with the wind, as the submarine sunk back into the depths.

"They wanted Barry," John said, working to breathe steadily as he felt blood from his wound mix with the water all around them. "Esteban."

"I'm messaging him now," Marcela said.

"He set us up," John said, raindrops clouding the corners of his vision. "He knew."

"We don't know that," Marcela said, sounding unconvinced.

John's vision was growing blurrier, and he wiped water from his eyes but found no improvement. It took him a moment to realize it wasn't the water.

"He messaged back!" Marcela said. "He says…*mierda*, half an hour. Another one-kay north for extraction."

"Barry? The Russians?" John hissed air through his teeth.

Marcela looked at him, noticing how pale and limp he'd become and crouching down next to him, checking his pulse.

"I told him. He said 'mission accomplished.'" Marcela turned her phone to show John the screen but John didn't look at it. He was fumbling for something in his pocket, feeble fingers prying at cloth.

Marcela patted down his pocket and helped him retrieve what he was struggling for.

It was a 'wig.

Not just any 'wig, of course, but the one they'd used to capture the Puentes laptop information and to help topple Pablo's command in their previous mission together. John had said he'd purged the data, but Marcela knew better. He'd been trying to find some connection to hunt down those who had betrayed his friend Brian.

"They wanted…Barry," John said through a heavy breath. "Barry's app."

Marcela took the 'wig as he thrust it at her. "John, what?"

"Downloaded it…the password entry," John swallowed, knowing Marcela was struggling to understand him. "They tried to get…a backdoor, but failed. I swiped it…"

"You…oh *María*." Marcela held the 'wig more carefully, as if it had grown more valuable in her hands. John had used the 'wig to steal the very thing his captors were after, from the man he was ordered to protect, all while in captivity. It was enough to make her head spin. And she reminded herself that she didn't give John enough credit.

Marcela tucked the 'wig away, making sure it'd be safe. "I see. Okay."

"I got a name…Antonio…Antonio Romero…*Isla de Anticipación*…"

"Okay, John, shush. We need to-"

She was trying to talk to him but he wasn't looking at her anymore. He was watching the sky. Felt the primal anger of rain on his face.

The helplessness of being tossed through cresting waves. He had always loved the ocean, ever since he was a boy growing up on the East Coast of Canada. Nature could be so angry.

Marcela lightly slapped his face. "John, not a good time for this."

She found the bucket and bailed furiously, checking on John in between emptying water. But eventually she had to jump on the engine and steer them further.

John lost consciousness as she took hold of the tiller.

An American Seawolf-class submarine surfaced twenty minutes later, and Marcela dragged John out of their boat that had all but sunk, collapsing onto a hull that was thankfully stronger than the remnants of their fishing boat. Two American sailors ran to their aid, nervously watching the storm in the sky grow heavier as the submarine was pushed around in the waves. They helped Marcela down the hatch and carried John to safety, uncertain if he was still alive.

EPILOGUE

Marcela hadn't heard from Esteban since she'd been extracted off the coast of Nicaragua. The American sailors who had picked her and John up were thankfully discreet and didn't prod her with their questions. She hadn't felt much like talking anyway. But she did ask where they were taking her. It wasn't a long voyage; they had been instructed to pick a course to Costa Rica after extraction.

Esteban had told her to go to Miami once she had landed and proceed to an address. No further instructions were given.

Increasingly disconcerted, Marcela had little choice but to book a flight and make her way to the address indicated. She assumed she was going to undertake debriefing, and perhaps a package needed to be collected along the way. But something felt off about the whole affair.

The address turned out to be a small sidewalk restaurant located in Little Havana East — two blocks from downtown Miami and five from Miami Beach and the Atlantic. The location made her travel easy at least. Esteban had required her to be there much faster than the usual timeline, but it wasn't as if she had plans coming out of the airport.

She didn't feel much like eating when the waiter swung by, but she ordered a beer and turned to survey the street. Little Havana had a huge population of Cubans, and it didn't seem coincidence that the meeting was to be here. She watched a vendor sell street meat to a family of eager customers and bicycles roll lazily down the road on their way to the beach, bells ringing as they faded into the coming sunset. A middle-aged man in a ball cap and sunglasses enjoyed a latte at the table in front of hers.

She was rudely interrupted by a man approaching her table head on. He had a slight limp that he was attempting to hide. He took the chair opposite her and dragged it across the concrete before sitting down.

Marcela arched an eyebrow at the man. He had a hefty build and dark skin, the lines on his face indicated he worked a stressful job. Marcela thought the man was attempting to hit on her before seeing the seriousness on his face.

"Kilo," the man said.

That was the weekly communications code to confirm someone working for the Firm.

"Zulu," Marcela said, giving the proper response for the week. It usually lifted the initial feeling of tension from meeting up with other agents. But Marcela didn't feel any ease this time around.

"It's nice to finally meet you Marcela," the man said in a low voice. "We have a lot of work to do."

Marcela didn't like that this man knew her name and used it upfront. She couldn't tell if he was flexing his knowledge or preparing a threat. The only operatives who knew her name were the ones she worked with on a mission. This man didn't strike her as an operative; she thought he was here to deliver something or retrieve information from her.

Marcela took a sip of her beer and kept her face blank as she decided to play it out.

"What does Esteban want?"

"We need to talk," the man said. "Where's John?"

"He's dead."

The man's eyes went wide in surprise, but Marcela's mind was moving into action. This man shouldn't know John's name or that they had worked together. Marcela kept her face blank as a professional poker player as she reached for her clutch. It was a casual motion, something anyone would do during conversation to retrieve some mundane item for use. But she was reaching for the Ruger LCR in her bag — a snub-nosed revolver she had picked up a few days ago to have in case of the worst.

Thank María for American gun laws, she thought.

The worst had arrived.

But the man in front of her didn't move. Didn't reach for a weapon, or make to attack, or to flee. "Don't pull out the gun," he said quietly instead, looking around and leaning forward as he spoke.

Marcela suppressed her surprise and the retort she had on her tongue. Instead she dropped the clutch back to her side and leaned in to meet the stranger's posture.

"Did Esteban send you or no?" Marcela asked. "Who are you?"

"Esteban didn't send me," the man said. "I *am* Esteban."

Two heartbeats flew by for Marcela in stunned silence before she sprang into action. Her Ruger LCR was out of the handbag and planted in her hands in a second, training on Mike under the table.

In the same instance, John appeared behind the man and loomed over him, pressing a gun hard into his back.

"Ah. Okay then," Mike said, unimpressed. He still hadn't moved. His expression changed from amused, to annoyed, to dead serious as their trap unfolded. "Let's take it easy. I needed to meet with you. In person." When neither of them responded, Mike continued. "You know how dangerous that is for someone in my position."

"I don't give a fuck who you are," John said calmly, taking off his hat and sunglasses and tossing them on the table. "We have questions. And you're going to answer them."

AUTHOR'S NOTE AND ACKNOWLEDGEMENTS

This year was hell for me. I got hit by a ton of bad luck and circumstance and found myself in a bit of a hole. There's a reason this book took so long to come out and I sincerely apologize to my readers for it. The reason we are reading this today is because I have an incredible support network to who this book is dedicated, with the most deserving honor possible. A writer never writes alone, as much as they like to pretend so. I thank my family, friends, and friendly strangers who picked me up when I fell, and urged me on as I stumbled. If you're not sure that this includes you because you only encouraged me in some small way, then yes it does — and you made all the difference.

I'd like to thank Chapin Kreuter, my go-to guy for surfing information. *Muchísimas gracias* to Carmen Cardenas, my dad's Guatemalan Spanish teacher for double checking all the Spanish in *Operation Nicaragua*. And many thanks to my book formatter Ruslan Nabiev for making everything fit together.

Mom — thank you for coffee and snacks, wakeup calls, and accepting that I have to work things out for myself. Your love and affection kept me from freezing over many days. And to Shawna Roberge– thank you for your patience and understanding, and for making the bad better.

To my beta reading team, you are fantastic and I hope you find words on the page inspired directly from your feedback. For Brian O'Riordan, who is honest and generous with his time. For Alex Colvin, who is a sharp reader and nobler friend. For Dave McAdams, who lends help without question and allows me to pretend I know how guns work. I used to think allowing readers to look at my work was a blessing to them; I have learned instead that it is a privilege for me.

I was fortunate enough to secure my editor-wizard Ross Mosher for a second time around. Ross, it is a joy to work with you and see how you spin my half-drunk words into a symphony of sentences worthy of publication. Thank you for your understanding, patience, and creativity. Some of the words you'll read are his.

And of course for my legend of a father who is the commander behind the scenes and master of the John Carpenter Series. Dad wrote an elaborate thirty-page outline detailing not only the general plot of this book, but also with plenty of description and dialogue that I cannot claim credit to. Dad, I was pleasantly surprised by how well the outline worked and you proved me wrong in your writing abilities. I hope you write some fiction one day — I think it'd be pretty good.

ENJOYED THIS BOOK?
YOU CAN MAKE A DIFFERENCE

Thank you very much for purchasing this book, Operation Nicaragua.

I'm very grateful that you chose this book from all the other wonderful books on the market.

I hope you enjoyed reading it. If you did, please consider sharing your thoughts on Facebook, Twitter, LinkedIn, and Instagram.

If you enjoyed this book and found value in reading it, please take a few minutes to post an honest review on your favorite site.

Reviews are very important to readers and authors — and difficult to get. Reviews don't have to be long: even a sentence or two is a huge help. Every review helps.

While on your favorite site, feel free to vote for helpful reviews.

The top-voted reviews are featured for display, and most likely to influence new readers. You can vote for as many reviews as you like.

Thank you for your support,
Collin

ABOUT THE AUTHOR

Collin Glavac is a Canadian born actor and writer who lives in Southern Ontario. He has written, directed, and acted in two original stage plays: In *Real Life* and *LoveSpell*. He completed his Dramatic and Liberal Arts B.A. and M.A at Brock University.

Operation Nicaragua is the second book in the John Carpenter trilogy. *Ghosts of Guatemala*, the first book in the trilogy is his debut novel. *Vaulter's Magic*, the first book in a new series will be available soon. Collin loves hearing from readers, so please don't hesitate to contact him by email at: collinglavac@gmail.com

Please sign up for our newsletter, watch the book trailer, and stay tuned for more at: www.collinglavac.com

Made in the USA
Columbia, SC
17 December 2022

74379566R00159